Battle for North Korea
2033

Praise for Tushingham's Novels

"Fast-paced ... Just ahead of tomorrow's headlines ... Able to recreate [modern warfare] vividly"
    – *New Brunswick Telegraph-Journal*

"A keen student of military matters ... Gripping"
    – *Charlottetown Guardian*

"A prophecy of things to come?" – *Ottawa Citizen*

"Brisk seller" – *New York Times*

"A bullet" – *Toronto Star*

"Rapid fire ... Unremitting" – *Gallon*

"A best seller" – *CBC News*

"Engrossing and suspenseful" – *DreamCatcher*

"For fiction lovers" – *Halifax Chronicle-Herald*

"Begging to hear more" – *Manotick Messenger*

BATTLE FOR
NORTH KOREA
2033

북한을 위한 전투 2033

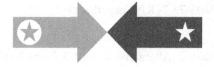

Mark Tushingham

Canadian Cataloguing Publication Data

Tushingham, Mark – 1962

Battle for North Korea 2033 / Mark Tushingham

ISBN 979-8-333805-73-7 (KPD paperback)

    I. Title.

        1. Fiction. 2. Alternative history. 3. North Korea.

        4. Military. 5. United States Air Force. 6. Nuclear war.

Editor: Dianne Tushingham

Typesetter: Mark Tushingham

Cover design, maps, tables and illustrations: © Mark Tushingham

FC 74454-78102

To Henry and Riley.

May your generation govern
our small and fragile planet wisely.

A Note to Readers

For readers of my other books in this series, *Battle for the Taiwan Strait 2033* and *Battle for the Baltic States 2033*, this present book is neither a sequel nor a prequel to those books, but rather a separate tale set within an alternative "history." The books are entirely independent and can be read in any order.

The characters, motivations, strategies and plans of military personnel and national leaders are products of my imagination or are used fictitiously in this speculative novel, but the weaponry and military technology described herein are not. The composition of the opposing armed forces—and all their vehicles, aircraft, ships and weapons—are (with a few minor exceptions for the benefit of the story) those that exist today or are announced to be in use by 2033. This is also true for the organizational structures of the armed forces and the locations of their bases.

This accuracy does not extend to North Korean facilities storing nuclear, chemical and biological weapons, or to the locations of underground artillery shelters. The locations of these top-secret facilities are not publicly known. For this story, I have cited disused nuclear facilities, suspected missile manufacturing facilities, and known submarine facilities, all of which might logically store weapons of mass destruction. Alternatively, I have cited locations that would be suitable for the distribution of such weapons to frontline troops or missile launching facilities, or that are within artillery range of the capital of South Korea. The exact location of these facilities is not critical to the story, but their existence is. No matter where these facilities are actually located, they would have to be neutralized before their devastating weapons could be used.

All this being said, and despite the novel being written in the format of a non-fiction history, the tale told is an imagined account of a truly horrific war that has not happened. And let us make sure that it stays that way.

M.T.

All leaders, eventually and inevitably, confuse their desires with the needs of the people who they govern. It is simply human nature.

In democracies, there are free elections, divisions of power, independent judiciary, unfettered media oversight, and other good-governance mechanisms to keep this delusion in check; in dictatorships, such mechanisms do not last for long.

Table of Contents

Maps

Tables, Diagrams and Documents

Romanization of the Korean Alphabet

한글 알파벳 로마자 표기

The Korean alphabet is called the Hangul in South Korea and the Chosŏn'gŭl in North Korea. It is converted into the Romanized alphabet using a different system in each country. Both countries began with the McCune-Reischauer system, a phonetic-pronunciation approach published in 1939.

South Korea's National Academy of the Korean Language devised a new system in 1995, and it was released to the public in 2000. The revised system dispenses with the use in the older system of breves (or accents) over some vowels. For example, the letter ŏ has been replaced by the letters *eo* and the letter ŭ by the letters *eu*. The use of apostrophes (which note changes in vocalization for the preceding letter) has been discontinued. The more Internet-friendly, tourist-friendly system is now in widespread use in South Korea.

In North Korea, the original McCune-Reischauer system was replaced by another system in 1992, and this was revised in 2002 and again in 2012. North Korea's latest system remains much closer to the original system (with its use of breves and apostrophes) than the system now in use in South Korea.

I have used the official system applicable to each country. Herein, this only impacts the names of places.

Time Zones

All dates and times in this book are those in the Korean peninsula, unless otherwise noted or obviously different from the context. South Korea and Japan are in the same time zone as North Korea, while Beijing is one hour behind. During the summer, North Korea is thirteen hours ahead the U.S. East Coast and sixteen hours ahead the U.S. West Coast. Guam is one hour ahead of North Korea, and Hawaii is nineteen hours behind. If it is evening in P'yŏngyang, it is morning in Washington, D.C.; if it is morning in P'yŏngyang, it is the evening of the previous day in Washington. All times are expressed in the twenty-four-hour format.

Metric Conversions

1 inch = 25.4 millimeters
1 yard = 0.9 meters
1 mile = 1.6 kilometers

1 pound = 0.45 kilograms (kilos)
1 U.S. ton = 0.9 metric tons (tonnes)

70°F = 21.1°C
90°F = 32.2°C
110°F = 43.3°C

Calendar of Significant Months in 2033

Sun	Mon	Tue	Wed	Thu	Fri	Sat
June						
			1	2	3	4
5	6	7	8	9	10	11
12	13	14	15	16	17	18
19	20	21	22	23	24	25
26	27	28	29	30		
July						
					1	2
3	4	5	6	7	8	9
10	11	12	13	14	15	16
17	18	19	20	21	22	23
24	25	26	27	28	29	30
31						

Sun	Mon	Tue	Wed	Thu	Fri	Sat
			August			
	1	2	3	4	5	6
7	8	9	10	11	12	13
14	15	16	17	18	19	20
21	22	23	24	25	26	27
28	29	30	31			
			September			
				1	2	3
4	5	6	7	8	9	10
11	12	13	14	15	16	17
18	19	20	21	22	23	24
25	26	27	28	29	30	

Regional Map of the Korean Peninsula

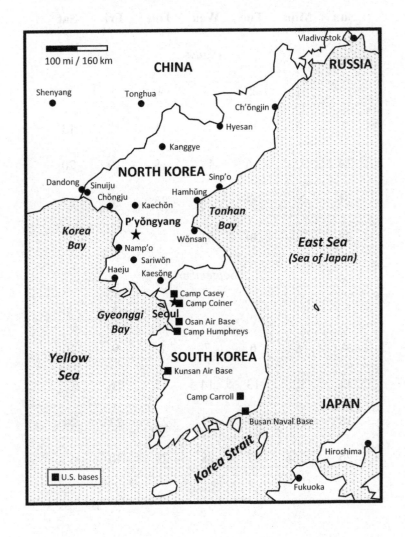

Preface

This book concerns itself with the battles that took place in and around the Korean peninsula during the summer of 2033. Many have claimed, with little justification, that the war against North Korea was primarily a combat between air forces, and that other forms of combat were merely afterthoughts. Others, with even less justification, insist that only the ground war mattered. More often than not, the complex and confusing political struggles that preceded combat have been completely ignored. Unlike those early books that concentrated on only one aspect of the war, this book examines the whole war from its political conception, through its air and naval battles, and finally to the ground war—all of which were fully dependent on the preceding phase.

By necessity, this history concerns itself with the actions of the armed forces of the United States and its allies. Information from the closed state of North Korea before and during the war is virtually non-existent, and given the current situation in that country, this scarcity is not likely to be remedied anytime soon. In contrast, the records regarding American actions are comprehensive and thorough, and growing by the day.

In my desire to capture the complexities of the war, I was assisted by many individuals. My particular thanks go to Dr. Cameron Luu of the Strategic Studies Institute, Dr. Park Kang-min of the Center for Strategic and International Studies, Mandy Clarkson of the International Institute for Strategic Studies, Jennifer Winslow of the National Museum of the United States Air Force, Barry Collins of the McDermott Library at the United States Air Force Academy, Mahmud Faizal of the Library of Congress, Teresa Mendez at the Marine Corps University Research Library, and Prof. Paul Norwich at the Canadian Center for Military, Security and Strategic Studies.

I would also like to thank my wife, Dianne, for her continued enthusiasm for this project, and for her boundless tolerance for my "focused distraction" on the complexities of the Korean peninsula.

It is now time to go back to the momentous events of the summer of 2033.

Mark Tushingham
Breckenridge, Colorado
2039

Foreword by General Lionel Dunn

North Korea had been our national boogeyman since the early 1950s. Eight decades of fear. It was a drab, secretive, scary place—a land that we could not understand, and in truth, did not want to. It was ruled by cruel dictators and populated by mindless fanatics or oppressed victims, depending to whom you were talking.

When, on June 17, 2033, our collective nightmare came true, we acted with rage in our hearts. As a nation, we needed justice for our dead, and no one was going to stop us. However, such unrelenting justice had a cost—and both sides paid it. A long time ago, the Chinese philosopher Confucius said, "Before you embark on a journey of revenge, dig two graves." There is a lot of truth in that. Like everyone else, I was caught up in our national thirst for vengeance, and I did my part in the great battles that followed. I am grateful that I was given the opportunity to serve my country in its darkest hour; but equally, I am horrified that the hour came on my watch, or that it came at all.

It was an extremely complex war where nothing was easy and where costly mistakes were inevitably made. The specter of Armageddon loomed over us constantly. That both tempered our actions and drove them with a desperate urgency—a duality that was difficult to reconcile. In his book, Dr. Tushingham has attempted to capture the enormous problems that the participants in this conflict had to overcome, and I believe that he has done so as well as humanly possible. As an American, this is a book that I needed to read, and I believe that others will feel the same.

L.A. Dunn, General, U.S. Air Force.

Part I

The Politicians' War

Chapter 1

Seattle

*Every war is going to astonish you in the way it occurred,
and in the way it is carried out.*

General Dwight D. Eisenhower,
U.S. Army, World War II.

Friday, June 17, 2033 was a beautiful day. Summer had
come early to Seattle. It was a rare cloudless day, with the
high forecasted to be 83°F. Traffic on the I-5 was lighter than
usual, because many had taken the day off work, either to
laze in their gardens or to make their way to the beaches. The
campus of the University of Washington was nearly
deserted. The few students still in attendance after the end of
spring term had abandoned their studies for the day, and
many were sunbathing in nearby parks. At Lumen Field
stadium, workers were setting up sound and lighting

equipment for the Tanya Rayn concert that night. All of Seattle was abuzz about the singer's extravagant performance in Los Angeles the previous week, and more of the same was anticipated for that night. No matter how nice the day, Union Pacific's Argo railyards and the Port of Seattle were still busy moving freight and cargo. Such work did not stop just because the sun was out and the day was pleasant.

At 11:07 local time, all was normal, a day like countless others. One minute later at 11:08, everything changed in Seattle, in America, and in the world. First, it was a white light, silent and blinding. Next, it was a burning heat that incinerated flesh. Moments later, a massive blast of air flattened everything in its path. Only then was the noise heard, deafening and indescribable. Across Puget Sound, those waiting for the ferry at Bainbridge Island Ferry Terminal saw a mushroom cloud billow high into the air. Not in eighty-eight years had such a cloud been seen above a city.

The atomic bomb that detonated on that day was not a large one. Its yield was measured in kilotons, not megatons.[1] Scientist later calculated that its explosive yield was twenty-five kilotons of TNT, only slightly larger than the atomic bombs that destroyed two Japanese cities nearly a century before. Damage to Seattle was somewhat less than to those other cities, due to the bomb being detonated at ground level and not at the optimal height in the air, which was the case in 1945. Much of the bomb's energy was directed upwards into the atmosphere, rather than downwards into the city.

---

[1] Nuclear bombs can be either atomic or hydrogen bombs. The former uses fission as the explosive process, while the later uses fusion. The Seattle bomb was an atomic (fission) bomb. Hydrogen bombs have much larger explosive yields. The largest hydrogen bomb ever was detonated by Russia in 1961. It had a yield of fifty megatons (or 50,000 kilotons) of TNT. The largest nuclear weapon in the U.S. arsenal in 2033 was the B83, which has a yield of 1.2 megatons. Prior to the late 1990s, the largest U.S. nuclear bomb available for use was the B53, which had a yield of nine megatons. It was withdrawn from service in 1997.

The buildings in Seattle in 2033 were better constructed than those in Japan in 1945, and so they offered more protection. The atomic bombs that destroyed Hiroshima and Nagasaki ended a war; the bomb that destroyed much of Seattle started one. The loss of life in Seattle was catastrophic. Over 85,000 died instantly, either vaporized or buried in rubble, and another 53,000 succumbed to radiation or other injuries over the next month. Tens of thousands more will have their lives cut short from cancer caused by the radioactive fallout. How many were injured has never been properly quantified, and the number of people afflicted with mental trauma will never be counted. However, this history is not about the tragic consequences to life, or the heroic efforts of the people of Seattle and the United States on that day and in the days, weeks and months that followed; it is about what happened next outside of Seattle. In short, panic. Global panic.

At Peterson Space Force Base near Colorado Springs, Colonel Felipe Rojas of the U.S. Air Force (USAF) was on duty in the operations center of the North American Aerospace Defense Command, universally known as NORAD. The command was tasked with the aerospace warning, the air sovereignty, and the protection of the continental United States and Canada. It had always been a joint two-nation command with an American commander and a Canadian deputy commander.

At 12:13 (Colorado time), Colonel Rojas was about to finish his noon-time rounds of the operation room and then return to his nearby office. Suddenly, there was a commotion behind him. He turned around and saw three young lieutenants standing in front of a computer terminal. One was talking loudly, almost shouting; the others were staring at the screen. Rojas's first reaction was anger at this lapse in discipline, but that quickly changed to concern when he saw the expressions on the lieutenants' faces.

Rojas later recalled:

I went over to the lieutenants and demanded to know what was going on. Lieutenant Bakker, the senior of the three, just pointed to the screen. It showed an image of mountains bathed in brilliant sunshine. The sky was a vivid blue. In the far distance, a thin pillar-like cloud was rising over the mountains. I asked what I was looking at. Lieutenant Bakker told me that a friend of his, who was stationed at McChord [Air Force Base] near Tacoma [forty-five miles south of Seattle], had called to tell him that there had been a huge explosion north of the base. Bakker had turned to a local news channel in Tacoma, and he saw what I was now seeing. My first thought was it was a local fire, but as I watched the image, a long-ago memory flickered vaguely in my mind. I couldn't quite grasp it, but I remember feeling a shiver run down my spine.

I ordered Bakker, who was the communications officer on duty, to get me the commander of the 62nd Wing at McChord. I spoke to Colonel [Bradley] Williams briefly. He had not seen the television images, and it soon became clear that I knew more than him, which was not saying much. I then attempted to contact the commander of Naval Base Kitsap [twenty miles west of Seattle], but there was no answer. That was highly unusual. It was at that moment when I became alarmed. I called for the attention of everyone in the operations room. I said that something had happened in the Seattle-Tacoma area, and I wanted answers. Lieutenant Bakker managed to contact a Globemaster [C-17 Globemaster III troop-transport plane] on route from Eielson [Air Force Base] in central Alaska to McChord. I remember Bakker shouting for the pilot to slow down [his talking]. I flicked on the speaker, and heard the pilot shouting. I couldn't make anything out of it. I took over from Bakker. In my most authoritative voice, I ordered that the pilot calm down and tell me what had happened. He shouted, "Seattle's gone!" I demanded that he explain. He just kept repeating those same two words: "Seattle's gone." I should've waited for confirmation, but my gut was screaming at me that something terrible had happened. Then and there, I ordered a full alert.

Captain Alan Smith was the pilot of the Globemaster to whom Colonel Rojas spoke. The large transport plane was part of the 8th Airlift Squadron of the 62nd Wing. He was returning empty from Eielson Air Force Base in Alaska where he had taken a detachment of special forces (from the 1st Special Forces Group) for a training exercise. Smith later recalled the conversation:

I was in shock. I couldn't believe what I was seeing. Zoey and Adam [his wife and eldest son] were down there somewhere in that horror. They had been on a school trip to the Space Needle [Seattle's iconic observation tower, built in 1962]. Adam was so looking forward to it. Zoey had taken a day off work to accompany him. The call [with Colonel Rojas] brought me back to my senses. I started to think again. Maria [his co-pilot, Captain Maria Evaretta] was sobbing. I spoke to her, and she too calmed down. I told her to take out her cellphone and take some pictures. I knew that it would be important.

I banked the plane towards Seattle, or what was left of it. I flew high, and never got closer than five miles from the center of the destruction. The mushroom cloud was like a thin column of grey smoke with a white boiling cloud at the top. There were frequent flashes of lightning in the cloud. The port and all around it were flattened. Fires were burning everywhere, and thick black smoke from the fires obscured much of what was below. Outside of the central devastation, I could see buildings still standing, or partially so. Many were on fire. Through all the smoke I was really looking for only one thing: the Space Needle. I can't tell you what relief I felt that day when I saw it emerge from the hellish smoke. It was still standing, and that gave me hope that somehow Zoey and Adam might still be alive down there.

Captain Smith returned to McChord Air Force Base where he was reunited with his two younger children. He then began to search for his missing wife and son. Captain Evaretta's photographs from the cockpit of the Globemaster became iconic images of that terrible day.

NORAD went on full alert at 12:19 (Colorado time), eleven minutes after the atomic bomb exploded. As NORAD's commander was at a meeting at the Pentagon, it was the task of Canadian Lieutenant General Kyle Denburgh, NORAD's deputy commander, to call the U.S. Chairman of the Joint Chief and the Canadian Chief of Defense Staff. This he did at 12:22.

By 12:30, distant images of the mushroom cloud were covered on every news channel—every channel that is except those in the Seattle area. The electronic pulse from the atomic detonation had destroyed sensitive electronic equipment in a wide radius around Seattle. Social media exploded with images of the deadly mushroom cloud and with every type of comment and wild theory. Speculation that it had been a nuclear explosion was already being openly discussed.

President Thomas Anders was on route to Camp David for a quiet weekend retreat. It would be a time for planning and renewal. He had been in office for 148 days. He believed that his first one hundred days had gone well, and the media and polls agreed with him. Many of his progressive reforms were already moving through Congress. Sixty-two-year-old Thomas Anders was a Democrat from Connecticut. He was from the progressive (far-left) wing of the party. After the harsh, hard-right policies of his predecessor, it was inevitable that the American public would swing the political pendulum equally far to the left. Anders had a long list of progressive policies with which he wanted to move forward. With majorities in both houses of Congress (albeit slim ones), he was optimistic that he could do so. Health care reform, gun control reform, meaningful action on climate change, action on immigration, tax reform, judicial reform, and much more. His platform was one of progressive reform and legislative action. The American people had given him a mandate to follow his dream of creating a better, kinder America. Anders's dream ended at 14:43 Eastern Daylight-savings Time.

The car phone rang, and a presidential aide picked it up and handed it to Anders. Secretary of Defense Carl Woodtke gave Anders the news that Seattle had been destroyed by a nuclear bomb, and that no one knew whether more nuclear attacks would happen. The President's immediate reaction was not recorded, but one can imagine that it was one of stunned horror. The catastrophe had happened on his watch. Anders continued on the few miles remaining to Camp David, where the Marine One helicopter was waiting. He was whisked away to a secret location.

At 15:14, via video, President Anders met with the Secretary of Defense and the four Joint Chiefs, all of whom were in the nuclear-hardened sublevels of the Pentagon. President Anders was informed that it had been "positively confirmed that much of central Seattle had been destroyed by a small nuclear device." According to those present, Woodtke had stressed the word *small* several times. The Joint Chiefs of Staff recommended that all armed forces of the United States go immediately from DEFCON 5 (Defense Condition 5) to DEFCON 2.[1] President Anders was having none of that. In his mind, a nuclear war had already begun. The dead and the dying in Seattle were testament to that. He ordered DEFCON 1. Never before had the U.S. gone to

---

[1] Since 1959, the U.S. armed forces have had five levels of readiness, or defense conditions. DEFCON 5 is the lowest level of readiness, and the normal one. DEFCON 4 means an increase in intelligence watch and a strengthening of security measures. DEFCON 3 means an increase in readiness of the armed forces. DEFCON 2 means prepare for war. DEFCON 1 means war is imminent or has already started. Each of the armed forces can be at a different defense condition.

DEFCON 1. It was unprecedented. In 1962, at the height of the Cuban Missile Crisis, President Kennedy had ordered DEFCON 2, but only for the Strategic Air Command; the rest of the U.S. armed forces had remained at DEFCON 3.

Back at NORAD headquarters, at 13:35 (Colorado time), the message came through that all United States forces had been placed at DEFCON 1. Eighty-six minutes had passed since the bomb exploded. Colonel Rojas was standing beside General Denburgh in the operations center when the message came through. Rojas later recalled their brief conversation:

The general said quietly, almost whispered, "DEFCON 1? Good God!"

To which I asked, "Yes, but who's the enemy? Who do we attack?"

The general paused for a moment and then replied, "I think that our job to find out."

I took that as my orders. I had a team set up within five minutes.

Destruction of Seattle

June 17

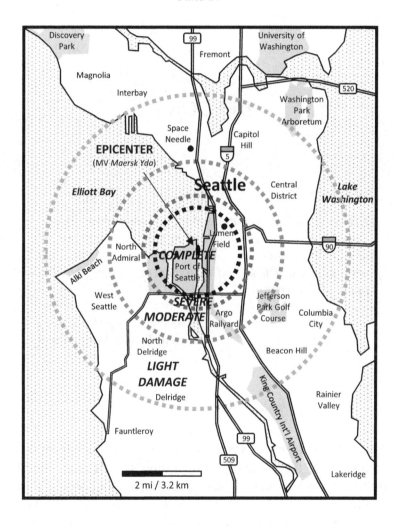

Chapter 2

DEFCON 1

History is not kind to nations that go to sleep. Pearl Harbor woke us up and we managed to win, although we are already forgetting the dark days when victory was uncertain, when it looked as though the scales might be tipped the other way.

General George C. Kenney,
U.S. Army Air Force, World War II.

The prevailing high-level winds on June 17 were from the south, and they pushed the bomb's radiation cloud northward. Some fallout landed on Burlington, less fell on Bellingham. The cloud crossed the border into Canada. The metropolis of Vancouver was only 140 miles from the bomb's epicenter. The Canadian government quickly advised the provincial government of British Columbia of the approaching danger. Public warnings were issued on television and radio and via cellphones. Two hundred thousand people in northwestern Washington and two-and-a-half million people in Canada found shelter in basements and any other structure that they deemed safe. There, they remained until the morning of June 20, when scientists announced that the fallout had been much less than first feared and it was now safe to resume normal activities. However, many terrified people did not emerge until several more days had passed. Despite many unsubstantiated claims to the contrary, there is currently no evidence that anyone died or even got sick from the limited radioactive fallout in those cities to the north of Seattle—not in Vancouver, and not in Burlington or Bellingham. Nevertheless, the prolonged fear seared itself into the collective minds of the inhabitants in those cities. Elsewhere in the U.S., people were terrified of more nuclear bombs exploding. Police telephone lines were choked by many thousands of tips of suspicious crates. The stock markets in the U.S. and Canada began to collapse and were quickly closed. As panic selling spread around the globe, other countries followed suit.

The Department of Homeland Security's Homeland Response Force and the Department of Energy's Nuclear Emergency Support Team joined teams from the Federal Emergency Management Agency and state agencies. They were all on the ground in Seattle before the sun set on the devastated city. It did not take them long to determine that the epicenter of the blast was the Port of Seattle. In the morning of June 18, the White House announced that all ships coming from other countries would not be allowed to get closer than ten nautical miles (11.5 miles) from the U.S. coast until they had been thoroughly inspected. At first, this Executive Order only applied to the Pacific coast, but by the afternoon, it was extended to cover the Atlantic coast as well. The Canadian government announced that it would refuse all maritime traffic that had been destined for U.S. ports.

Shipping traffic ground to a halt, and hundreds of ships began to sail in slow circles just outside of the ten-mile limit. The Coast Guard was swamped with calls from the captains of those ships desperately begging to be inspected. At 00:34 (West Coast time) on June 19, a second atomic bomb exploded offshore of Los Angeles. Its yield was the same as the earlier one. It was immediately evident that the bomb had been on board a large containership called MV *EML Doudart*, owned by the French CMA CGM Group. No other vessels were within two miles of the doomed ship. Besides the ship's crew, who died instantly, no one else died, although there were some injuries on two containerships that were two-and-a-half and four miles away, respectively. The eastward winds blew the bomb's radioactive cloud over Los Angeles. Its terrified inhabitants sought shelter wherever they could find it. This second attack drove panic in the U.S. to frantic levels.

President Anders spoke before a joint session of Congress later that day at 10:30 (East Coast time). His speech lasted thirty-seven minutes. In it, he described the destruction of Seattle and the horrors inflicted on its population, and he justified his decision to go to DEFCON 1. Anders struck a defiant and resolute tone. Gone was the thoughtful reformer, and in his place, there emerged a vengeful commander-in-chief. His speech received thunderous applause from both parties. It galvanized the nation and turned shock and fear into anger and a thirst for revenge. Military leaders, who initially had considerable reservations about the new left-wing President, were now firmly by his side.

An extract of the President's speech follows:

We have been attacked. A horrendous attack. A cowardly attack. An evil attack. Think not of 9/11 [the terrorist attack in 2001]. Think not of Pearl Harbor [the Japanese attack in 1941]. The destruction wrought on our country is a hundred-times worse, a thousand-times worse, and so will be our response. This is a time for a national commitment—an unwavering vow to ensure that the persons or countries perpetrating this atrocity on us will be brought to justice. Our retribution will be swift, and it will be terrible. ...

I ask that Congress vote for war against those who committed this terrible crime against us and against humanity. We will find out who they are—that I pledge to Congress and to the American people. ... Such evil must be utterly destroyed. ... Search your consciences and your love of our great nation, and ask yourself what the dead of Seattle would demand of you.

The President had captured the vengeful mood of the nation. Although a few news commentators and reporters questioned his state of mind, no one ask whether going to DEFCON 1 was an overreaction, and no one asked for cool second thoughts. Subsequent polls found that between eighty-seven and ninety-one percent of Americans supported the President's actions. The vote in Congress was almost unanimous. In the House of Representatives, the vote was 432 to two, with one notable absence. The representative of the Seventh Congressional District of Washington, Jamal Heff, had been attending the birth of his second child at Virginia Mason Medical Center in Seattle. The hospital was one-and-a-half miles from the epicenter of the blast. Satellite images showed that there was nothing left of the hospital except for some scorched steel frame. In the Senate, the vote was ninety-nine to zero, also with one absence. The senior senator from Oregon, Susanne Bonman, had died from a massive stroke after viewing the scenes from Seattle. Her son and his young family, who lived in Seattle, had gone to Alki Beach on the sunny morning of the explosion. The beach was three miles west of the epicenter. Bonman's son and daughter-in-law survived, but her two grandchildren, girls of seven and three, did not. They were blown out to sea by the resulting blast.

In Canada, at 14:00, Eastern time, on June 18, the day after the first bomb exploded, the government of Blake Farr sat in an emergency session of Parliament in Ottawa. Prime Minister Farr rose and first explained what steps had been taken to aid the people of Vancouver and the Lower Mainland of British Columbia in dealing with the radioactive fallout. Emergency teams, supported by medical and security units from the armed forces, had been sent. He then went on to detail the steps his government was taking to stop any nuclear bombs coming to Canada. All U.S.-bound ships would not be allowed to enter Canadian waters. All ships bound for Canadian ports would be searched by the Canadian Coast Guard, backed up by the warships of the Royal Canadian Navy. Airports and the border with the U.S. would be closed for two days while new security procedures were developed. The various Canadian stock markets would remain closed until 9:30 a.m. on Monday, June 27. Farr's precision on the time of the opening of the markets was deliberate; it was intended to provide a drop of certainty in an ocean of confusion.

Unlike President Anders speech of the following day, Farr's tone was moderate and his words implied caution and patience. He was attempting to calm a panicking nation, not to incite it into action. In Vancouver, two-and-a-half million Canadians were still hiding in their basements and fearing that they were going to die slow deaths by radiation poisoning. Farr reassured his people that no Canadians in Canada had died because of the attack, and that radiation levels were not as high as previously thought. Nevertheless, he urged them to stay at home for two more days. He then acknowledged that "several thousand" Canadians were likely to have been in Seattle at the time of the explosion, and that many may have died. It was later determined that nearly six thousand Canadians had been in Seattle on that day, either visiting or traveling through, and 1,565 of them had died either in the initial blast or shortly thereafter from their wounds or their exposure to the bomb's radiation.[1] Prime Minister Farr then solemnly pledged "complete support" for the U.S. in helping it "bring to justice those who killed so many of our friends and neighbors." It has been reported that President Anders was much moved by this immediate and unreserved support for the U.S. in its hour of need.

Over the next few days, messages of condolences and promises of aid came in from nations across the globe. However, among these messages, there was a tone of restraint and caution. The nuclear "genie" had been let out of its bottle, and everyone wanted the genie put back in. The fear that the United States, in its all-consuming wrath, would unleash a nuclear holocaust on someone was widespread in the world's capitals.

One statement was missing from all these international messages: no one claimed responsibility. Known terrorist organizations were silent. No one chanted "Death to America" or burned American flags. Fear of America's retaliation, fueled by rage and blinded by grief, chilled the world.

---

[1] A tally (certainly an incomplete one) of the deaths of citizens of other nations was not available until early 2034. Besides the 1,565 Canadians who died in the nuclear explosion, there were citizens of many other nations who also died: 589 Filipinos, 432 Chinese, 342 Japanese, 322 South Koreans, 232 Australians, 188, Pakistanis, 134 British, 122 Germans, 112 French, 82 Thais, 32 Vietnamese, 23 Indians, 14 Dutch, 10 Italians, 5 Danes, 4 Greeks, 4 Malaysians, 4 Singaporeans, 3 Saudis, 3 Kenyans, 3 South Africans, 2 Icelanders, 2 Russians, 2 Iranians, 1 Iraqi, 1 Chilean, and 1 Swiss. Many of the international deaths occurred among the crews of the ships in the Port of Seattle or at King County International Airport, when the terminal's roof collapsed. The number of serious injuries or of later deaths from cancer among of non-Americans has never been centrally quantified, and it is never likely to be.

Chapter 3

"Who do we attack?"

Retreat, Hell! We're just attacking in another direction.

Major General Oliver P. Smith
at the Battle of Chosin Reservoir, North Korea, 1950,
U.S. Marine Corps, First Korean War.

On June 19, Congress voted for war, but who was the enemy? Speculation was rampant in the media, and all the usual suspects were blamed: China, Russia, Iran, North Korea, and Islamic fundamentalists. The list of those who had, or could acquire, nuclear weapons was a short one; the list of those willing to use them was shorter still. All those blamed professed their innocence. With the attack occurring on the West Coast, China was first on many people's list of prime suspects.

The Chinese president, Guan Zixuan, was adamant that China had nothing to do with the attack. Since Guan had taken leadership of China in 2030, he had done much to repair China's relationship with its largest trading partner. Although he was frequently rebuffed by the previous American administration and its hardline trade policies, early indications were that President Anders was much more amenable to thawing relations between the two countries. That optimism was "vaporized" on June 17.

Scientists combed through the radioactive rubble. Measurements of isotopes were taken and compared to known nuclear-material manufacturing sites. The bombs were definitely not of American manufacture, and many sighed with relief at that news. Britain and France were immediately ruled out as sources, as was Israel. The process took longer for the other possible sources, but one by one, they were dismissed. Russia, China, India and Pakistan—all were eventually ruled out. That left Iran and North Korea. Concurrent with the scientific analysis, thorough inventory checks were claimed to have been done by all the nuclear powers, and all announced that no bombs were missing from their arsenals. The Anders Administration believed the assurances from Britain, France and Israel, but it was less certain about the others and completely distrustful of any claims coming out of Iran and North Korea. When America's vengeful eyes turned on Iran, the Iranian government did the unthinkable and allowed inspectors from the United Nations into its nuclear storage facility to confirm the veracity of its claims. North Korea made no such offer. The isotopic analyses of the bomb's fallout and the stocktaking of foreign nuclear arsenals were suggestive, but not conclusive.

National Stockpiles of Nuclear Warheads

2033

Country	First test	Warheads	
		Total	Deployed
United States	1945	4,884	1,470
Russia	1949	5,400	1,475
Britain	1952	260	192
France	1960	290	240
China	1964	500	< 40?
Israel	c. 1970	90	0
India	1974	180	0
Pakistan	1998	180	0
North Korea	2006	~ 130?	< 30?
Iran	c. 2027	6	0

Notes:
- In 2033, the U.S. and Russia were the only countries that were known to have nuclear warheads with yields of greater than one megaton.
- China claimed that none of its nuclear weapons were ever deployed, but the veracity of this assertion was questioned by the U.S.
- Neither Israel nor Iran have ever detonated a nuclear device, so the year of the first successful test is actually the year of first production.
- The total for Iran is the number confirmed by U.N. inspectors. The estimates for North Korea are based on multiple U.S. and allied intelligence sources.

While the media was busy speculating (irresponsibly so, in the opinions of many), the intelligence agencies of the United States began their work. In the evening after the first bomb exploded, President Anders tasked the Secretary of Homeland Security, Evelyne Vogtle, to coordinate the efforts to identify who was responsible for the attack on Seattle.[1] Anders met with Vogtle again after the second atomic bomb exploded off the coast of California. Intelligence efforts focused on the epicenters of the two explosions. The second one obviously came from the large containership MV *EML Doudart*. Using marine vessel traffic tracking systems, it did not take long to discover that at the epicenter of the first explosion was the newer and slightly larger containership MV *Maersk Yda* owned by the Danish shipping company Maersk Line. The *Doudart*'s destination had been Long Beach, south of Los Angeles; the *Yda*'s destination had been Seattle. What was of particular interest was where their voyages originated. For both, it was Shanghai, a major port in China. Once this became known, public anger at China exploded. President Guan personally called President Anders to strongly deny any role in the attack and to calm America's fury. He promised his nation's full cooperation and unfettered access for American intelligence officers to the Shanghai's port facilities and dock personnel. Both shipping companies and the French and Danish governments promised their full cooperation and access to the cargo manifests and crew rosters.

---

[1] The Department of Homeland Security was created by President Bush after the 9/11 attacks in 2001, and it began operations in 2003. Its creation was in direct response to the lack of interagency coordination that allowed the terrorists' plans to go undetected. The department's mission was "to develop and coordinate the implementation of a comprehensive national strategy to secure the United States from terrorist threats or attacks," and "to coordinate the executive branch's efforts to detect, prepare for, prevent, protect against, respond to, and recover from terrorist attacks within the United States."

The MV *Maersk Yda* was a new Y-class containership. It was rated to carry 17,000 twenty-foot-equivalent container units. There might have been a maximum of 17,000 units on that ship when it arrived in Seattle, but almost certainly less. Ships were rarely loaded to their rated capacities. Units generally came in either twenty-foot or forty-foot lengths, with the latter being more common. The MV *EML Doudart* (named after Ernest-Marc-Louis Doudart de Lagrée, a Nineteenth-century French explorer of Southeast Asia) was rated to carry 14,770 twenty-foot-equivalent container units.

Although the atomic bombs could have been placed in the ships themselves, the initial focus of the investigation was on the container units. From the shipping manifests, the *Yda* carried into the Port of Seattle 7,312 of the standard forty-foot units and 1,244 of the shorter twenty-foot units. The smaller *Doudart* was carrying 5,922 forty-foot units, 1,018 twenty-foot units, and 116 of the uncommon forty-five-foot units. A total of 15,612 units had to be investigated: what each contained, who owned what was inside, and who loaded the unit and when. The *Yda* had a crew of seventeen: a Danish captain, four more Danes, two Italians, four Greeks, and six Filipinos. The *Doudart* had a crew of fourteen: a British captain, four more Brits, three French, four Thais, and two Malaysians. Thirty-one deceased individuals were about to have their personal lives invaded and sifted for every small detail. The grieving families were interrogated relentlessly by security officials and hounded by the media.

Theresa McAdams, the widow of Bruce McAdams, the *Doudart*'s engineering officer, remembered the "heartless" invasion of her life:

> I was lying in my bed crying. My parents were downstairs looking after my two boys. I'd told them that Daddy was never coming home, but they were too young to understand properly. Bruce was often away for long stretches at a time.
> There was a knock on the door. I could hear my dad talking to someone. Then, there was a loud commotion

downstairs. I tried to collect myself, but before I could, my bedroom door burst open and in walked three policemen and one policewoman. I was told that I had to go downstairs and sit with my parents in the front room. I was in such a state that I didn't even ask them what they were doing in my home. I just started to sob. I went downstairs and sat on the chesterfield [sofa] next to my parents, who were holding my boys. Jimmy, my youngest, was crying. Robby, my oldest, was wide-eyed and terrified. I took him from my dad and hugged him.

The policewoman sat down in front of me, and starting asking me questions. I can't remember what they were now. Lots of things about money and bank accounts. I cried the whole time. They searched everywhere, and they took my mobile [cellphone] and my computer. They even took the boys' tablet. It was awful.

There has been a lot of speculation in recent years on how the two bombs were triggered. The *Doudart* had been delayed in Shanghai by engine problems. It was some forty hours behind schedule. It is widely believed that timers were not involved, at least not as the primary trigger mechanism, as implied by the two-day delay in detonation of the second bomb. One possibility is that the detonations could have been triggered by a cellphone call to a receiver on the bomb. However, because the bombs were inside steel container units, reception would have been poor to non-existent. Such a tenuous situation would not have been satisfactory to the planners of the attack. A much more promising line of speculation was that the trigger mechanisms might have been somehow tied to engine vibrations. It is suggestive that remote tracking of the *Doudart*'s movements shows that the ship was slowing down just prior to the bomb exploding, while such tracking showed that the *Yda* had docked ten minutes before its bomb detonated. Although such postulating is an interesting academic exercise, how it was done was not on the minds of most Americans; what

America was going to do about it was a much more relevant question.

The investigation focused on the port of origin of the two ships: Shanghai, China. A senior agent in the Federal Bureau of Investigation (FBI), Terrance Lindstrom, arrived in Shanghai on June 21 after an eighteen-hour flight from Dulles International Airport, near Washington, D.C. He was one of fifteen FBI agents from various branches. The executive assistant director of the National Security Branch, Fred Whitt, was in charge of the delegation. Lindstrom, however, was in the Criminal Investigation Division of the Criminal, Cyber, Response and Service Branch. He was a criminal investigator, with twenty-two years of experience in catching criminals.

Lindstrom recalled his arrival in China:

We landed [at the airport] in Shanghai where we were met by a large delegation of Chinese officials. EAD Whitt [Executive Assistant Director Fred Whitt] led our delegation, which also included a NEST team [Nuclear Emergency Support Team] of four scientists. Three officials and six translators from the State Department were also with us. I think one of them was CIA [from the Central Intelligence Agency]. But even if he wasn't, the head of the CIA's Weapons and Non-proliferation Center accompanied us in his official [public] capacity.

It was my task to run the investigation itself. I had decided on the plane to run it as though it was any other case. I had to keep my anger in check. You can't be emotionally engaged in a case, because you can lose perspective and objectivity, but it would have been impossible to find an agent who was not angry and upset about what had happened in Seattle. I tried to put my emotions aside. Facts and evidence, witnesses and testimonies—that was where my priorities lay. I drilled that into the six agents who reported to me.

The Chinese took us directly to the port [of Shanghai], where they had set up a command center of sorts in a large warehouse. I dumped my carryon [suitcase] in a corner with the others and got down to work. The Chinese thought that we would want to get stuck in straightaway, and they were right. Translators were all over the place—ours from the State Department and theirs. I was lucky because my counterpart, Inspector Jin Kai of their Criminal Division [of State Security], spoke fluent English. He told me that he'd been born in Hong Kong.

While Agent Lindstrom was interviewing dock workers, back in Washington, D.C., teams of FBI agents were scrutinizing the specifics of each container unit on the two ships. The records of the Bureau International des Containers et du Transport Intermodal in Paris, France, were compared to the manifests. A container unit's unique registration number consists of a three-letter owner's code, a one-letter product-group code (usually a U for freight), a six-digit serial number, a one-digit "check" number, and a size and type code of four letters and digits. The registration numbers of each container were compared to the container's check digit. In all cases, they matched, so no container was unregistered. Next, the owner of each container was contacted and the details of what the container carried was discussed. The information was then verified with the owner of the cargo. As the investigation developed, thirteen container units became "items of interest": five on the *Yda* and eight on the *Doudart*. The owners of the cargo could not be found.

A list of these units and the names of the owners of the cargo that they contained was forwarded to Lindstrom, who shared them with Inspector Jin. Jin informed Linstrom that three of the names on the list were suspected to be fronts for Chinese criminal organizations. Lindstrom recalled:

When Inspector Jin told me this, I realized that such organizations could easily be involved, at least as unwitting middlemen. They may not have known what they were being asked to smuggle [into the U.S.]. However, I had a gut feeling that it was too obvious a lead. During my career, I had come to rely on my gut. Since I was in Shanghai, I decided to start with the local shippers. There was one local company that had one of the suspect containers on each ship: Ding-Willis Shipping.[1] Jin told me that it was small company, but seemingly legit [legitimate]. No known criminal connections.

Jin and I went to company's headquarters, which was just a short car ride from the port. We met with the general manager—a man called Lin Chao. Lin was very sympathetic to America's agony, and he was eager to help. If the man was acting, he'd have won an Academy Award. We ran the two container numbers in his computer system. They were loaded on the same day. I asked Lin who loaded them and he replied that in both cases the owners of the cargo had loaded it themselves. He volunteered that this was common, but the cargo was always inspected by his company's inspectors before the [container] doors were closed. I asked to talk to the inspector who inspected each one. I remember what happened next vividly.

Lin replied, "Sadly, one was in a tragic car accident. He died, I'm sorry to say."

"And the other one," I asked.

Lin replied, "He's been off sick for a while. He hasn't been back to work in weeks."

I think my heart stopped beating. My gut certainly twisted itself into a knot. I immediately called in the NEST team. Lin showed the scientists where the two containers had been loaded. He was clearly getting concerned that something bad was going on, and that somehow, he and his company were right in the middle of it. The NEST team found slightly elevated radiation levels on the ground. Not

---

[1] The registration numbers of the container units on the MV *Maersk Yda* and the MV *EML Doudart* were DWSU-007381-3-45G1 and DWSU-003845-7-45G1, respectively. Both were standard forty-foot general product freight units. The manifests listed "construction machine parts" for the former and "power turbine parts" for the latter.

much, but enough. We had discovered which containers, and now we had to found out who loaded them.

We went to the apartment of Dong-Willis's sick inspector. He was missing. Jin and I, through a female FBI interpreter, interviewed his wife. She claimed that three men from Dong-Willis has come to their apartment and told her husband that the company needed him in Qingdao [a large port city north of Shanghai] for an extended period. She had not heard from him since then, and she was getting worried. He didn't answer his cellphone.

I had to find those three men. From the wife, I had a date, a time, and a starting point: her front door.

Lindstrom and his team scoured through hundreds of hours of video footage from road and store cameras, which the Chinese authorities made available. They noticed a car leaving the area at the right time. There were four men in it, and the missing inspector was one of them. The faces of the others could not be discerned clearly enough, but the car's license plate could. The car was a rental from Beijing. More video footage was reviewed, and now they had the faces of the three men. One was recognized by the Chinese as a North Korean operative, and the CIA confirmed this.

The border between China and North Korea immediately became the focus of the investigation. Video tapes of border crossings were made available, and border guards were interviewed. All of them that is but one. He had apparently hung himself, but no suicide note was ever found. The focus narrowed to the border crossing at Dandong during times when the suspect guard had been on duty. Two trucks were noted to enter China from North Korea on April 29 at 05:33. The video footage showed the guard walking up to the first truck, but he did not look inside its trailer. He spoke to the driver of the first truck and then waved both trucks through. Using traffic cameras, the route of the two trucks could be followed from Dandong on the North Korean border all the way to Dong-Willis's warehouse. It was, according to Agent

Lindstrom, "as close to an open-and-shut case as I've ever had. The bastards did it, and now we knew. But we didn't know why. What was their motive? That question really got under my skin."

The conclusion that North Korea was behind the nuclear attack on Seattle moved quickly through the FBI bureaucracy. The director of the FBI, Cameron Filburn, briefed President Anders at the White House on June 29. It had been twelve days since the first atomic bomb destroyed a large part of Seattle. He explained the investigation and its findings. He could confidently state who attacked Seattle, but he could not explain why.

Unbeknownst to Director Filburn, Agent Lindstrom, and almost everyone else in America, a few in the CIA and the State Department suspected a reason. Once it became known that North Korea was behind the destruction of Seattle, CIA Director Valerie Ullman briefed President Anders of a significant development regarding relations with North Korea that had occurred just prior to Anders becoming the President. The briefing took place early on June 30.

During the briefing, Ullman, laid out the events of Christmas Day, 2032. On that day, a man and a women entered the U.S. embassy in Abu Dhabi, the capital of the United Arab Emirates. Both held North Korean passports and both wanted asylum in the United States. The embassy, which had been running in holiday mode, was quickly transformed into "a madhouse of frantic activity." The man was General Cho Nam-jun, the commander of the Supreme Leader's bodyguards, a very important position, but it was the woman who sent the embassy staff into a frenzy. She was Kim Sang-hui, the younger sister of the Supreme Leader of North Korea.[1]

---

[1] In North and South Korea (and China), surnames are placed first and given names are placed last. Two-syllable Korean given names are officially either one word or more commonly hyphenated, not two

Twenty months before the defection of Kim Sang-hui and her husband, the previous Supreme Leader, Kim Jong-un had died under mysterious circumstances. For three tumultuous weeks, Kim Jong-un's daughter and heir, Kim Ju-ae, attempted to rule with the assistance of her aunt, Kim Yo-jong. After a bloody palace coup, Kim Ju-ae's half-brother, Kim Ji-ho, emerged as the new Supreme Leader. Prior to his seizing of power, Kim Ji-ho was virtually unknown in the West. He was the fourth Kim to rule North Korea (not counting the brief and chaotic reign of Kim Ju-ae). Kim Il-sung, the founder of the modern authoritarian state of the Democratic People's Republic of Korea, ruled from 1948 to 1994; his son, Kim Jong-il, ruled from 1994 to 2011; and the third son of Kim Jong-il, Kim Jong-un, ruled from 2011 to his mysterious death in 2031.

Kim Ji-ho was the illegitimate son of Kim Jong-un. On Kim Ji-ho's twenty-fifth birthday in 2027, the former Supreme Leader had officially adopted his son. After Kim Ji-ho seized power in 2031, he was brutally ruthless, even by North Korean standards. There was a great purge of the Kim family. Uncles, aunts, half-siblings—all disappeared from view. Western analysts assumed that they were either in prison or dead, and most assumed the latter.

Kim Sang-hui was the full sister to Kim Ji-ho. Their mother was the same mistress of Kim Jong-un. Kim Sang-hui and her husband were initially trusted by the new Supreme Leader. Her husband, Cho Nam-jun, was immediately promoted in rank from captain to general and placed in charge of the Supreme Guard Command, the personal bodyguard force for protecting the Supreme Leader. Kim Sang-hui watched as her brother became more vicious, more paranoid, and more unpredictable. She began to fear for her life, and for the life of her husband and unborn

---

separate words (although they are frequently and incorrectly written that way in the West). For consistency, I have used hyphenated names herein.

31

child. She was secretly three-months pregnant at the time of her defection.

As privileged members of North Korean society, Kim Sang-hui and her husband were permitted to travel to some international destinations, and the mecca for the ultra-rich, Dubai in the United Arab Emirates, was one of them. On December 25, 2032, husband and wife slipped away from their security detail and drove just over an hour from Dubai to the capital, Abu Dhabi, where they immediately sought asylum in the U.S. embassy. The couple were secretly flown back to the U.S. and were extensively debriefed. General Cho knew a treasure trove of state secrets. The CIA was ecstatic with the intelligence that he provided. Kim Sang-hui provided an alarming picture of her brother's growing paranoia and his deteriorating mental state. The couple's defection was not announced by either country, because both sides wanted it to be kept a secret, but for different reasons.

The North Korean government quietly demanded the couple's return through back-channel intermediaries, but in the waning days of the previous U.S. administration, the answer was firmly no. When Thomas Anders became the President on January 20, 2033, the North Koreans stopped asking. The CIA and the State Department assumed that they had given up. With the evidence of the bombing of Seattle pointing directly at North Korea, it became clear that Kim Ji-ho's demands for the return of his sister had been replaced by a craving for revenge on the American people for giving her sanctuary. Over 138,000 had died to satisfy his lust for revenge, and in the months that followed, more would die.

Chapter 4

NATO and Article 5

The friend of my adversity I shall always cherish most. I can better trust those who helped to relieve the gloom of my dark hours than those who are so ready to enjoy with me the sunshine of my prosperity.

General Ulysses S. Grant,
Union Army, Civil War.

The United States had been attacked, horribly so, and the President had pledged to respond. However, America's allies had to be consulted, and the broader international community had to be considered. This chapter will examine how the North Atlantic Treaty Organization (NATO) responded to the crisis. Subsequent chapters will discuss the deliberations of the United Nations, and America's bilateral meetings with China and Russia.

In the eight decades of NATO's existence, the call for collective defense under Article 5 of the North Atlantic Treaty had been invoked only twice—and both times it was invoked by the United States. The first time was in response to the 9/11 terrorist attacks in 2001; the second was in response to the nuclear attack on Seattle in 2033. Neither call for action was what Article 5 had originally envisioned when it was signed back in 1949.[1] Back then, NATO was intended to contain the expansionist Soviet Union. In 2001, the North Atlantic Council (NATO's principal political decision-making body) had taken over three weeks to debate whether Article 5 applied. In the end, it concluded that it did. In 2033, debate was again needed, at least that was how the non-U.S. members of NATO saw it. The debate at NATO's headquarters in Brussels, Belgium, was not about the invocation of Article 5 due to a major terrorist attack on a NATO member, because the decision in 2001 had resolved that ambiguity; the debate was about the retaliatory use of nuclear weapons.

The first meeting of the North Atlantic Council took place on June 22, before it was known that North Korea was responsible for the attack on Seattle. Barry Finick, Canada's permanent representative on the council (equivalent to an ambassador), remembered that first meeting:[2]

---

[1] Article 5 of the North Atlantic Treaty states: "The Parties agree that an armed attack against one or more of them in Europe or North America shall be considered an attack against them all and consequently they agree that, if such an armed attack occurs, each of them, in exercise of the right of individual or collective self-defense recognized by Article 51 of the Charter of the United Nations, will assist the Party or Parties so attacked by taking forthwith, individually and in concert with the other Parties, such action as it deems necessary, including the use of armed force, to restore and maintain the security of the North Atlantic area."

[2] The U.S. permanent representative on the North Atlantic Council, Alec Wilson, a holdover from the previous administration, ignored my many requests for an interview.

I had received instructions from my government to support the invocation of Article 5 [by the U.S.]. Canada would support the United States to the fullest extent possible, but with one non-negotiable caveat. Canada would not support any use of nuclear weapons. Although I'm not aware of any behind-the-scenes discussions, it soon became clear that all the other [non-U.S.] representatives were of the same view. Destroying another city was not the answer. That was my government's view, and for what it's worth, that was—and still is—my personal view as well.

Representative Wilson [of the United States] didn't take this show of unity very well. He repeatedly stated that the United States had been attacked by nuclear weapons, and that the United States should be able to respond in kind. His view was that NATO was limiting itself, and more importantly to him, it was attempting to limit America's response. He became very angry and used considerable profanity. Much of his rage was directed towards [the representatives of] Britain and France, the other two nuclear powers [in NATO]. The French representative kept asking for translations of Mr. Wilson's many colorful words— deliberately, I suspected at the time. The British representative just looked down at his notes. Many other representatives argued with Mr. Wilson. At one point, both the Polish and Romanian representatives were shouting at him. Sweden and Finland joined in. It was clear to me that all the Eastern European countries were terrified of opening Pandora's nuclear box, a box that the Russians might open next. Mr. Wilson threatened to … No, I won't discuss that.

I had been on the Council for three years. This was the most fractious meeting that I had ever attended. Mr. Wilson stormed out, and the Secretary General, who had by now lost all control of the meeting, called for an adjournment.

We met twice more, both without Mr. Wilson in attendance. At those much calmer meetings, we solidified NATO's position that nuclear weapons were not to be used. It was not until after North Korea had been identified as the perpetrator [of the attack] that Mr. Wilson returned.

The united rebuff by NATO of the retaliatory use of nuclear weapons was a significant setback to President Anders. He was not prepared to take any military options "off the table."

Independence Day on July 4 was a somber affair; it was more like a national wake for those lost than a celebration of nationhood. During the first week in July, rumors that North Korea was responsible for the destruction of Seattle swirled around Washington. The media fanned the flames by wildly speculating about what President Anders was going to do to North Korea. After initially attempting to downplay the rumors, the White House announced that the President would address the nation at 21:00 on Tuesday, July 12.

In hindsight, it is now clear that the rumors had forced President Anders to act prematurely. He would have preferred to have formulated a solid plan of action and found unity with America's allies before announcing who was responsible for the destruction of Seattle. The President's speech explained who did it, but not why. The defection of Kim Ji-ho's sister and her husband was not revealed, then or for months afterwards. After the President's strident speech, it was never in doubt that North Korea was to be attacked— not by anyone in the White House, in Congress, at the Pentagon, on Wall Street, or on Main Street—and not in the North Korean capital. There was, however, considerable doubt about how it was to be done. Anders called for patience as the United States "readies its forces to smite the evil Kim regime." Much has been made of Anders use of the word *smite*. It has strong religious overtones, which many at the time thought noteworthy given Anders's tepid views on religion. The speech gave no indication of how America's forces would be used. The use of nuclear weapons was not mentioned, but neither was it dismissed. In the absence of any announced plan, the media freely speculated how it was to be done.

Into this media frenzy, the news broke about NATO's "dictate" that nuclear weapons were not to be used by the U.S. in its retaliation. Many were indignant and thought that it was none of NATO's business how the U.S. responded, but others were horrified that nuclear weapons might be used. They agreed with NATO's premise that destroying a city full of millions of innocent people was not something Americans should be doing. The unity of purpose that President Anders had enjoyed was fractured by this divisive national debate.

While all of this was going on, U.S. diplomats were talking to their allies in the region. It was obvious to all that a war against North Korea would require the support of South Korea and Japan. Significant U.S. forces were already stationed in those countries, but to use them would require the approval of the host country. Both countries were in range of North Korea's ballistic missiles. Worse, the capital of South Korea, Seoul, was less than thirty-five miles from the border and well within range of artillery. The northern suburbs of Seoul were less than half that distance.

Before the President's public denunciation of North Korea as the nation responsible for the Seattle attack, the American ambassadors in South Korea and Japan met with the South Korean president and the Japanese prime minister. In Seoul, Ambassador Kevin Todd and President Yeon Ki-moon met first on June 20, just after the destruction of Seattle, and again on July 3, when it was known but not yet publicly announced that North Korea was behind the attack. Ambassador Todd remembered the stark contrast between the two meetings:

> The first meeting was simply me informing President Yeon about what had happened and what steps the United States government was taking to find out who was responsible. President Yeon and the others in the room listened, and they were clearly upset and outraged about what had happened. President Yeon was very supportive and offered whatever

help his government could give. No outcome was expected from this meeting. My task was to simply reassure our ally that the U.S. government would soon discover who was responsible.

The second meeting was quite different. There was only President Yeon and myself in the room, as I had requested. I officially informed President Yeon who we believed committed the atrocity. From his reaction, I suspected that Yeon already had his suspicions. I had hoped for a show of angry defiance at North Korea and a strong commitment of support for us. Instead, he was much more circumspect than I expected. He frequently mentioned how close Seoul was to the border [with North Korea].

When the news broke in South Korea that the U.S. was blaming North Korea for the attack, initially there was outrage at North Korea, but this was quickly replaced by fear and in some cases panic. Visions of nuclear missiles and chemical artillery shells raining down on Seoul were vividly described in the South Korean media. "Scientifically projected" casualty estimates were commonplace, and each day the estimates grew larger.

When Ambassador Gerald Freeman met with Japanese Prime Minister Hajime Shimazu in Tokyo, the Prime Minister was even more cautious than President Yeon. The horrific nuclear attacks on Hiroshima and Nagasaki at the end of World War II were deeply engrained in the Japanese psyche. The scenes from Seattle distressed the people of Japan even more than the peoples of other nations. Many in Japan could find an ancestor in their family tree who had died from, or lived through, the atomic bombs of 1945. No one wanted another Japanese city to suffer such a terrible fate.

After President Anders had publicly denounced North Korea, Secretary of State Cheryl Bowes traveled to South Korea and then to Japan. Ambassador Todd accompanied

Secretary Bowes to her meeting with President Yeon on July 14. Todd later recalled the tension in the room:

> The [South] Koreans sat on one side of the [conference] table and we sat on the other. President Yeon had with him key cabinet ministers and military leaders. Secretary Bowes had with her me, some aides, and General [Alexander] Sweeny, commander of the United States Forces Korea. To undertake a meaningful attack on North Korea, we had to have the support and cooperation of the South Korean government.
>
> The discussions were testy. Although I cannot get into the specifics of what was discussed at the meeting, the outcome was that South Korea would not declare war on North Korea and its forces would play no role in our impending attack, at least not initially. The government would, however, allow American forces to operate from our bases in South Korea and American naval forces to operate inside their territorial waters.

The South Korean government had decided on a policy of limited logistical support but no active participation. It announced this "non-participation" policy in an effort to calm the growing fears of its citizens. The government of North Korea stated that if this policy was "to change in any way" there would be "serious consequences." That overt threat was the only statement that North Korea made towards South Korea. All its other official statements were directed towards the U.S. In every one of those statements, North Korea denied any involvement in the attack on Seattle.

The non-participation policy of South Korea did not apply to its extensive intelligence networks (both military and civilian) or to its special forces. Both would be completely, but secretly, available to the U.S. One other element of South Korea's involvement was deliberately left vague. The U.S. Second Infantry Division in South Korea comprised of a U.S. combat brigade, with air and artillery support units, plus an assigned South Korean brigade, which rotated in and out of the division on an irregular schedule. The purpose of this rotation was to provide South Korean soldiers with the opportunity to train alongside American soldiers, and for both militaries to become familiar with the other's procedures and tactics. In the summer of 2033, the assigned brigade was the 16th Mechanized Brigade, with its K1 main battle tanks and K200 armored personnel carriers. It had been assigned from the Capital Mechanized Division, which in turn was part of South Korea's VII Maneuver Corps. The status of the brigade was purposefully not discussed at the meeting between President Yeon and Secretary Bowes. As a consequence of this calculated omission, the brigade remained under U.S. command as part of the Second Infantry Division. General Sweeny and the South Korean military leadership were content to leave the issue for another day. For now, the South Korean brigade would continue to follow the orders of the division's American commander, Major General Walter Brum.

When Secretary Bowes arrived in Tokyo on July 15, the reception was more restrained than it had been in Seoul. "Frosty" was how several participants described it. Initially, the Japanese government, fearful of North Korea's long-range nuclear missiles, was not going to allow the U.S. forces to operate from its country or provide any logistical assistance. Bowes later testified before the Senate Committee on Foreign Relations that "the ghosts of Hiroshima and Nagasaki haunted the room." Bowes nimbly adapted to this reality, and she pivoted to arguing for the same approach that she had argued against in Seoul. In the end, the Japanese government permitted U.S. forces to operate from their country. It provided all the intelligence that it had on North Korea, but it offered no military support. The best outcome that Bowes could obtain from the reluctant Japanese government was a promise to "actively re-assess" its policy as developments unfolded.

Chapter 5

United Nations

I am tired and sick of war. Its glory is all moonshine. It is only those who have neither fired a shot nor heard the shrieks and groans of the wounded who cry aloud for blood, for vengeance, for desolation. War is hell!

General William T. Sherman,
Union Army, Civil War.

Concurrent with the meetings with America's allies, President Anders had to navigate the churning waters of the United Nations. He greatly desired to have international condemnation of North Korea and have the U.N.'s blessing of his war of revenge upon the nation that had killed over 138,000 Americans. It was abundantly clear at the time that the U.S. was going to take its revenge regardless of what the U.N. did or did not do, but the idea that the world supported the U.S. was a politically attractive one. It would also avoid diplomatic problems later if (or more likely when) unfriendly nations started accusing U.S. military personnel of war crimes.

The first significant meeting at the U.N. building in New York did not happen until after North Korea had been publicly identified on July 12. Prior to this date, the focus was on condemning the attack and expressing alarm about the decision of the United States to got to DEFCON 1. The phrase "nuclear war is imminent," which accompanied the elevation to DEFCON 1, sent shockwaves through the international community. However, until an enemy had been identified, the war was viewed as hypothetical. One unidentified U.N. representative was overheard expressing the wish that "the culprit never be discovered." Once the "culprit" was identified, concern in the international community grew rapidly. The vengeful language coming out of Washington did much to cause this escalation.

The fifteen members of the Security Council met on July 13 to discuss the issue.[1] A resolution was proposed by China that nuclear weapons should not to be used in any attack on North Korea. This resolution was strongly supported by Japan and Romania. The council voted on the resolution the next day. Twelve voted in favor, France and the United Kingdom abstained, and the U.S. used its veto, which caused the resolution to fail. The debate then moved to the General Assembly, which in 2033 comprised of 193 member states. An emergency special session of the General Assembly was

---

[1] The Security Council comprises of five permanent members and ten non-permanent members which change every two years. The five permanent members are China, France, Russian Federation, the United Kingdom and the United States. In 2033, the ten non-permanent members were Cameroon, El Salvador, Ethiopia, Japan, Kuwait, the Netherlands, Romania, Thailand, Tunisia, and Uruguay. North Korea, as an affected party, attended the Security Council meetings and took part in the debate, but it could not vote. Canada also claimed to be an affected party and attended the meetings, but its representative said little.

scheduled for July 18. It was only the thirteenth such session in the U.N.'s eighty-eight-year history. [1] A similar non-nuclear resolution was to be proposed by China in the General Assembly where it would certainly pass, and where the U.S. could not veto it.

The Canadian Minister of Foreign Affairs, Glen Rathwell, met with Secretary of State Cheryl Bowes in Washington on July 15, the day after the vote in the Security Council. The Canadian and American U.N. representatives, Thomas Boyd and Tyler Vinka, were also in attendance. In 2034, on the first anniversary of the attack on Seattle, Minister Rathwell provided details of this meeting in a television interview on Canada's CBC:

> Secretary Bowes was adamant that all military options had to be left open. However, I pointed out that the U.N. was certainly to reject the use of nuclear weapons, and that meant that the U.S. would have to go to war without the approval of the U.N. Secretary Bowes understood the geopolitical risks of that. Nevertheless, she argued that the American people would not accept limitations to their response to the destruction of Seattle imposed by the outside parties. ...
>
> I had carefully read the report on the Security Council vote by our U.N. representative [Thomas Boyd]. I immediately understood how much fear was present [at the Security Council meeting]. It was a real fear—a fear that [Canadian] Prime Minister Farr and I both shared—that the use of nuclear weapons, once begun, could not be stopped. It would set a dangerous precedent. I described this fear to Secretary Bowes, and she understood. I believe that it was a fear that she privately held. I then observed that the United

---

[1] The thirteenth emergency session was the first such session that was in regards to an Asian country. Earlier emergency sessions were in regards to issues in the Middle East or Africa, except the second, which involved the Soviet invasion of Hungary in 1956, and the eleventh, which involved the Russian invasion of Ukraine in 2022.

Nations would, in my opinion, give the United States broad support if the United States agreed not to use nuclear weapons. Secretary Bowes asked me to clarify what I was proposing. This I did. My formula was for a fully U.N.-sanctioned non-nuclear war against North Korea.

The Anders Administration was skeptical, but it did not object to the Canadian proposal. President Anders had to balance national desire to punish North Korea against a growing American sentiment that, as one commentator on MSNBC succinctly argued, "nuking children is un-American."

On July 16, Representative Boyd submitted the Canadian proposal in a letter to the president of the Security Council. The meeting of the General Assembly was delayed one day to allow all the representatives time to review the proposal and suggest amendments and revisions. After many intense behind-the-scenes discussions, a draft resolution was ready to be tabled. The most significant amendment to the original proposal was that the North Korean leader had to be given the opportunity to voluntarily surrender himself to the International Criminal Court in The Hague, Netherlands. [1] No one believed at the time that Kim Ji-ho would do this; nevertheless, the opportunity was to be provided. A second significant amendment was added that, in addition to nuclear

---

[1] The International Criminal Court (ICC) prosecutes individuals for the international crimes of genocide, crimes against humanity, crime of aggression, and war crimes. It is distinct from the International Court of Justice, which adjudicates disputes between countries. Ironically, in 2033 neither North Korea nor the U.S. accepted the jurisdiction of the ICC. In 2000, the U.S. signed the Rome Statute of the International Criminal Court, which established the ICC, but President Clinton never submitted it to Congress for ratification. In 2002, Congress enacted the American Servicemembers' Protection Act, which had the "overriding purpose" of inhibiting the U.S. government from supporting the ICC. Since then, American views on the ICC have alternated between cautious cooperation and open hostility, depending on the administration. North Korea never signed the Rome Statute.

weapons, chemical and biological weapons could not be used. Representative Vinka, on behalf the U.S., insisted that the final resolution remove those restrictions if North Korea used them first. There were a series of fractious behind-the-scenes debates about the exact wording and the time allowed for Kim Ji-ho to surrender. By the morning of July 19, the final wording of the resolution was ready for voting.

Immediately after Representative Boyd introduced the Canadian proposal to the General Assembly, Secretary Bowes gave the American speech. In it, she made numerous references to the horrific deaths and terrible suffering of the people of Seattle. She reiterated the proof of North Korea's involvement—proof that the U.N. had been sifting through for a week. After Bowes finished, North Korea's U.N. representative (and the *de facto* ambassador to the U.S.), Mun Do-hyun, made an angry denunciation of how his country was being made a scapegoat for something that "Americans did to themselves." This was a common theme in the denials coming from the North Korean government. Their argument (without submitting any proof) was that the destruction of Seattle was done by American terrorists. A more bizarre theme was blaming Japan. Here, the argument went that Japan wanted to destroy the hi-tech industry of Seattle for commercial reasons. The Japanese government never responded to these accusations.

Life in New York was not easy for Representative Mun; in fact, it was very dangerous. He claimed "many thousands" of death threats and "numerous" attempts on his life, one of which was certainly real. On July 16, Representative Mun stepped out of his limousine in front of his Manhattan residence when Kyle Bonner, a 33-year-old electrician living in Staten Island with no prior criminal convictions, stepped forward and pointed a loaded handgun at Mun. Mun's security detail wrestled Bonner to the ground and later turned him over to New York City police. Bonner was convicted of second-degree criminal weapon possession, and sentenced to three-and-a-half years in prison (the minimum sentence for the charge). He was paroled after serving fifteen months. Mun and his small staff returned to North Korea immediately after the U.N. vote.

The vote gave overwhelming support to the Canadian formula of an internationally sanctioned non-nuclear war. Of the 193 member states in the General Assembly, 180 voted to support the resolution, including the United States. There was a round of applause when Representative Vinka of the United States voted in the affirmative. One representative from Morocco was absent; he was in a New York hospital after suffering a mild heart attack caused by overwork. Six countries abstained and six voted in the negative, including unsurprisingly North Korea. The concern of those countries' governments (all authoritarian dictatorships) focused on the precedent-setting demand by the United Nations for a leader of a sovereign nation to surrender and face international justice.

The United States had now received the approval of the United Nations for its war against North Korea. All that remained was to wait and see if Kim Ji-ho would surrender himself. The date set by the U.N. resolution was August 1. To no one's surprise, the deadline came and went without the surrender of North Korea's Supreme Leader. On August 2, Kim made a defiant speech in P'yŏngyang in front of a huge cheering crowd. There were many promises of "a swift and terrible retaliation" to any attack by the U.S. with "every means available." The clear implication was that North Korea would not hesitate to use the nuclear and chemical weapons in its arsenal.

The United States had international approval for its war against North Korea. There was, however, two major obstacles around which President Anders had to navigate: North Korea's longtime supporter, China, and North Korea's new ally, Russia.

U.N. Resolution ES-13/1

Page 1 of 2 – July 19

 United Nations
A/RES/ES-13/1

General Assembly

Distr.: General
25 July 2033

Thirteenth emergency special session
Agenda item 2
Letter dated 16 July 2033 from the Permanent
Representative of Canada to the United Nations
addressed to the President of the Security
Council (S/2033/272)

Resolution adopted by the General Assembly on 19 July 2033

ES-13/1. Nuclear attack on the United States of America

The General Assembly,

Reaffirming the paramount importance of the Charter of the United Nations in the promotion of the rule of law among nations,

Condemning all violations of humanitarian law and violations of abuses of human rights,

Condemning any use of nuclear weapons, chemical weapons, and biological weapons,

Condemning the nuclear attack on the city of Seattle in the United States of America on 17 June 2033,

33-09388 (E)   250733

Please recycle

47

U.N. Resolution ES-13/1

Page 2 of 2 – July 19

A/RES/ES-13/1	**Nuclear attack on the USA**

Condemning the attempted nuclear attack on the city of Long Beach in the United States of America on 19 June 2033,

Expressing grave concern that the United States of America might, going forward, use nuclear weapons in retaliation for the noted nuclear attacks,

Finding that Kim Ji-ho, President of Democratic People's Republic of Korea, is widely suspected of authorizing the noted nuclear attacks,

1. *Demands* that Kim Ji-ho, President of the Democratic People's Republic of Korea, surrenders himself to the International Criminal Court in the city of The Hague in the Kingdom of the Netherlands no later than 16:00 local time on 1 August 2033;

2. *Supports* all subsequent diplomatic, economic and military actions by the United States of America and its allies after the noted deadline to enforce the noted demand of the United Nations, except for the use of nuclear and chemical weapons unless they are first, going forward, used by the Democratic People's Republic of Korea or its allies or agents;

3. *Condemns* the use of biological weapons going forward by any party under any circumstance;

4. *Decides* to adjourn the thirteenth emergency special session of the General Assembly.

1st plenary meeting
19 July 2033

33-09388

2/2

48

Chapter 6

Dancing with the Dragon

Be careful what you choose. You may get it.

General Colin L. Powell,
U.S. Army, Gulf War.

China and North Korea share an 880-mile border, which almost entirely follows two rivers: the Yalu in the northwest and the Tumen in the northeast. Since establishing relations in 1949, the two countries had been generally close. China was North Korea's largest trading partner. China came to North Korea's aid during the First Korean War and thereby saving the Kim regime—something that the United States has never forgotten. During the famine in North Korea during the late 1990s, China provided substantial food aid to North Korea. However, when North Korea started its nuclear program, China grew concerned about having another nuclear power on its border, and relations between the two countries cooled. Relations reached a nadir in 2017, but under President Xi Jinping, relations steadily improved throughout the 2020s. Military cooperation was always close. The Mutual Aid and Cooperation Treaty of 1961 had been in place for seven decades, and it was the only mutual defense treaty that China had.

Nevertheless, the drain on the Chinese economy of the never-ending financial aid to North Korea was a constant irritant to the Chinese government. The financial turmoil during and after the COVID pandemic of the early 2020s worsened the burden. In 2014, polling by the British Broadcasting Corporation found that only twenty percent of the Chinese people viewed North Korea positively. Fifteen years later, in a 2029 poll this number had fallen to fourteen percent. The mysterious death of the previous North Korean Supreme Leader and the rise of the young and unpredictable Kim Ji-ho caused the Chinese people much anxiety. Although no polls were done in China after Kim Ji-ho took power in North Korea, it can safely be assumed that his country's approval rating among the Chinese people would have fallen below fourteen percent, perhaps substantially so.

When Guan Zixuan took control of the Communist Party in 2030 and became its General Secretary and the President of China, he sought to improve relations with the United States—relations which had significantly deteriorated under his predecessor, Xi Jinping, and his fixation on absorbing Taiwan. However, North Korea's growing arsenal of nuclear weapons "poisoned the well," as one unidentified American diplomat described the situation. When Thomas Anders took office as President of the United States, Guan again expressed his desire to improve relations. President Anders was amenable, and the future of Sino-American relations seemed to be heading in the right direction. The Anders Administration had begun to plan a state visit for the Chinese president.

Then, Seattle happened.

At first, President Guan, like almost all leaders around the world, expressed outrage at the destruction of Seattle and sympathy for the survivors. Guan offered any aid that China could supply. When it became clear, through both American investigations and the Chinese own inquiries, that North Korea was behind the bombing, Guan's problems multiplied. He faced either abandoning the 1961 treaty of mutual defense (China's only such treaty) or supporting a pariah regime that had used nuclear weapons to destroy one city and attempted to do the same to another.

It was into this complex internal debate that American diplomats started to arrive. On July 13, the day after President Anders's denunciation of North Korea, U.S. Ambassador, Morris Carver, met with Qin Xiaobo, the director of China's Office of Foreign Affairs. Carver later testified before the Senate Committee on Foreign Relations:

> I met with Director Qin in his office. He asked me about the current situation in Seattle, which I briefly described. He wanted me to convey the Chinese people's deepest condolences to all those who had lost family in the bombing. … I then came straight to the point. I asked him what China's position was on North Korea. Director Qin was evasive and rambling in his reply. I got the distinct impression that he wasn't deliberately hiding something. It was just the Chinese government didn't know what its position was. I asked for a meeting with President Guan, and Director Qin said that he would be happy to arrange it. My meeting with him never happened because later that day Secretary [of State] Bowes announced that she would be traveling to Beijing to meet with President Guan.

Secretary Bowes arrived in Beijing very late on July 15, and she met with President Guan the next day. Bowes came with an entourage of staff and advisors. Ambassador Carver and two of his staff attended the meeting as well. President

Guan had an even larger entourage. It was a packed conference room. Secretary Bowes later testified to the Senate Committee on Foreign Relations:

> It became immediately apparent that the Chinese were very alarmed about us going to DEFCON 1. They asked for my assurances that the United States would not use nuclear weapons in North Korea. I told them that the United States was at war and that all military options were being actively considered. I then asked President Guan what China's stance was in regards to North Korea in its war with the United States. I used very strident language, which I felt was appropriate given the situation. Rather than reply, President Guan again repeated his question about our use of nuclear weapons. He mentioned fallout and prevailing winds. He seemed remarkably well versed on weather-related issues. We got nowhere in the morning, so we broke for lunch.
>
> By the afternoon, word had reached me of the approach that was being proposed by the Canadians at the U.N. I called President Anders and discussed the situation in Beijing and the Canadian approach. ... When we resumed [the meeting with President Guan] in the afternoon, I informed President Guan of Canada's proposal, and our administrations possible support for it, at least in principle. I asked him how China would vote on such a resolution if it was tabled. President Guan remained silent for some time. He then asked if we could meet in private. I agreed. The room emptied, leaving President Guan and I alone in the conference room.
>
> President Guan paced around the room in silence. Eventually, he stopped his pacing. He turned to me and said that he felt that a regime change would be good for the North Korean people. This statement greatly surprised me. I could only agree him. He then asked whether the President [Anders] had thought of the endgame, although he didn't use that word. He asked something like what North Korea would look like afterwards. I had no response. Frankly, I don't believe anyone in Washington at that time had thought about what would happen *after* the war. ... He said, and I

believe I noted his words correctly, "China will support such a resolution at the United Nations and remain neutral in this crisis, as it did during the prior crisis on the Korean peninsula, provided that the Democratic People's Republic of Korea is returned to China's sphere of political influence after the present crisis has been resolved."

As I saw it at the time, President Guan wanted us to solve his problem in North Korea, and then hand the country back to him. I didn't know how the President [Anders] would react to that. Also, the reference to the prior neutrality during the First Korean War filled me with doubt and concern.[1] Nevertheless, I balanced this against the concrete result—and deafening message to the North Korean leadership—of China's public support in the U.N. for an American attack on North Korea. I told President Guan that I would confer with President Anders and return tomorrow with his reply.

Secretary Bowes returned to the American embassy in Beijing and talked to President Anders over a secure video link for "well over an hour." The next day, Bowes again met privately with President Guan. The gist of the American reply to the Chinese proposal was a four-part plan, which the American media later dubbed the Anders Plan. First, the Kim regime would be ended, and Kim Ji-ho would be arrested and brought before the International Criminal Court. Second, North Korea would be disarmed, and all weapons of mass destruction would be destroyed or removed. Third, the U.S. and its allies would remove all fortifications and landmines from the North Korean side of the 160-mile-long, two-and-a-half-mile-wide Demilitarized Zone (DMZ),

---

[1] During the First Korean War, China remained officially neutral, but that diplomatic status did not stop it sending three million soldiers of the People's Volunteer Army into North Korea. The "unofficial" Chinese involvement prolonged the war by three blood-soaked years, and it saved the authoritarian regime of Kim Il-sung and his successors.

which separated the two Koreas.[1] Fourth, once these first three steps were complete, U.S. forces would withdraw all forces from North Korea, except that it would continue to occupy the southern border region for an unspecified period. This was to ensure that South Koreans living in Seoul and other northern cities in South Korea would no longer be living "under a constant threat of annihilation." The exact delineation of the southern border region was left vague.

President Guan agreed to first three points "without hesitation," although he requested that the destruction and removal of weapons of mass destruction be undertaken jointly with Chinese experts. Bowes indicated that she believed that would be acceptable to President Anders. On the fourth point, Guan asked for clarification regarding the status of the capital, P'yŏngyang. Bowes clarified that the capital was not part of the southern border region as far as the United States government was concerned. Guan accepted the plan provisionally, pending a detailed delineation of the southern border region and a more precise estimate of the length of time that the U.S. planned to stay there.

Secretary Bowes departed Beijing with Chinese support for an American war in North Korea. On July 19, this support was made public when China voted in favor of the U.N. resolution. The North Korean U.N. representative, Mun Do-hyun, who had many cameras recording his every gesture, was visibly shaken when the Chinese representative voted in the affirmative.

---

[1] The Korean Demilitarized Zone, or the DMZ as it was universally known, was a border buffer zone that separated North and South Korea. Although the zone itself was demilitarized, the lands on either side of the border were in 2033 (and for many decades prior) one of the most heavily militarized areas in the world. Officially, landmines were removed by both sides in 2018, but forgotten and misplaced mines were speculated to exist in large numbers. In the late 2020s, rumors and some anecdotal evidence suggested that the North Korean military was again planting landmines just north of the DMZ.

Bowes traveled from Beijing to Moscow. It was the last stop on her hastily arranged four-country trip. Russia shared a short eleven-mile border with North Korea at the mouth of the Tumen River. The Russian economy was suffering from the costly Ukraine War and the Western sanctions placed upon it as a result of that war. Its leader, the ailing eighty-year-old President Vladimir Putin, remained an international pariah. He had an outstanding warrant against him issued by the International Criminal Court in 2023 for "the war crime of unlawful deportation" and "unlawful transfer" of children from the occupied areas of Ukraine to Russia during the Ukraine War.

During the Ukraine War, North Korea had supplied the struggling Russian army with weapons. In 2024, while that war still dragged on, Putin traveled to P'yŏngyang to meet with Supreme Leader Kim Jong-un. During the visit, the two leaders signed the Treaty on the Comprehensive Strategic Partnership. The treaty renewed the lapsed 1961 mutual defense agreement that North Korea had with the Soviet Union. Both politically isolated countries benefited from the new treaty. It was a mutual defense treaty, but only if aggression was committed against one of the two countries.[1] Although Kim claimed the treaty was a military alliance, Putin was more restrained. Western analysts at the time thought that the wording left room for the Russian government to avoid helping North Korea if it so chose, particularly if North Korea was the aggressor.

---

[1] Article 4 of the Treaty on the Comprehensive Strategic Partnership stated: "In case any one of the two sides is put in a state of war by an armed invasion from an individual state or several states, the other side shall provide military and other assistance with all means in its possession without delay in accordance with Article 51 of the U.N. Charter and the laws of the DPRK [North Korea] and the Russian Federation." The reference to Article 51 of the U.N. Charter recognized a member state's right to self-defense.

Putin refused to meet with Bowes, and instead she met with the Russian minister of Foreign Affairs, Viktor Abashkin. Abashkin was an astute diplomat, who Bowes had met many times before and once after she became Secretary of State. Both shared a mutual respect of each other's abilities. Bowes needed to know how far Russia would go in supporting North Korea. Would Russia respect the treaty and come to the aid of North Korea militarily, or would it limit itself to protests and threats?

Abashkin opened the discussion by casually noting that the long-awaited international bridge joining Russia to North Korea might be soon approved by the State Duma (the Federal Assembly's lower house). Because of their long association, Bowes understood what Abashkin was not saying. The bridge over the Tumen River, which was promised by Putin at the 2024 meeting with Kim Jong-un, was seen by many Western analysts as a bellwether of the depth of commitment of Russia to the treaty. By raising the subject of the unbuilt bridge, Abashkin was implying that Russia's commitment to the treaty under the current situation could be assessed by the unbuilt status of the bridge. Abashkin then hinted that Russia might support the U.N. resolution if the United States lifted its economic sanctions and stopped its ongoing financial support to Ukraine. Bowes replied that neither were possible, but she understood that such a hint would never have been made if Russia was fully committed to the treaty.

Bowes, sensing an unspoken reluctance to support North Korea, asked whether Russia would support the upcoming U.N. resolution. Abashkin replied that Russia "would honor its debt of friendship to North Korea," which was an oblique reference to the weapons that North Korea had supplied to Russia during the Ukraine War. Abashkin's statement did not reference the treaty, which again implied that the Russian government was distancing itself from the nine-year-old agreement. He then curtly stated that Russia would vote as it saw fit and abruptly ended the meeting.

Secretary Bowes trip had resulted in two allies moving from positions of no involvement at all to providing vital logistical and intelligence support. No less important, it had reached a non-interference understanding with North Korea's long-time defense partner, China. That alone was a remarkable diplomatic achievement! As for Russia, Bowes had gained a sense that its government would not support North Korea. Military analysts at the Pentagon and in the CIA agreed with her. They concluded that the Russian armed forces were rebuilding after their near destruction during the Ukraine War and were not ready to go to war against the U.S.

Bowes communicated her beliefs to President Anders, but events had moved past diplomatic nuances. She testified to the Senate Committee on Foreign Relations:

> The United States was already at war, and Russia would have to decide whether or not to support in such a war its treaty obligations with North Korea—a country that was no longer strategically relevant to Russia and one that complicated its weakening relations with China under President Guan. ... Nobody in the State Department thought that the Russian armed forces were ready for another war.

When asked what would happen if Russia did support North Korea militarily, Bowes replied:

> President Anders was committed to serving justice on those who bombed Seattle and killed over one hundred thousand of our citizens. Congress had supported that commitment by overwhelmingly voting for war. We as a nation could not— and would not—back down from our solemn promise to the dead of Seattle. ... If Russia intervened, we would be ready.

Russia was one of six countries that voted against the U.N. resolution, but that was the extent of its support for

North Korea. It remained silent on the buildup of American forces in South Korea and Japan until after combat had begun. At that time, Foreign Minister Abashkin (and notably not President Putin) announced that because North Korea had "unlawfully attacked" the United States first, the 2024 treaty was "not applicable," and Russian armed forces would "not support" North Korea in its conflict with the United States.

North Korea had been abandoned by its allies.

Chapter 7

"Just pieces on a chessboard"

Always mystify, mislead, and surprise the enemy, if possible; and when you strike and overcome him, never give up the pursuit as long as your men have strength to follow; for an army routed, if hotly pursued, becomes panic-stricken, and can then be destroyed by half their number.

General Thomas J. Jackson,
Confederate Army, Civil War.

In the evening of Thursday, June 23, six days after the Seattle bombing, two off-duty Air Force colonels met at Amuse, a chic restaurant atop of the Le Méridien Hotel in Alexandria, Virginia. Its elevation gave its patrons a splendid view of the Potomac River, the Mall, and the political heart of Washington. Because it was within walking distance of the Pentagon, it was frequented by senior officers, politicians, top managers in the Department of Defense, defense contractors, and defense lobbyists. The two colonels were lifelong friends. They had attended the United States Air Force Academy in Colorado together, graduating in the Class of 2009. Both had seen action in Afghanistan early in their careers, but their passion was for planning. It was that aspect of their characters that had brought them together at the Academy in the first place.

Colonel Jonathon Cole was on the planning staff of Indo-Pacific Command, headquartered at Camp H.M. Smith, a Marine Corps base in Hawaii. He was in Virginia for meetings with officers from the Transportation Command regarding his command's future fuel requirements. Colonel Gilford Frizell was on the planning staff of Global Strike Command, headquartered at Barksdale Air Force Base in Louisiana. He was in town to attend a meeting with senior air force officers on the status of the Air Force's tactical nuclear ordnance. Cole had arrived from Hawaii that morning, and after a nap to recover from jetlag, he had arranged to meet his friend. As the two were in the same place at the same time, they had to "find time to catch up" on each other's lives. Frizell had suggested the expensive restaurant, and Cole agreed, but mindful of his tight family budget, he did so with some trepidation.

There was only one subject that everyone was talking about in the latter half of June 2033: Seattle. The two friends settled into the comfortable atmosphere, ordered the cheapest meal on the menu, and then speculated about who was responsible for the destruction of Seattle. Both agreed that, as the attack was on the West Coast, the most likely suspect was North Korea. They believed that Iran or Islamic terrorists would have attacked sites on the East Coast. By the end of the delicious meal, they had formulated a strategy to defeat North Korea, if that is, the United States chose to attack it. Cole later recalled:

We both thoroughly enjoyed our stimulating debate. It was like being back at the Academy. It was late by the time I returned to my hotel room, but I couldn't sleep. My sleep patterns were entirely messed up by jetlag. As I lay there, I reflected on our debate. We had convinced ourselves that North Korea was the most likely suspect [in the bombing of Seattle], and I thought that what we had discussed that night might have some future utility. I got out of bed and jotted some of our points on a hotel notepad. The next day, I arrived at my temporary office in the Pentagon and fired off an email to Gil [Colonel Frizell].[1] Gil thought that we had something. We each started to make some calls and put some flesh on the bare bones of our strategy. It was all corner-of-the-desk work [unauthorized work done on one's spare time], and networking with friends and longtime colleagues. Colonels talking to colonels for the most part.

Just before Independence Day [July 4], rumors started flying around the Center [Nimitz-MacArthur Pacific Command Center at Camp H.M. Smith] that North Korea was indeed behind the bombing. I took a summary of our work to General Yarok [Air Force Major General Karl Yarok], who then discussed it with Admiral Sentsey [Admiral Lawrence Sentsey, the commander of Indo-Pacific Command]. After that, things started to get real really fast.

The gist of Cole and Frizell's strategy for defeating North Korea was a six-part plan:

1. Discover the locations of all nuclear and chemical weapons;
2. Conduct a large bombing raid by stealth aircraft with the goal of destroying those weapons before they could be used;

---

[1] The remarkable prescient email was later supplied by the Air Force to the House Armed Services Committee as evidence of proactive planning after the attack on Seattle. It was leaked to the media soon thereafter.

Initial Email on U.S. Strategy

June 24

AIR FORCE   Cole, Jonathan, Col. <jecole@airforce.mil>

RE: Initial thoughts on NK
2 messages

Classification: UNCLASSIFIED
Encryption: N.A.
From: Frizell, Gilford K., Col. <gkfrizell@airforce.mil>
Sent: June 24, 2033 9:38 AM
To: Cole, Jonathan, Col. <jecole@airforce.mil>
Subject: RE: Initial thoughts on NK

Tx. Good idea. I agree. Check scenario inventory to see if this is covered. If not, flesh out and then send ideas up both command chains. Discuss with PACFLT what port would be best. Who in the 82A or the 101A is best to talk to? Suggest you contact them. I'll talk to 8AF and TRANSCOM. Gil.

Classification: UNCLASSIFIED
Encryption: N.A.
From: Cole, Jonathan, Col. <jecole@airforce.mil>
Sent: June 24, 2033 8:12 AM
To: Frizell, Gilford K., Col. <gkfrizell@airforce.mil>
Subject: Initial thoughts on NK

I've put down in writing our thoughts on NK. I see 6 sequential steps: 1. Find WMDs. 2. Massive stealth strike. 3. Achieve air superiority. 4. Capture airport/seaport with airborne landings. 5. Clear path thru DMZ. 6. Move on capital in force.

Can you discuss with 8AF the actual stealth capabilities of B21. And B2 and F35 too? Lets see what the B21 can really do!

Any more thoughts on this? Jon.

3. Conduct an aerial campaign on the North Korean air force with the aim of achieving complete air superiority;
4. Capture an airport or a seaport, or both, with airborne forces to enable reinforcements to arrive in North Korea;
5. Open a path through the DMZ to enable more reinforcements to arrive; and
6. Advance on the capital of North Korea, P'yŏngyang.

Their plan tended to focus on the role of the Air Force and airborne forces (not surprising for two Air Force officers). Significantly, it did not plan for a large role for South Korean forces, and it was this aspect of the plan that became of paramount importance as international events unfolded. Colonels Cole and Frizell each received an Achievement Medal from the Air Force for their initiative and "meritorious service."

On June 17, just over an hour after the nuclear attack on Seattle, President Anders ordered all U.S. armed forces to DEFCON 1. The armed forces scrambled to action stations. Although there was no one to attack on that day, the military did mobilize. Personnel were recalled from leave and weapons and machines were inspected and fueled. When the second bomb exploded offshore of Los Angeles, the commander of the Third Fleet, Vice Admiral Bertran Hankel, believed that it was an attack on America's ports, and in particular, ports located in his command area. He immediately ordered all carrier strike groups on the West Coast out to sea.

He had three carrier strike groups (CSGs) at his command: CSG-9 based at Naval Station San Diego, CSG-11 based at Naval Station Kitsap, and CSG-12 also based at Kitsap. A fourth carrier strike group (CSG-3) had been temporarily deactivated while the USS *Abraham Lincoln* underwent a major two-year refit. CSG-12, which was based around the aircraft carrier USS *Gerald R. Ford*, was already at sea and on its way back to Kitsap from Pearl Harbor. Hankel ordered the strike group to remain at sea. CSG-9, centered around the USS *Theodore Roosevelt*, departed San Diego at 06:30 on June 20. However, the USS *John F. Kennedy* and the rest of CSG-11 could not leave Kitsap. The naval base, which was eighteen miles west of Seattle, was not significantly damaged in the attack, however the blast caused a series of gigantic waves to travel outwards across Puget Sound. The ships in the naval base were thrown against the piers. The *Kennedy*, two destroyers, and two ballistic submarines of Submarine Squadron 17 (the Pacific Fleet's strategic deterrent squadron) were damaged, as were several patrol boats. The damage to the hulls of the two ballistic submarines, the USS *Maine* and the USS *Kentucky*, was extensive.[1] The damage to the *Kennedy*'s hull could be repaired in two to three weeks under normal circumstances, but it was not normal circumstances. Many sailors had been on leave in Seattle and feared dead. This, as it was later discovered, included the captain of the *Kennedy*, Captain Peter Chazelle. Many more were frantic about their families in Seattle. The rest had fallen under a presidential order to assist in the rescue operations.

The Federal Emergency Management Agency and other national and state disaster organizations were overwhelmed by the destruction in Seattle. Late on June 18, when the tremendous scope of the disaster became more evident, President Anders ordered all military personnel in the Seattle area to assist in the rescue operations. This order affected all military and civilian personnel at Naval Base Kitsap, Fort Lewis Army Base, and McChord Air Force Base, plus those at smaller bases in the Seattle area.

On July 1, the Secretary of Defense briefed the Joint Chiefs of Staff on the findings of the FBI investigation in Shanghai. The U.S. military now had an enemy on which to focus its attention. Contingency plans were activated. The

---

[1] The damage to the USS *Kentucky* was never repaired, and the submarine was scrapped in 2035. The newly commissioned USS *Wisconsin* took its place in Squadron 17.

two carrier strike groups at sea in the Pacific Ocean, CSG-9 and CSG-12, were ordered to sail to Yokosuka Naval Base in Japan. This was the home port of the USS *George Washington* and the rest of CSG-5. The Navy also ordered the four attack submarines of Submarine Squadron 1, stationed at Pearl Harbor, to make their way to Guam to reinforce Submarine Squadron 15. The four of the six surviving ballistic submarines of Submarine Squadron 17 (three of which were already at sea) were ordered to move to positions in the far western Pacific. The Air Force had already dispatched a squadron of fighters from Hawaii and another one from Alaska to reinforce the Seventh Air Force in South Korea.

At Indo-Pacific Command, contingency plans were reviewed and scenarios were considered. All that changed after Secretary of State Bowes visited Seoul on July 14. The caution of the South Korean government and its announced policy of non-participation in the conflict sent pre-existing plans into disarray. Colonel Cole explained:

Up to that moment, all our contingency plans involved us defending against frontal attack across the DMZ by North Korean forces. There was only one plan for attacking into North Korea, and that was with us playing a supporting role to South Korean forces after a large-scale incursion by the North. Prior to Seattle, the notion of us attacking North Korea by ourselves was laughable. As it turned out, the only plan we had—if you want to call it that—was the few points that Gil [Colonel Frizell] and I had developed at the fancy restaurant in Alexandria.

Prior to mid-July, I had had a few discussions with Admiral Sentsey, but nothing substantive. Two carrier groups were on their way to us from Third Fleet, as well as some fighter squadrons from the Eleventh Air Force. I made some calls to NORTHCOM [Northern Command, the command covering North America] to discuss the availability of airborne troops. After South Korean forces stood down and we were on our own, I was regularly meeting with three-star and four-star generals and admirals. I was placed in charge of expanding our high-level concepts into an implementable plan of operation. Many other groups became involved, including Global Strike Command, where Gil [Frizell] played a key role.

Before long, I was working directly for Admiral Sentsey. Another team was finding a suitable location [in North Korea] to land our forces. They were working under General Rodriguez [Marine Lieutenant General Emilio Rodriguez, deputy commander of Indo-Pacific Command]. I would meet often with him. He would give me his requirements, and I had to find units to fill them. The task was dauntingly complex. At times, it seemed like they [the units] were just pieces on a gigantic chessboard. I had to stop to remind myself that these were real people who I was choosing to put into harm's way.

More units were sent to Indo-Pacific Command. Two additional carrier strike groups were transferred from the U.S. East Coast (Second Fleet) to the western Pacific (Seventh Fleet). It would take nearly four weeks for them to cross the Atlantic Ocean, traverse the Suez Canal, and make their way to the waters off the Korean peninsula. For decades, U.S. aircraft carriers had been too large to pass through the Panama Canal, but they could transit the Suez Canal. Combat strike teams (effectively brigade-size units) from various divisions were assigned to Indo-Pacific Command.[1] They all had to be transported across the Pacific Ocean to U.S. bases in South Korea and Japan. These units included strike teams from three airborne and two infantry divisions, plus units from the First Marine Expeditionary Force based in California. Teams of special forces were also to be sent to South Korea. Of particular need were units with expertise in finding and dismantling nuclear and chemical weapons. The truly Herculean efforts by Transportation

---

[1] A complete order of battle for all U.S. and allied combat forces deployed to the Korean peninsula is provided in the appendices.

Command of transporting this army and all its supplies across the Pacific Ocean will be discussed in a later chapter.

In addition to U.S. forces, forces of allied nations were on their way to the Korean peninsula. In Canada, the political fallout from the Seattle bomb was far more extensive than the actual radioactive fallout. Prime Minister Farr vowed that Canada would be involved in "punishing" North Korea and "fulfilling the U.N. mandate." A Canadian squadron of fighters was immediately sent to reinforce the U.S. Seventh Air Force. A battalion of light infantry was promised, as were two of Canada's newest frigates. After discussions with President Anders, where America's need for transport planes was made "abundantly clear," Farr placed three squadrons of transport planes for the use of Transportation Command.

The Canadian military was thoroughly familiar with American processes and combat tactics. Joint training exercises were commonplace, and most of its officers had attended advanced courses in U.S. military training establishments. Through NORAD, the two air forces were fully integrated. President Anders readily accepted Canadian involvement, and he frequently referred to the neighboring country as "a fellow sufferer in the evil attack," but he was strangely reluctant to accept aid from other nations. There has been much speculation as to why. General John Jaynes, Chair of the Joint Chiefs, stated that U.S. supply chains were "already tight" and transport planes were "at a premium," but many have not accepted this explanation. Some believed that it was due to security concerns, while others believed that President Anders simply wanted America to punish North Korea by itself (more or less). Despite these psychological theories of a self-reliant justice, President Anders did welcome the addition of two carrier strike groups: one from France and one from Britain. South Korean special forces were already secretly working alongside U.S. special forces inside North Korea.

The French carrier strike group, its only one, was centered around the aircraft carrier *Charles de Gaulle*. The carrier and its escort of four Aquitaine-class frigates had been conducting an air-defense exercise with the Italian air force off the coast of Sardinia in the western Mediterranean Sea. From Portsmouth Naval Base in England, the British Royal Navy sent the aircraft carrier HMS *Prince of Wales*, the air-defense destroyer HMS *Defender*, and three of its new City-class frigates. Because the HMS *Queen Elizabeth*, Britain's only other carrier, was undergoing a lengthy refit, this represented the country's entire available carrier force. Both the French and British carriers had completed many exercises with the U.S. Navy. It is believed that the Navy's persistent lobbying to have these two carriers overcame the odd reluctance of President Anders to utilize allied forces, other than those from Canada. It would take three weeks for these two carrier strike groups to arrive offshore of the Korean peninsula.

On July 28, the French and British government jointly announced that they each had sent a "nuclear deterrent submarine to the seas around the Korean peninsula." The joint statement stated that the "devastating destructive power" of those submarines would only be used if North Korea "used nuclear weapons on any ship, installation, or territory of France or the United Kingdom." The submarines were the French *Terrible* and the new HMS *Dreadnaught*. The next day, the world's media solemnly recorded their departure from their respective home ports (Brest and Clyde). Flags were flying, but no one was cheering.

Two days later, President Anders, following the Anglo-French example, announced that three (actually it was four) nuclear-armed ballistic submarines were "already on station near North Korean waters," and that any nuclear or chemical attack by North Korea would be "met with a massive retaliation." These deterrent submarines were the USS *Nevada*, the USS *Nebraska* and the USS *Louisiana*, all

1980s-vintage Ohio-class submarines. Not announced to the world, the USS *District of Columbia* (the first of the new Columbia-class of ballistic submarines) was also dispatched in secret. It was exceedingly rare for the U.S. government to announce the locations of its strategic deterrent submarines, but those were unprecedented times.

As the days passed, it became obvious to all in Indo-Pacific Command that destroying North Korea's nuclear and chemical weapons before they could be used was easier said than done. Step 1 of the Cole-Frizell plan, find the weapons of mass destruction, was proving to be far more difficult than its designers had originally supposed. Before the search for these weapons is described in this history, a comparison of the military forces of the United States and those of North Korea is warranted.

Chapter 8

Comparison of Armed Forces

If we desire to avoid insult, we must be able to repel it; if we desire to secure peace, one of the most powerful instruments of our rising prosperity, it must be known, that we are at all times ready.

General George Washington,
Continental Army, War of Independence.

The Second Korean War was asymmetric. It was so by design—by North Korean design. By the early 1980s, it became obvious to the regime of Kim Il-sung that his country could no longer compete with the growing military might of South Korea, which was funded by a rapidly expanding modern economy. The North Korean leadership decided that it had to change to a deterrent strategy, and it did this by developing and deploying nuclear and chemical weapons. The programs that developed these weapons will be reviewed in the next chapter. As a consequence of its deterrent strategy, North Korea's armed forces withered, particularly those that required advanced technologies, such as its navy and its air force. Before the conventional weapon platforms are examined, the military command structure of the two combatants will be reviewed.

Command structures

The armed forces of North Korea were controlled by the General Staff of the Korean People's Army. The General Staff reported to the Workers' Party Central Military Committee. The chair of that committee, and also the general secretary of the party, was the Supreme Leader; and in 2033, that leader was Kim Ji-ho. In theory, the Supreme Leader shared control of the government with the Premier, who managed domestic affairs, and the Assembly President, who managed legislative affairs. In reality, the Supreme Leader controlled the party, the government, the military, and the country. The power of the General Staff had diminished significantly during the regime of Kim Jong-un, and his successor, Kim Ji-ho, continued the regime's tight grip on the military.

The Korean People's Army controlled five forces: the ground force, the naval force, the air force, the strategic force (which operated the ballistic missiles), and the special operations force. An astounding thirty percent of the population were part of the active military, the military reserves, or various paramilitary organizations. This was the largest per-capita participation in the world. Five percent of its population were part of its active military, also the largest per-capita participation in the world. For comparison, South Korea had 1.2 percent of its population in the active military, and the U.S. had 0.4 percent. On a numerical basis, North

Korea's active military was the fourth largest in the world, behind China, India and the U.S., and just ahead of Russia.

The U.S. also had a large military, the third largest in the world, and of primary importance, it had a truly massive technological advantage over North Korea. The U.S. military was organized into seven unified combat commands and four functional commands. The combat commands were Northern (North America), Southern (South and Central America), European, African, Central (Middle East), Indo-Pacific, and Space. The functional commands were Strategic, Transportation, Cyber and Special Operations.

It was Indo-Pacific Command that planned and managed the Second Korean War. In the theater of operations, the command had at its disposal the United States Forces Korea (which comprised primarily of the Eighth Army and the Seventh Air Force), the Fifth Air Force from the U.S. Forces Japan, the Third Marine Expeditionary Force (stationed on the Japanese island of Okinawa), and the Pacific Fleet's Seventh Fleet and Submarine Fleet. As the war progressed, reinforcements from other commands were integrated into the applicable ground, naval and air forces under Indo-Pacific Command's control. Assets from Strategic and Transportation commands were also employed, particularly the bombers from Global Strike Command's Eighth Air Force and the large airlift aircraft from Air Mobility Command's Eighteenth Air Force. Units from Special Operations Command were also deployed for a wide range of missions.

Air forces

During and after the Second Korean War, two American aircraft captured the public's imagination: the B-21 Raider and the F-35 Lightning II. Both were technologically advanced stealth aircraft, and both were used to great utility.

North Korea's Military Command Structure

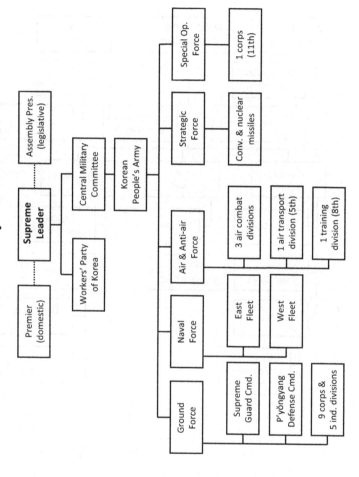

U.S. Combat Command Structure

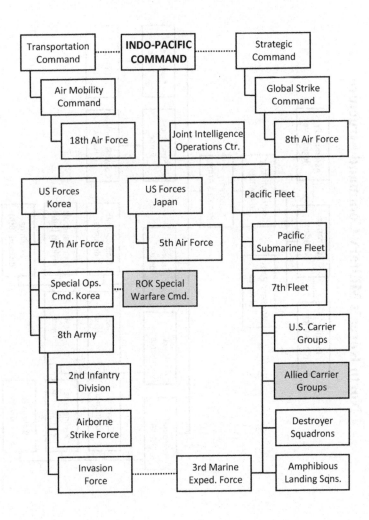

The delta-wing Northrop Grumman B-21 Raider first flew in 2023, and by 2033, it had been deployed in two bomber squadrons of the Eighth Air Force (the 9th and the 34th). The Raider was a stealth bomber that had a weapon load capacity of ten tons. It had a wingspan of 132 feet and a cruising speed of Mach 0.8. The Raider had a crew of two, and although it had the capability of being unmanned, all missions during the Second Korean War were manned. Originally, the Air Force had intended that the Raiders would replace its 1980s-vintage B-1 Lancers by the late 2030s and its 1990s-vintage B-2 Spirits by the early 2030s. There was even talk of it eventually replacing the venerable B-52 Stratofortresses—a plane that first flew in 1952 and had been frequently updated and retrofitted ever since. In 2033, due to cost overruns and production delays, the Air Force had only twenty-four Raiders in two squadrons of twelve each. As a consequence, the retirements of the Lancers and the Spirits were delayed.

The delta-wing Northrop Grumman B-2A Spirit was the immediate predecessor of the Raider. It was similar in appearance and speed, but its weapon load capacity was twenty tons, twice that of the Raider. Its wingspan was 172 feet, some forty feet wider than the Raider. The Spirit had a crew of two. The planes were very expensive to build and maintain. As a consequence, the production program was canceled in 1998. Twenty-one were built, but one (the *Spirit of Kansas*) crashed in 2008. In the summer of 2033, two Spirits were undergoing extensive maintenance. Eighteen Spirits flew missions during the war.

The Rockwell B-1B Lancer was a supersonic bomber with a maximum speed of Mach 1.25. The B-1B was the production variant of the B-1A prototype and had a smaller radar signature than the prototype. The Lancer had a variable wingspan of 137 feet in extended mode and 79 feet in swept mode. One hundred were made, but due to several crashes and many retirements, by 2033 only forty-one remained to participate in the war. The bomber's weapon load capacity of twenty-five tons was larger than that of the Spirit and the Raider. It had a crew of four.

The long-serving Boeing B-52 Stratofortress was the other bomber used during the war. The last Stratofortress was built in 1962. Because of underinvestment during the 1990s in a replacement bomber, the old bomber remained in service until its replacements were available in large numbers. The Stratofortress was a large subsonic aircraft with a wingspan of 185 feet, and as non-stealthy as a modern bomber could be. It had a crew of five. Two variants flew during the war: the B-52H and the newer B-52J. The latter had more powerful retrofitted engines and newer radar and communications equipment. The B-52J was considered a complement to the Raider's capabilities, and so allowed for diverse missions. Only two squadrons had received the retrofitted aircraft (the 11th and the 23rd). The Stratofortress had three distinct advantages over the more modern bombers: a larger weapon load capacity (thirty-five tons), a longer range, and a much cheaper operational cost than any of the more modern bombers (which was a major consideration in the endemically cash-strapped Air Force). Of the seventy-two Stratofortresses in the Air Force's fleet, which included those in reserve and used for tests, all fifty in Global Strike Command participated in the war.

The other American aircraft to capture the public's attention was the Lockheed Martin F-35 Lightning II. This versatile stealth fighter was a joint Anglo-American project, co-funded by many other NATO countries. It had significantly advanced electronics and avionics. It could act as a standoff launch platform, or it could be used as a sensor node in data gathering. It did, however, require frequent and careful maintenance, but by 2033, the serious reliability issues of the early 2020s had been resolved. The Lightning came in three variants. The primary variant, the F-35A, was used by many NATO air forces. The F-35B could take off and land vertically, but it had a smaller weapon load capacity than the F-35A. It was used by the Marine Corps and by some allied navies on their smaller carriers. The F-35C was specifically designed to be used on U.S. carriers. It had a longer range and reinforced landing gear, but it had a smaller weapon load capacity than the F-35A. By 2033, the Lightning had replaced most of the Air Force's older fighters, and it had entirely replaced the fighters used by the Navy and the Marine Corps.

During the war, the British aircraft carrier flew the F-35B Lightning II, while the French carrier flew the older Dassault Rafale M (the marine variant of the French air force's Rafale with a substantially reinforced landing gear to cope with the increased stresses of carrier landings). It was a multi-role fighter, but it was not as stealthy as the F-35B and it did not have the ability to take off and land vertically.

Two other fighters saw action during the war: the older F-22 Raptor and the newer F-15EX Eagle II (often called the Super Eagle by its pilots). Both were multi-role strike fighters and both were much faster than the Lightning (Mach 2.5 versus Mach 1.6), but the agile Eagle lacked the Lightning's stealth and its complex sensors, but it was more affordable. The older Raptor was considered even more stealthy than the Lightning, but it lacked the sophisticated onboard sensors of the newer aircraft.

The odd-looking Fairchild Republic A-10C Thunderbolt II, affectionately nicknamed the Warthog, was a subsonic close-support attack aircraft. It mounted a 30-mm rotatory cannon and a wide variety of bombs, missiles and rockets. The 1970s-vintage aircraft was in the process of being retired from the Air Force, and only one squadron remained: the 25th, which happened to be stationed at Osan Air Base in South Korea. The squadron saw considerable action during the latter part of the war. The last Thunderbolt was retired in 2035, and it is currently on display at the National Air and Space Museum in Washington, D.C.

USAF Aircraft

Bombers

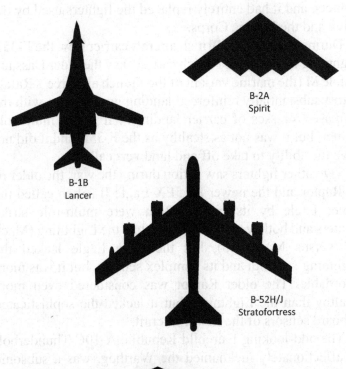

B-2A
Spirit

B-1B
Lancer

B-52H/J
Stratofortress

B-21
Raider

50 ft / 15 m

USAF Aircraft

Fighters, transports and UAVs

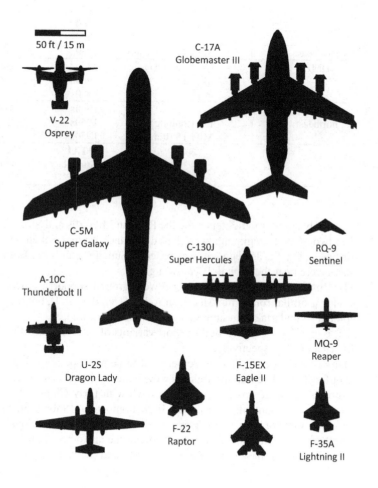

50 ft / 15 m

V-22
Osprey

C-17A
Globemaster III

C-5M
Super Galaxy

C-130J
Super Hercules

RQ-9
Sentinel

A-10C
Thunderbolt II

MQ-9
Reaper

U-2S
Dragon Lady

F-15EX
Eagle II

F-22
Raptor

F-35A
Lightning II

North Korean Fighter Strength

Air div.	Region	No. of regiments	Type of fighters	Vintage	No. of fighters
1	West coast	2	MiG-29	1980s	35
		1	Su-25 (support)	1980s	34
		1	MiG-23	1970s	56
		1	MiG-21	1960s	20
		2	F-6	1960s	97
2	East coast	4	MiG-21 & F-7 mix	1960s	68
3	DMZ	1	Q-5 (support)	1970s	30
		1	MiG-21	1960s	8
		4	F-5	1950s	56
8	Far northeast	2	F-7	1960s	60
		1	F-5 (training)	1950s	50
		1	MiG-15 (training)	1950s	4
				TOTAL	**518**
				Operational	~ 450
				"Modern"	69

Notes:
- Relatively "modern" fighters were the Russian MiG-29s and Su-25s. The two MiG-29 regiments were based at Sunch'ŏn and Pukch'ang air bases. The Su-25 regiment was based at Sunch'ŏn air base. Both bases were near the capital, P'yŏngyang.
- The Russian Su-25 and Chinese Q-5 were ground-support fighters, having a similar role to the American A-10C Thunderbolt II, but they could also undertake air-supremacy missions if required.
- F-5, 6 and 7 are Chinese-build export variants of the Russian MiG-17, 19 and 21, respectively.
- Many of the older fighters were believed to be non-operational and kept for show. The training fighters were believed to be unarmed.
- A bomb regiment was on each coast, each with forty Chinese H-5 bombers, a variant of the Russian Il-28 bomber (a 1950s-vintage aircraft). Some of these bombers were believed to be non-operational.
- Another air division (the Fifth) was home to the air force's transport aircraft. It was based on the west coast and headquartered in Taech'ŏn.

Naval Forces of the Korean People's Army

	West Fleet	East Fleet
Headquarters	Namp'o	T'oejo Dong
Number of bases	6	9
Frigates (2013+)	-	1
Frigates (pre-2013)	1	-
Corvettes (2013+)	-	3
Corvettes (pre-2013)	3	3
Stealth missile boats	-	7
Missile boats	10	10
Torpedo boats	30	57
Patrol boats	77	110
Submarine bases	Pip'a-got	Ch'aho
Submarines (ballistic)	-	6
Submarines (attack)	20	40
Submarines (midget)	24	12

Notes:
- The KPA navy was a riverine or "brown-water" navy. It was intended to operate within 50 kilometers (27 nautical miles or 31 miles) of the coast. It was primarily used for guarding the coast and for supporting infiltration mission into South Korea. The two fleets could not support each other during wartime due to the range limitations of their warships.
- The five of the six ballistic submarines were built between 2023 and 2030. The first one was built in 2014 as an experimental prototype, and in 2033, it was believed to be non-operational. Most of the attack submarines were old and considered obsolete. All submarines were powered by diesel engines when on the surface and electric batteries when submerged.

In 2033, the Air Force had three large transport aircraft: the propeller-driven Lockheed C-130J Hercules, the Boeing C-17A Globemaster III, and the giant Lockheed C-5M Galaxy. The load capacity of these aircraft was 21 tons, 85 tons and 140 tons, respectively. The Globemaster could also aerially deploy up to 102 paratroopers, and this capability was used during the war. Air Mobility Command's Eighteenth Air Force had three types of refueling aircraft: the McDonnell Douglas KC-10 Extender, the Boeing KC-46 Pegasus, and the Boeing KC-135 Stratotanker. These aircraft gave the Air Force its global reach, and they were extensively employed during the war.

The Air Force also deployed many types of unmanned aerial vehicles (UAVs or drones) in a number of roles: most notably, the stealthy, delta-wing Lockheed Martin RQ-170 Sentinel for reconnaissance, and the General Atomics MQ-9 Reaper to provide a remote-controlled offensive option.

In glaring contrast to the modern U.S. Air Force, the air force of North Korea was obsolete, and many of its older aircraft were non-operational and kept just for show. Most of its fighters were built before 1980, and its bomber fleet dated from the 1950s. Its most modern fighters were the Mikoyan MiG-29 and the Sukhoi Su-25 (the latter of which was primarily a close-support aircraft, similar in role to the Thunderbolt). Both were introduced into service in Russia in the early 1980s, and North Korea acquired them after the fall of the Soviet Union. The North Korean air force had over five hundred fighters, but only the sixty-nine MiG-29s and Su-25s could in any way be considered modern; the rest were obsolete or non-functioning.

The North Korean air force was divided into three combat divisions, one training division (the Eighth), and one transport division (the Fifth). The combat divisions covered the west coast (the First), the east coast (the Second), and the DMZ (the Third). In the far northeast of the country, besides its primary role in training, the Eighth Air Division had some old fighters that were capable of combat. All the best fighters were kept close to the capital.

Navies

Like its air force, the North Korean navy was old. It was designed to be a riverine (or "brown-water") navy, as it was not intended to operate more than thirty miles from the coast. Its primary tasks were to guard North Korea's coasts and to support infiltration missions into South Korea. The navy was divided into two fleets: one on the west coast and one on the east. Due to the range limitations of the North Korean warships, the two fleets could not support each another in wartime.

In 2033, the North Korean navy had only two frigates (only one of which could be considered modern), nine corvettes, and many smaller boats. It had sixty old diesel-electric attack submarines, most of which dated from the 1960s to the 1990s, with a few newer ones dating from the early 2010s. It did, however, have six modern diesel-electric ballistic-missile submarines that could launch nuclear-armed missiles. They were integral to North Korea's deterrent strategy. At the start of the war, five of these submarines were operational and at sea.

In stark contrast, the modern and powerful U.S. Navy was a potent symbol of America's global reach. Its offensive power was centered around the carrier strike group, which consisted of a large, nuclear-powered aircraft carrier, four or more destroyer escorts, and several support ships. The U.S. Navy had eleven carrier strike groups, nine of which were operational in 2033, and four of those were in the Pacific Ocean. Of those in the Pacific, two were based in the Puget Sound area of Washington State, one was based in San Diego, California, and one was forward based in Yokosuka, Japan. The carriers were either of the Nimitz class or of the newer Ford class. Each carrier had four squadrons of ten F-

35C Lightning II fighters each, plus squadrons of other aircraft used for electronic warfare, reconnaissance, early warning, refueling, search-and-rescue, and logistics.

Each aircraft carrier was escorted by four or more destroyers. All but one were variants of the Arleigh-Burke class: specifically, Flights IIB and III. They were armed with ninety-six missile cells, a five-inch gun, and a number of machine guns. The sole exception was the USS *Norman Scott*, which was the first, and in 2033, the only destroyer in the Scott class—a class that was developed out of the Next Generation Guided Missile Destroyer (DDGX) program of the 2020s. The Navy also had three "experimental" stealth destroyers of the controversial Zumwalt class, two of which saw action during the war.

The U.S. also had a large, modern submarine fleet. All its attack submarines were various "blocks" (variants) of the nuclear-powered Virginia class. The latest block, Block V, had the Virginia Payload Module, an extra compartment just aft of the conning tower that contained additional missile silos. It also had a deterrent fleet of submarines armed with nuclear-armed ballistic missiles. They were all of the 1980s-vintage Ohio class, except one that was of the new Columbia class.

Armies

Unlike its air force and its navy, North Korea's army had not withered. It had a mix of modern and obsolete equipment, but its real strength was its sheer size. In absolute numbers, its military was the fourth largest in the world, with over 1.2 million active soldiers, sailors and pilots, 600,000 reservists, and nearly six million men and women who participated in various paramilitary organizations. Combined, the U.S. armed forces had almost 1.4 million servicemembers, but it was logistically impossible and politically inconceivable to transport all of them to North Korea. As tensions rose prior to the war, the North Korean reservists were called up, and the U.S. faced a military force of 1.8 million men and women, plus more in local paramilitary units.

The quality of the North Korean army varied widely. Its special forces were well equipped and highly motivated, whereas its regular infantry had a mix of equipment and a mix of morale levels. Those closest to the capital, such as III Corps and the P'yŏngyang Defense Command had the best equipment and the highest morale. The soldiers in the Supreme Guard Command, whose duty was to guard the Supreme Leader, were considered fanatical in their loyalty.[1] Those units guarding the DMZ had a mix of equipment, but morale was believed to be high. Those units assigned to the northern part of the country had old equipment and little support. Rumors of northern units starving or having to use forced civilian labor were rampant in the West, and more likely than not these rumors had some foundation in fact. Morale in the more remote units was anticipated by American planners to be low, and the fighting quality of the paramilitary units was generally thought to be poor. Given the authoritarian system in which the North Korean military existed, American planners anticipated that the battlefield initiative of low-level and mid-level officers would be poor to nonexistent, and that the high-level officers would be rigid and formulistic in their strategies and tactics. The war painfully demonstrated that this optimistic appraisal was often false.

---

[1] This command was known by several designations over the years, including Escort Bureau, Bodyguard Command, General Guard Bureau, and Unit 936. (Nine is considered a lucky number in Korean society, so double nine—9 and 3+6=9—is doubly lucky; conversely, the number 4 is considered unlucky and is avoided, because in Korean, it sounds like the word for death.) General Cho Nam-jun, Kim Sang-hui's husband, was the commander of the Supreme Guard Command before he and his wife defected in December 2032. After Cho's defection, General Nang Ha-joon, a close confidant of Kim Ji-ho, was given the command.

The army's four independent mechanized divisions and its one independent tank division were well equipped and morale was anticipated to be high. The four mechanized divisions were the 108th, the 425th, the 806th and the 815th, and the tank division was the 820th. Only the 425th was based on the east coast; all the others were located on the west coast.

Domestically produced tanks varied from the Ch'ŏnma (an older design based on the Soviet T-62) to the P'okp'ung-ho (a mix of T-62 and T-72 technology). The latest tank was the M2020 (a U.S. designation), which was based on the new Russian T-14 Armata tank, but only a few were ever made, and those that were available were kept near the capital. The North Korean army also fielded some imported Soviet tanks (T-54, T-55, T-62 and T-72).

Armored personnel carriers were available in large numbers. Domestically produced models included the M2010, which copied its design from the Russian BTR-80, and the M2023, which appeared to be a copy of the Canadian-made M1126 Stryker—a vehicle widely used in the U.S. Army. Imported Russian BTR-80s and the smaller BTR-60s were also used.

North Korean artillery had many older towed howitzers and some newer self-propelled artillery using Ch'ŏnma chassis or those of old Soviet tracked vehicles. Caliber sizes ranged from 120-mm to 180-mm guns. The army had a number of older rocket-launching vehicles, plus the modern KN-09 and KN-15 guided rocket systems.

Although its air force was obsolete, its air defense network was not—or not as much. Its domestically made KN-06 mobile air defense missile launcher was available in large numbers, plus there were many air defense systems imported from Russia and China. It also fielded a network of antiquated anti-aircraft guns that had been upgraded to be radar controlled. Domestically produced man-portable systems were widely dispersed throughout the army. Most were based on Russian or Chinese designs, but one appeared to be based on the American FIM-92 Stinger air-defense missile system.

In contrast, the American soldiers and marines who participated in the war were well equipped, and after Seattle, highly motivated. All the units involved were good and many were considered to be elite. For the U.S., the ground war in North Korea was largely an infantry battle, and few vehicles were involved, at least initially. The M1126 Stryker infantry carrier vehicle, the M3 Bradley cavalry fighting vehicle, and the M1 Abrams main battle tank (with its 120-mm main gun) were the primary American combat vehicles used in the war.

The U.S. also fielded a variety of helicopters in the roles of combat support, transportation and logistics. The Boeing AH-64 Apache was outstanding in its combat support role. The Sikorsky UH-60 Black Hawk was used extensively in its troop-transport capacity, while the tandem-rotor Boeing CH-47 Chinook was used as a heavy-lift cargo transport and logistical support. The tiltrotor Bell Boeing V-22 Osprey was used by the Marine Corps for combat transport, and by the Navy for logistical support.

With this brief overview of the two combatants complete, it is now time to see how the military forces were used during the war.

Part II

The Air Force's War

Chapter 9

Searching for WMDs

The truth is no one knows exactly what air fighting will be like in the future. We can't say anything will stay as it is, but we also can't be certain the future will conform to particular theories, which so often, between the wars, have proved wrong.

Brigadier General Robin Olds, Jr.,
U.S. Air Force, Vietnam War.

Weapons of mass destruction, or WMDs, include nuclear, chemical and biological weapons. The phrase was made famous (or infamous) in 2003 during the Iraq War. The Bush Administration insisted that Iraq had WMDs, specifically chemical weapons (which the Iraqi military had in the past used against its own population). [1] President Saddam Hussein, Iraq's dictator, did not definitively deny the American claim, and he refused to let U.N. inspectors verify the nonexistence of the WMDs. After the U.S. military invaded Iraq, an extensive search was conducted for WMDs, but none were found, much to the political embarrassment of President Bush and his administration. American analysts had failed to appreciate the pathological need of dictators to always appear powerful to the people who they rule. To a dictator, weakness—real or perceived—means the dictator's rapid downfall and subsequent death or incarceration. In 2033 and for decades before that, there was *absolutely* no doubt at all that North Korea had WMDs.

North Korea began its nuclear weapons development program in the early 1980s. After some pauses and missteps, the program finally achieved its goal. On October 9, 2006, North Korea became the world's ninth nuclear power when it successfully exploded a small nuclear device in an underground test. The yield of the devices was less than one kiloton, but that did not matter because larger weapons would come—and they did. By 2013, it was estimated that North Korea had some ten nuclear warheads. By 2020, this number had risen to between thirty-five and sixty-five, and by 2033, it was estimated that the country had around 130 warheads. Most of the warheads were believed to have yields of between ten and thirty kilotons of TNT. North Korea attempted to develop larger yields using hydrogen fusion,

---

[1] On March 16, 1988, in the final year of the Iraq-Iran War, the Iraqi military attacked the Kurdish town of Halabja, in northeastern Iraq, with chemical weapons. Between 3,200 and 5,000 people (mostly civilians) died and another 7,000 to 10,000 were injured. Rates of cancer and birth defects increased for years after the attack. Prior to this attack, there had been at least twenty-one smaller-scale chemical attacks on Iraq's Kurdish minority. The chemicals used on the inhabitants of Halabja were likely a combination of mustard gas (a sulfur-chlorine compound) and the nerve agents Tabun, Sarin and VX (all of which are organophosphorus compounds).

but there was no evidence of such warheads in North Korea's arsenal in 2033. Throughout the 2010s and 2020s, North Korea developed the missiles to deliver the warheads. By 2033, nuclear-armed missiles could easily hit South Korea, Japan and Hawaii, and cities on the west coast of the United States were achievable targets. Throughout the 2020s and early 2030s, spirited debates occurred in the U.S. about the accuracy of these missiles, but there was a general consensus that they would hit somewhere near the targeted city.

North Korea began its chemical weapons manufacturing program in 1954, just after the First Korean War. The program greatly expanded in the 1980s, and by 2009, North Korea had become the third largest possessor of chemical weapons in the world, behind the U.S. and Russia. By late 2023, North Korea, which never signed the U.N.'s Chemical Weapons Convention of 1992, was the only country in the world with confirmed stocks of chemical weapons.[1] North Korea was generally believed to have between 3,000 and 7,000 tons of chemical weapons in its arsenal in 2033, up slightly from what it had a decade before.

North Korea once had a nascent program to develop biological weapons, but the program never had the same priority as the development of nuclear and chemical weapons. After the global COVID pandemic of the early 2020s demonstrated the inherent mutagenicity (and hence uncontrollability) of viruses and bacteria once released into

---

[1] The Chemical Weapons Convention (officially called the Convention on the Prohibition of the Development, Production, Stockpiling and Use of Chemical Weapons and on their Destruction) was passed in 1992 and came into force in 1997, with prescribed deadlines and allowable extensions. All signatories to the convention, along with all countries that later acceded to it, committed to destroy their stocks of chemical weapons. As required by the Convention, the U.S. declared that it once had 33,600 metric tons of chemical weapons. Its last chemical weapon was confirmed destroyed in July 2023. Over ninety-eight percent of the world's chemical weapons have been destroyed since the Convention was enacted.

the general population, North Korea realized its own vulnerability and the feebleness of its healthcare system. Starting in 2026, North Korea's government began to make public denouncements condemning the use of biological weapons. Sometime around that time, it is believed that the government closed down all its bio-weapons research. The country did, however, have a modern post-COVID medical research facility in Kaech'ŏn, which was completed in 2027. The facility was known to store many dangerous biological samples—samples which could (in theory) be weaponized in the future. The P'yŏngyang Biotechnical Institute in the capital was, since 2015, suspected of storing such samples. It was uncertain whether it continued to do so in 2033, because samples would have likely been transferred to the newer facility in Kaech'ŏn.

The issue of supreme importance facing American planners during the summer of 2033 was identifying the locations of these weapons of mass destruction. They had to search a secretive country of 46,541 square miles. At the Pentagon and at CIA headquarters in Langley, Virginia, decades of data were sifted and analyzed. Discovering the storage locations of North Korea's nuclear and chemical weapons had always been a high priority. Many facilities were suspected to various degrees of confidence. To reduce the number of possible targets, the National Reconnaissance Office, headquartered in Chantilly, and the National Geospatial-Intelligence Agency, headquartered at the Fort Belvoir Army Base (both in Virginia), analyzed hundreds of thousands of satellite images.

In a heavily redacted report to Congress, the CIA described its work with the special forces and intelligence organizations of South Korea to refresh and confirm the data. It is now known that South Korea's 9th Special Forces Brigade (the "Ghost Brigade") undertook infiltration missions to visually reconnoiter suspected facilities. How many missions is not publicly known. On at least one of the missions, a team from the U.S. 23rd Chemical Battalion accompanied a squad from the 51st Battalion of the Ghost Brigade. This mission involved a reconnaissance around a suspected chemical weapons storage facility near Sariwŏn, a city halfway between the DMZ and P'yŏngyang. Those U.S. soldiers could have been the first Americans to enter North Korea during the war. That mission will be described in more detail later in this history.

Although little is publicly known about all these clandestine efforts (because many of the tactics used remain closely guarded secrets), the end result is known. Twelve probable nuclear weapons storage facilities and five probable chemical weapons storage facilities were identified with various levels of confidence. Two storage facilities for dangerous biological samples, which could be weaponized in the future, were identified as well. It was assumed by American analysts that the management of WMDs in North Korea would be very tightly controlled, and more relevantly, highly centralized with only a limited number of well-guarded facilities. Consequently, it was likely that only a few of the identified facilities would actually store WMDs.

More well known by the public are the efforts by the Air Force and the Navy to identify the locations of the weapon platforms that could be used to deploy the WMDs. These platforms were long-range artillery hidden in numerous shelters near to the DMZ and the modern ballistic submarines operating out of Ch'aho Naval Base on the East Sea.

Possible WMD storage facilities

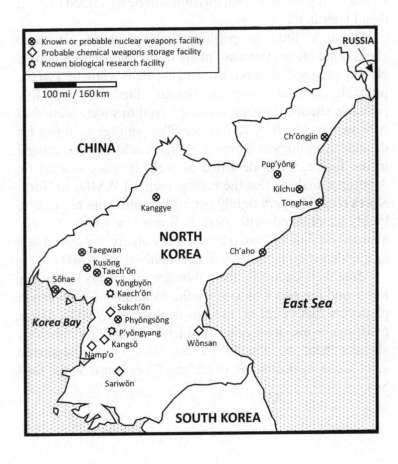

- ⊗ Known or probable nuclear weapons facility
- ◇ Probable chemical weapons storage facility
- ✿ Known biological research facility

100 mi / 160 km

RUSSIA

CHINA

Ch'öngjin ⊗

Pup'yöng ⊗

Kilchu⊗

⊗ Kanggye

Tonghae ⊗

NORTH KOREA

⊗ Taegwan
Kusöng ⊗
⊗Taech'ön
Söhae
⊗ Yöngbyön
✿ Kaech'ön
△
Sukch'ön
◇
Korea Bay
⊗ Phyöngsöng
✿ P'yöngyang
◇◇ Kangsö
Namp'o
◇
Sariwön

Ch'aho ⊗

East Sea

◇ Wönsan

SOUTH KOREA

Confidence on Possible WMD Sites

WMD	Location	Confidence	Remarks
Nuclear	Ch'aho	High	Naval base for ball. subs
	Ch'ŏngjin	Low	Undgrd. nuclear fuel fac.
	Kanggye	High	Adv. weapons prod. fac.
	Kilchu	Very high	Based on classified intel.
	Kusŏng	Low	Weapons testing facility
	Phyŏngsŏng	Medium	Research facility
	Pup'yŏng	Low	Fac. near nuclear test site
	Sŏhae	Low	Satellite launch complex
	Taech'ŏn	Very high	Undgrd. nuclear fuel fac.
	Taegwan	Low	Missile production facility
	Tonghae	Medium	Missile launch complex
	Yŏngbyŏn	Medium	Nuclear research facility
	Deployed	*High*	*Ballistic subs at sea*
Chemical	Kangsŏ	Medium	Near a chemical plant
	Namp'o	Medium	Near a chemical plant
	Sariwŏn	Very high	Based on classified intel.
	Sukch'ŏn	Low	Near a chemical plant
	Wŏnsan	Medium	Underground air force fac.
	Deployed	*Medium*	*Shelters for artillery*
Biological	Kaech'ŏn	Very high	New bio-research facility
	P'yŏngyang	Low	Old bio-research facility
	Deployed	*Very high*	*No bio-weapons deployed*

Notes:
- The chemical storage facilities at Sariwŏn and Wŏnsan were believed to store chemical artillery shells. The facilities were not too far away from the underground artillery shelters near the DMZ.
- U.S. and allied air forces were ordered not to bomb the two biological research facilities due to concerns that some of the samples might escape.

North Korea's two satellite-launching complexes, Sŏhae on the west coast and Tonghae on the east coast, might also have had nuclear warheads stored for immediate use. In addition to launching satellites, these facilities tested regional and intercontinental ballistic missiles. Sŏhae had been active since 2012. The older complex at Tonghae was mothballed in 2014, but it was reopened and refurbished in 2028. It was believed that the refurbished site's sole purpose was to launch regional and intercontinental missiles at Japan, Hawaii, and the U.S. mainland. No satellites were ever known to have been launched from the refurbished facility.

To augment the analyses of satellite images, the Air Force sent two of its last remaining U-2 spy planes close to the DMZ, but not over it. The Air Force had planned to retire the 1950s-vintage Lockheed U-2Ss in 2025, but the retirement date was delayed several times. The ability to rapidly respond to urgent surveillance requirements was something that satellites simply could not do. The spy plane could take off and climb to its mission altitude of 60,000 feet in twelve-and-a-half minutes. In 2033, only two reconnaissance squadrons of U-2s remained: the 1st based at Beale Air Force Base in California and the 5th based at Osan Air Base in South Korea. Each squadron only had two U-2s left. The final two U-2s assigned to the 5th had been scheduled to retire in October 2033, and the pair in California a month later. After that, the Dragon Lady (as the U-2 was affectionately known) would end its remarkable seventy-six years of service with the Air Force. The bombing of Seattle postponed that retirement.

Colonel Dale Cormack later remembered his first U-2 flight after Seattle:

I took the Lady [the U-2] up to mission altitude [60,000 feet]. My flight plan did not authorize me to cross over the DMZ. I paralleled the DMZ from west to east and then back again. I took oblique photos and videos of road movement and suspected artillery shelters. The 411 [intelligence] was that there a number of them in the Mount Taedun area. I did five circuits before returning to base. As soon as I landed, Tailor [the call sign of Colonel Anthony Francesco] took up the other Lady. Between the two of us, we had near-continual coverage of the terrain just to the north of the DMZ. It was good to take her [the U-2] back up for some last missions. I didn't think I'd get the chance again, but I sure wished it had been under happier circumstances.

Reconnaissance deeper into North Korea was undertaken by stealthy RQ-170 Sentinel drones from the 44th Reconnaissance Squadron. The drones had been airlifted to Kadena Air Base in Japan, although their operators remained at Cheech Air Force Base just outside of Las Vegas, Nevada. The drones could not go as high as the U-2, but they were far stealthier, virtually undetectable. Their radar cross-section was like that of an insect. For comparison, the radar cross-section for a Lightning was comparable to a medium-sized bird, while that of the Raptor was like a small bird. The radar cross-sections of a Spirit and a Raider (which were larger aircraft) were a little larger than a bird. The older Lancer had a radar cross-section about one hundred times larger than that of a Spirit. The venerable Stratofortress and the propeller-driven Hercules both had radar cross-section one hundred times larger than that of a Lancer and ten thousand times that of a Spirit.

Lieutenant Christine Yellen was one of the Sentinels' operators. She later recalled:

At the start of my duty, I walked across the base to the portable control hut. It was desert-hot outside, but as soon as I got inside, I was blasted by the a/c [air conditioning]. The electronics were sensitive to the heat. Because all my missions were without weapons, I was alone in the hut, although I was in constant communications with Flight

Control [at Cheech]. I logged on and waited for Kadena [air traffic control at Kadena] to give me clearance [to take off].

I had a [fuel] duration of five to six hours, depending on how I handled her [the drone]. It took me about an hour-and-a-quarter to get across the Sea of Japan, more if there were strong headwinds. Being at Kunsan or Osan [air bases in South Korea] would have been optimal for the mission, but I heard that those bases were crazy busy. The distance [from Japan to North Korean airspace] did, however, give me time to get to mission altitude [50,000 feet] at a leisurely rate of climb, and that saved a lot of fuel.

Once in hostile [North Korean] airspace, I kept the Wraith [the unofficial nickname for the Sentinel] steady. No tight turns. Most of my missions were on the other side of the peninsula, north or south of P'yŏngyang. Dangerous airspace, but I never got hassled. The 411 [intelligence] was that [North Korean] radar coverage was weaker to the northeast of the capital, so that was the direction I approached. Once I was over the mission's target, I started the cameras. I don't know how many shots I took. Must have been many thousands, but I never saw any of them. After I landed the Wraith back at Kadena, I logged off and left the hut. It was always hot outside. A real dry heat. Others found it stifling, but I liked it. Usually, I went straight to the canteen to get some coffee and something to eat.

Once the ground crew at Kadena had prepped the Wraith for the next mission, either I returned to the hut, or Jen [Lieutenant Jennifer Tully], the other operator, took over. If we ever had some downtime together, Jen and I compared missions. She thought she'd been locked on once [detected by radar]. Exciting, but nothing happened.

I flew all over the enemy without ever leaving my base. Occasionally, I got a twenty-four-hour pass, which I spent in [Las] Vegas. That was my war.

By the first of August, the Air Force believed that it had an excellent understanding of where the artillery shelters were located. Many of them were dug into the southern foothills of Mount Taedun. Others were found to the west of

Kaesŏng, and a few were found to the northeast of the village of Ch'olwŏn. In all, nineteen shelters for long-range artillery were located. The Air Force was confident that it had found them all, and that was what it told President Anders.

While the Air Force and special forces attempted to identify WMD targets inside North Korea, the Navy was tasked with finding North Korea's ballistic submarines. There were six of them, and all were capable of launching three Pukguksong-3 (or KN-26) missiles with nuclear warheads. One of the submarines was in port at Ch'aho Naval Base. It had been tied up at its berth for years. It is believed that this submarine, the *8.24 Yongung* (the *August 24th Hero*), was the original prototype of the Sinpo class of ballistic submarines. Built in 2014, it was nearly a decade older than the next submarine in the Sinpo class. It was assumed that the prototype had been placed in North Korea's naval reserves. Five more of the Sinpo-class submarines had been built between 2023 and 2030. It was the Navy's mission to find them, and when the order was given, to sink them.

The three Virginia-class attack submarines of the Navy's Submarine Squadron 15 (based in Guam) were the first to arrive offshore of the Korean Peninsula. The USS *Vermont* was already there when Seattle was attacked. It had been conducting a routine patrol in the deep waters of the East Sea.[1] It was tracking one of the new ballistic submarines, which could not be confused with the older and noisier attack submarines. Commander Anton Zeligs, the captain of the *Vermont*, described it as "like listening to a computer hum compared to the noise from a distant washing machine, but

---

[1] This sea is called the East Sea by Koreans, because it is to the east of the Korean peninsula, and the Sea of Japan by the Japanese. Herein, it is called the East Sea. It is a deep sea with a maximum depth of 12,276 feet and an average depth of 5,700 feet. The sea to the west of the peninsula is the Yellow Sea, a very shallow sea with a maximum depth of 499 feet and an average depth of barely 150 feet.

with the superb acoustical sensors we had on board, we could find both [types of submarines]."

By the end of June, the USS *Washington* and USS *Arizona*, which had both been moored at Polaris Point Submarine Base in Guam, had joined the *Vermont*. The four submarines of Submarine Squadron 1, based at Pearl Harbor in Hawaii, arrived near the peninsula in mid-July. They focused their search in the shallow Yellow Sea and the Korean Strait. Although the modern North Korean submarines were believed to have a range of 1,500 nautical miles (1,700 miles), in the past they had not strayed too far from waters around the Korean peninsula.

Commander Bain Williston, the captain of the USS *Hawaii*, recalled arriving on station to the west of the Korean peninsula in the Yellow Sea:

We arrived on July 12. The shallow sea was a bitch for us to work in. The acoustics were awful. The sea had a maximum depth of 500 feet, but most places it was barely 150 feet! It was an excellent place for the North Koreans to hide their boomers [ballistic submarines]. They could just sit on the bottom and wait for orders. North Koreans thought that we wouldn't dare risk our boats [submarines] in those shallow waters—and perhaps they'd have been right if the Chinese had been involved [in the war].

We immediately discovered two of the older [attack] submarines, even with all the poor acoustics of the shallow sea. They were noisy fuckers. My deaf grandma could've heard them. None of those old subs were [nuclear missile] launch capable. We noted their location, course and speed, and then moved on. On July 15, we found one of the new [ballistic] subs. We tracked it closely. From that moment on, I was running silent with only one mission. My orders were to stay on its ass and blow it to hell if it opened its [silo] hatches.

As it turned out, the Sinpo-class submarine that the *Hawaii* found was the only one found in the Yellow Sea. The

Vermont had already found one in the East Sea, and the *Washington* and the *Arizona* found two more, also in the East Sea. By the end of July, only one Sinpo-class submarine remained undetected, and that caused much anxiety within the Navy.

Possible Long-range Artillery Shelters

August 1

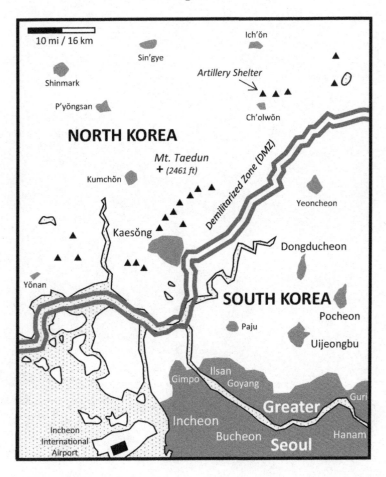

Chapter 10

TRANSCOM

Men without weapons in modern war are helpless, but weapons without men are nothing.

General Omar N. Bradley,
U.S. Army, World War II.

It is over 5,500 miles from the U.S. West Coast across the Pacific Ocean to South Korea, and nearly 7,000 miles from the East Coast. In order for America to attack North Korea and bring justice for the dead of Seattle, tens of thousands of personnel and millions of tons of materiel had to be transported over that long distance. The task fell to Transportation Command, or TRANSCOM, one of the U.S. military's functional commands. Much of the burden was placed on Air Mobility Command and on the pilots, technicians and aircraft of the Eighteenth Air Force.

One of the first tasks was to get reinforcements of fighters to the Seventh Air Force in South Korea. A squadron of Lightnings and a squadron of Raptors flew from their bases in Hawaii and Alaska, respectively, and headed out across the Pacific. Five KC-135 Stratotankers of the 93rd Refueling Squadron (based at Fairchild Air Force Base near Spokane, Washington) took off to rendezvous with them. Major Manfred Wiltz remembered his first flight after Seattle:

Being based near Spokane, on the other side of the state from Seattle, we weren't caught up in the aftermath of the Seattle attack or in the Presidential order to assist in the rescue efforts. Everyone on the base was in a daze after the attack. No one from the Wing King [Colonel Charles Kenchester, the commanding officer of 92nd Wing] down to the most unpolished nugget [raw first-time pilot] had a fucking clue what we were supposed to do. It was such a relief when orders finally came through.

My flight [of three Stratotankers] took off at 12:30 on June 26 [West Coast time] to rendezvous with the F-22s [Raptors] of the 525th flying out of Elmendorf [Air Force base near Anchorage, Alaska]. We had almost a full squadron to ferry across the Pacific. Twenty-two planes in all [another two were undergoing maintenance and remained at Elmendorf]. We stayed with the F-22s until we handed over the mission to the 909th [Refueling Squadron based at Kadena Air Base, Japan]. They took the F-22s the rest of the way to Osan [Osan Air Base, South Korea]. After the handoff, we headed back to Elmendorf to refuel. The F-22s had drained us dry [of fuel]. Jesus Christ, it felt good to be doing something.

Captain John Albright of the Canadian 437th Transport Squadron had a similar experience. He flew an Airbus CC-150T Polaris (one of two refueling aircraft converted from an Airbus A310-300). His squadron was based at CFB Trenton, a Canadian Forces Base in Ontario. He later recalled:

I departed CFB Trenton on Canada Day [July 1] and headed to CFB Cold Lake [in Alberta], with the other Polaris following behind. We refueled and then took off in the company of eight Lightnings from 401 Squadron. The flight across the Pacific was uneventful, and we landed in South Korea on-time and without incident. We then flew back to Cold Lake, filled up [with fuel], and escorted the squadron's final eight Lightnings. Once that was done, we returned to Trenton. Upon my arrival there, I was informed that our entire wing [the 8th Wing] had been put on call for the Americans to use. My squadron was busy enough, but I heard that 429 [squadron] was working nonstop. Their Globemasters [CC-177 Globemaster III, the Canadian variant of the American C-17A] were always in the air. No downtime at all.

Once the Anders Administration became convinced that the attack on Seattle was undertaken by North Korea, the movement of materiel to South Korea and Japan moved into high gear. In June, the reinforcement of two fighter squadrons was undertaken only as a prudent contingency; in July, the endless movement of materiel was done with a grim determination. After the President's public denouncement of North Korea on July 12, everyone in Air Mobility Command wanted to be involved.

Brigadier General Benjamin Crossman of Air Mobility Command was given the task of planning the movement of personnel and materiel from the U.S. to South Korea, Japan and Guam. General Crossman remembered it as a daunting assignment:

It was an enormous undertaking, made worse by the fact that plans were nebulous and ever-changing. I had to foresee every contingency. It quickly became clear, at least to me, that there would be a prolonged air campaign [over North Korea] before the army became involved, so I put my priority there. I had ordnance of all kinds transported to the

Seventh [Air Force in South Korea]. And parts too. Food, fuel, computers. Everything from nuts and bolts to missiles and helicopters. At one time, all our C-5s [Lockheed C-5M Galaxies] from both Travis and Dover [air force bases in California and Delaware, respectively] were in the air at the same time. I can't remember that ever happening before.

On the receiving end of this aerial conveyor belt of reinforcement and supplies, the commander of the Seventh Air Force, Lieutenant General Lionel Amos Dunn (a Californian and universally known by his callsign "L.A."), had to find a place for everything. He recalled:

The runways at both Kunsan and Osan [air bases] were busy 24/7 [all the time]. Both bases were jammed with equipment. If we could send anything to Camp Humphreys [the large army base nearby], we did. Space was at a premium. Fortunately, until plans solidified, we weren't bringing in additional personnel, other than the fighter pilots and some extra maintenance technicians. Finding quarters for them all would've been a nightmare in those early days. My staff needed time to arrange things. It was eighteen-hour days for everyone.

It was not just the air bases in South Korea that were working nonstop, but also the U.S. bases in Japan, Guam and the United States. Transport planes were constantly taking off and landing at bases all across the U.S.—bases such as Little Rock, Travis, Fairchild, Dyess, Dover and Charleston. All this activity was in addition to the humanitarian aid that was being flown to Seattle. McChord Air Force Base in Tacoma was the hub for receiving this aid.

The Air Force was not alone in this heightened level of activity; the Navy was also moving assets across the Pacific. It was clear to everyone in the Navy that one carrier strike group would not be nearly enough. Seventh Fleet and Carrier Strike Group 5 (CSG-5), which was centered around the

USS *George Washington*, had to be reinforced—and substantially so. Already part of the Pacific Fleet, CSG-9 and CSG-12 from Third Fleet were ordered to sail to Yokosuka Naval Base in Japan. Half a dozen oilers and replenishment ships sailed with them. Damage to the USS *John F. Kennedy* from the mountainous waves caused by the nuclear explosion, and the loss of a significant portion of its crew, precluded sending the carrier and the rest of CSG-11 to Japan—a significant loss. To compensate for this loss and to provide additional offensive power, two carrier strike groups from Second Fleet on the East Coast were dispatched: CSG-8 and CSG-2, which centered around the USS *Harry S. Truman* and the new USS *Enterprise*, respectively. The *Enterprise*, the latest Ford-class carrier, had only just completed her post-commission shakedown cruise. These two Atlantic-based carrier strike groups left port on July 9, and it would take them four weeks to reach the waters around the Korean peninsula.

In San Diego, the landing ships of Amphibious Squadron 7 were loaded with vehicles and equipment. If an invasion of North Korea was ordered, the single marine brigade on Okinawa would not be enough. The marines based at Camp Pendleton, just north of San Diego, would be air transported to Okinawa later, once plans matured. There, they would be reunited with their equipment.

The United Nations's deadline of August 1 came and went without Kim Ji-ho surrendering himself—to no one's surprise. Immediately afterwards, the airlift began to transport soldiers in larger numbers. Army and marine personnel were bused to nearby air bases and flown to South Korea, Guam and Okinawa. They flew primarily on Boeing C-17A Globemaster IIIs, but other military and civilian aircraft were also used, including six Boeing 777s requisitioned from American Airlines and United Airlines (three each).

On August 2, immediately after the U.N. deadline expired, Major Wiltz of the 93rd Refueling Squadron noticed a sudden change:

> Everything moved into high gear. I felt on edge for the first time since the operation began. Everyone around the base [Fairchild Air Force Base] was speculating about when something big would start. Such talk was discouraged, but it happened anyway. You don't move all that stuff across the ocean and then do nothing with it. Everyone knew that the attack would come soon. We [in the United States] did. The North Koreans did. The world did. You only had to turn on the news to hear someone taking a guess as to when. It was a circus out there.

Relevant Military Bases in the U.S. and Canada

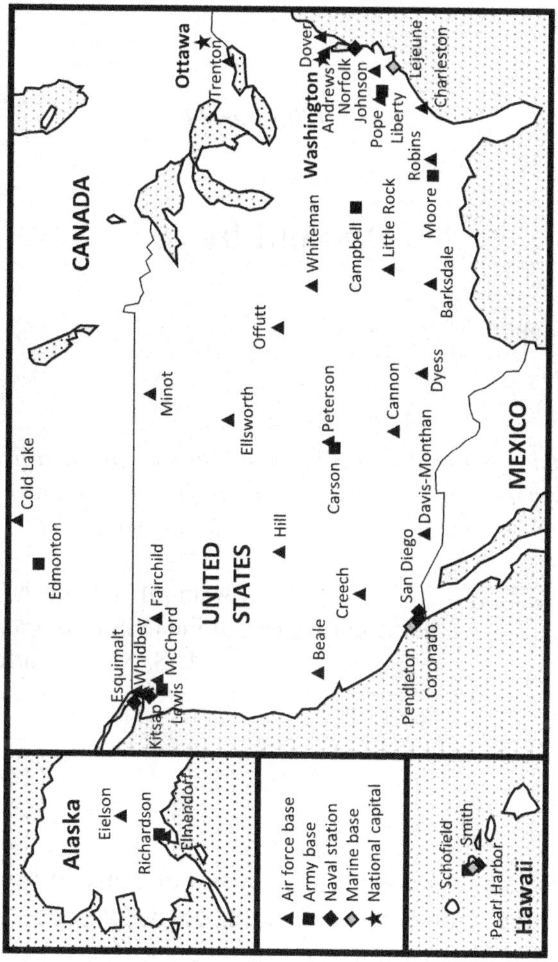

Chapter 11

"Stand by ..."

I am convinced that a bombing attack launched from such carriers from an unknown point, at an unknown instant, with an unknown objective, cannot be warded off.

Rear Admiral William A. Moffett
at the christening of the USS *Lexington*, 1925,
U.S. Navy, World War I.

August 2 and 3 were a time of frantic activity in the Eighth Air Force. Bombers were being loaded at bases all across America. The Air Force's entire fleet of Lancers, Spirits and Raiders were being loaded with a wide variety of bombs and missiles. In South Korea and Japan, Lightnings and Raptors were being loaded, as were the Navy's Lightnings on board the aircraft carriers in the seas around the Korean peninsula.

H-hour had been set for 22:00 on August 4 Korean time (09:00 in Washington, D.C., and 06:00 in Seattle), and everything had to be ready. The Air Force intended to fly its entire fleet of stealth bombers from their bases in the U.S., across the Pacific, and arrive over targets in North Korea in a carefully timed and tightly coordinated attack. The margin for error or mischance in this ambitious operation was tiny. Depending on the base from which the bombers departed, the flight times to the targets in North Korea were between ten and fifteen hours. The speed of the bombers was limited by the speed of the command-and-control and refueling aircraft which accompanied them. The demands placed upon the limited number of refueling aircraft meant that the bombers flew without fighter escort. The last stealth bomber in the aerial armada took off from Ellsworth Air Force Base in South Dakota at 07:45 on August 3, local time. The opening move in Operation Retribution was underway.

Colonel Charles Trang, the commander of the 28th Wing based at Ellsworth, recalled:

It was a tremendous achievement by my ground crews. We got all thirty of the wing's bombers [ten Raiders and twenty Lancers] into the air, fully loaded and on time. The schedule was unforgiving. All my bombers and the bombers from two other wings [the 7th and the 509th] had to arrive over their targets precisely on time. The logistics of that were daunting. I took great satisfaction that the men and women in my wing had achieved precisely what I had asked of them. My pilots were well trained, and the aircraft were in great shape. The ground crews had made sure of that. We all knew the stakes, and everyone was fully committed to the mission. It was payback time.

I watched the last of my wing take off with mixed emotions. I was proud of my staff, but I envied the two squadron commanders. I wish I could go with them. All I could do now was wait. For me, that was the hardest part. After the ceaseless activity and clear purpose of the past few weeks, the quiet and stillness of the base seemed somehow unnatural. When the last B-1 [Lancer] took off, I had a moment of dread when I realized that some of them might not return. Such brooding was counterproductive, so I tried to get some sleep. It would be fourteen hours before my bombers were over their targets. I flopped down in my bed in my uniform and immediately fell asleep. I had been awake for nearly thirty-two hours.

Master Sergeant Amilia Emon of the 37th Bomb Squadron in Colonel Trang' wing remembered the intensity of the loading work:

The loading schedule was really tight! When we started, I didn't know how we were going to do it. It was just insane. The hangers were a mess of equipment and ordnance. I had to take extra care that everything was tracked. We couldn't just load the ordnance in any order, it had to be done right. It was mission-critical that the most precise bombs were dropped first.

All the bombs were guided units [laser-guided or GPS-guided bombs], mostly 31s and 24s, but we also had to deal with the larger 28s and some of the older 10s. No dumb [unguided] bombs were allowed. Precision was absolutely mission-critical. The Wing King [the wing commander, Colonel Charles Trang] had really pounded that into us. The deep pens [massive GBU-72 and GBU-79 deep penetration bombs] were a bitch to load. Fortunately, there were only a few of those. The old B-1s [Lancers] were easier to load than the new B-21s [Raiders]. Those new birds [aircraft] were unforgiving, but there was less to load [because their weapon load capacity was less]. Me and my squad of load toads [ordnance loaders] really did our jobs on that day. It was real sat [satisfactory] to see all our birds take off on time.

Virtually all of the Air Force's fleet of stealth bombers were airborne—six squadrons, an armada of forty Lancers, eighteen Spirits and twenty Raiders. One Lancer did not take off due to a major mechanical failure, and two Spirits were left behind because they were undergoing extensive maintenance. In total, seventy-eight stealth bombers headed towards targets in North Korea.

The bombers carried a variety of guided bombs. The most common were the 2,000-pound GBU-24 laser-guided penetrating bombs and the GBU-31 GPS-guided bombs. There were also twenty 4,000-pound GBU-28 laser-guided penetrating bombs. Ten of the Spirits each carried advanced penetrating bombs for deep targets. The 5,000-pound GBU-72 and the new 10,000-pound GBU-79 were specifically designed to destroy deep underground facilities storing weapons of mass destruction.

No sooner had the bomber fleet left U.S. airspace than it was joined by a fleet of refueling aircraft from the Eighteenth Air Force. Major Manfred Wiltz of the 93rd Refueling Squadron out of Fairchild Air Force Base recalled his flight that day:

We rendezvoused with the 393rd [a squadron of ten Spirits out of Whiteman Air Force Base in Missouri]. There were two of us [two Stratotankers]. Everyone had a back-up on that day.

The flight was routine for the most part. There was one terrifying moment when the bomber that I was refueling developed a mechanical issue with its fuel-intake system. My [refueling] overpressure alarm sounded and we had to abort immediately. That certainly scared the crap out of me. It had never happened in training, except on simulators. The bomber [the *Spirit of Missouri*, the oldest Spirit] had to disengage and change course to Elmendorf [Air Force Base in Alaska]. A second bomber [the *Spirit of Texas*], developed an engine problem near the end of the flight, and it had to land in Japan [at Misawa Air Base].

USAF Ordnance Used in North Korea

bombs

Ordnance	Nom. weight (lbs.)	Description
Unguided bombs		
BLU-109	2,000	Penetrating for fortified targets
BLU-111 Mk 82	500	General-purpose bomb
BLU-116	2,000	Advanced penetrating for deep targets
BLU-117 Mk 84	2,000	General-purpose bomb
BLU-118/B11	2,000	Thermobaric ("vacuum") bomb
Unguided cluster bombs		
CBU-87 CEM	1,000	202 bomblets
CBU-89/B Gator	1,000	72 AP mines and 22 AT mines
CBU-97 SFW	1,000	40 target-seeking "skeets"
CBU-103/4/5 WCMD	1,000	CBU-87/89/97 with wind-correcting kit
CBU-112 Hammer	2,000	36 incendiaries for chem/bio targets
Guided bombs		
GBU-10	2,000	Laser guided
GBU-12	500	Laser guided
GBU-15	2,500	TV and infrared guided
GBU-24	2,000	Laser guided, penetrating
GBU-28	4,000	Laser guided, penetrating
GBU-31 JDAM	2,000	BLU-117 with GPS-guided JDAM kit
GBU-43/B MOAB	20,000	Airburst for large-area targets
GBU-57 MOP	30,000	Deep penetration for very deep targets
GBU-72 A5K	5,000	Adv. penetration for deep targets
GBU-79 NGP	10,000	Adv. penetration for very deep targets

Notes:
- Many unguided BLU-117 bombs were retrofitted with a JDAM "bolt-on" packages to make them into guided bombs. They were then redesignated as GBU-31s.
- Many cluster bombs were retrofitted with a wind-corrected munitions dispenser, a tail-mounted kit that improved accuracy. When this was done, the bomb's designation changed from CBU-87, 89 and 97 to CBU-103, 104 and 105, respectively.
- The maximum effective launching range for bombs was around ten miles.
- Abbreviations: BLU – bomb live unit; CBU – cluster bomb unit; GBU – guided bomb unit.

USAF Ordnance Used in North Korea

missiles

Ordnance	Nom. weight (lbs.)	Max. Range (miles)	Description
Air-to-ground missiles			
AGM-65 Maverick	500	14	Tactical targets
AGM-88 HARM	800	180	Anti-radar
AGM-114 Hellfire	100	7	Precision armored targets
AGM-154 JSOW	1,000	80	Precision defended targets
AGM-158 JASSM	2,200	575	Stealthy cruise missile
AGM-187 LRSO	2,200	1,800	Long-range cruise missile
Air-intercept missiles			
AIM-9X Sidewinder	188	22	Short range
AIM-120 AMRAAM	356	112	Medium range
AIM-260 JATM	253	120	New medium range

Note: Numerous variants of the missiles were deployed, which vary in warhead, targeting systems, range, speed, vintage, and other characteristics.

We also left the squadron over Japan and landed to refuel. I remember watching the bombers fly away from us as we started our descent into Misawa. The sun had just set, but I could make them out against the fading evening glow. They were heading into enemy territory. At the time, I still couldn't quite grasp it. It was just too big. We were going to bomb the hell out of a country. Then, I remembered Seattle.

At Nimitz-MacArthur Pacific Command Center (the headquarters of Indo-Pacific Command at Camp H.M. Smith in Hawaii), Colonel Jonathan Cole watched the progress of the aerial armada. He later recalled:

I stood with Admiral Sentsey and General Yarok. None of us spoke. The operation was underway, and there was nothing any of us could do now. A hundred bombers and refueling aircraft were heading to North Korea. Screens graphically showed their progress. It was up to the [bomber] crews as to whether the op [operation] was successful or not. In no small way, I had set this op into motion, and I felt completely responsible for its success. I was so keyed up. The margin of error was non-existent. Everything had to work right today—and that certainly wasn't the norm for military operations, not in my experience anyway.

The bombers were on their way, so I turned my attention to the naval situation. Confirmation reports started coming in from task force commanders. Fighters from seven carriers, when you include the British and French [carriers], were due to be launched. Next, it would be the turn of the fighters from bases in South Korea and Japan. Soon three hundred aircraft would be entering North Korean airspace. When that happened, there was no turning back. I remember thinking at the time that it might take a long time to win the war, but we could lose it on that one night. No pressure there!

In the seas around the Korean peninsula, seven carrier strike groups began to launch their fighters, electronic-warfare planes and command-and-control aircraft. In the East Sea, the USS *George Washington*, the USS *Theodore Roosevelt*, the USS *Gerald R. Ford* launched their aircraft. It took over an hour for the strike groups to launch and assemble. To the west in the Yellow Sea, the USS *Enterprise* and USS *Harry S. Truman* did the same. Fighters from HMS *Prince of Wales* and the French carrier *Charles de Gaulle* joined them. Each aircraft had a mission to perform, and there were back-ups for each of them. It was assumed by military planners that some things would go wrong, so planners at Indo-Pacific Command had built in redundancy in every one of those missions.

Lieutenant James Wu was a catapult officer (or "shooter" in Navy jargon) on board the *Roosevelt*. He remembered the evening of August 4:

> The action never stopped. Plane after plane, squadron after squadron. I don't remember ever sending so many planes airborne at the same time. I was responsible for launching the Fists [the Fists of the Fleet, F-35C Lightning IIs of the 25th Strike Fighter Squadron] and some of the Rooks [EA-18G Growlers of the 137th Electronic Attack the Squadron]. Fourteen planes in all. One of the catapults malfunctioned near the end of my shift, but I used the other one until it was fixed, which took maybe ten minutes. Everyone was on their game that night.
>
> Afterwards, I returned to my squadron's [the 25th] operations room. Jesus, it was crowded. Everyone wanted to see what was going to happen. Our CO [commanding officer] let everyone stay, provided they kept out of the way and remained quiet. You could've heard a pin drop in that room.

The air officer (or "air boss") on board the *Ford*, Commander Martin Baquer, also recalled hectic activity of that evening:

We had all of our fighters in the air, plus our Growlers and both Hawkeyes [electronic warfare planes and command-and-control planes, respectively]. We had three missions that night. There were two targets to attack: the submarine base at Ch'aho and a possible nuclear weapons storage site near Kilchu. We were also providing CAP [close air patrol] over the *GW* [USS *George Washington*] and the *Roosevelt*, as well as ourselves. The mission board was full. One Lightning had an aileron issue and had to return, but otherwise, everything went okay. We had trained relentlessly for this. Thank God we did, because if we hadn't, it would have been a Charlie Foxtrot [clusterfuck] for sure.

Back at the Nimitz-McArthur Pacific Command Center on Hawaii, one issue was giving Admiral Sentsey and his subordinates considerable anxiety: the missing North Korean ballistic submarine. North Korea had six ballistic submarines. The oldest was in port and had been for years; it was widely assumed that it was non-operational. The whereabouts of four others had been discovered by U.S. Navy's attack submarines. The USS *Hawaii*, the USS *Vermont*, the USS *Washington* and the USS *North Carolina* were stealthily following these four submarines, ready to sink them when ordered. The recently arrived *North Carolina* had taken over from the USS *Arizona*, because that Block V submarine had another mission to complete that night. One enemy submarine was left unaccounted for: a submarine that could potentially launch three nuclear-armed missiles at targets in South Korea or Japan, or at the American fleet.

According to Colonel Cole, Admiral Sentsey was "visibly relieved" when, at 01:16 Hawaii time (20:16 Korean time), he was informed that the USS *Delaware* had finally found the missing submarine hiding on the shallow bottom of Korea Bay, not far from the Chinese coast. Cole remembered that "We were told that the *Delaware* was closing in on its target and would be within attack range within half-an-hour. What a relief!" At that time, H-hour was less than two hours away. History might have been very different—and possibly horrific—if that submarine had remained undetected for just a few more hours.

Meanwhile, elsewhere under the sea, five Block V Virginia-class submarines were preparing to launch a massive volley of Tomahawks cruise missiles. Their launches would be coordinated with the aerial attack by the bombers and fighters currently approaching North Korean airspace.

Far away in North Carolina and in the equatorial region of the Indian ocean off the African coast, another operation was underway: Operation Negate. Two destroyers from Fifth Fleet, the USS *Quentin Walsh* and the USS *Delbert D. Black*, had been detached from their escort duties for the aircraft carrier USS *George H.W. Bush* in the Arabian Gulf. The destroyers had reached their assigned location earlier that day, where they awaited orders from Space Command, headquartered in Peterson Space Force Base, Colorado. Both destroyers had been assigned to that command for this particular operation. Later that day, two F-15EX Eagle IIs took off from Seymour Johnson Air Force Base in North Carolina and headed out over the Atlantic Ocean. They too were assigned to Space Command. The objective of these two disparate forces was to destroy North Korea's two known reconnaissance (spy) satellites.

Between 2023 and 2025, North Korea launched four military satellites. One was destroyed when the rocket exploded just prior to leaving the atmosphere. Another one made it to orbit, but failed to turn on. However, the other two worked perfectly. The North Korean government proudly announced the fact, and it went as far as publishing photographs of the White House and the Pentagon to demonstrate the operational status of their two satellites. Space Command had been carefully monitoring these two satellites for a decade. It had been decided by President Anders, upon the advice of the Joint Chiefs, to destroy these enemy satellites, despite that the U.S. would be reneging on an international treaty it signed and originally sponsored.

In 2022, the United Nations adopted an anti-satellite weapon testing ban, a ban that the U.S. promoted and the European Union endorsed. Prior to that date, the U.S. had been the only nation to successfully destroy a satellite in space. Throughout the 2020s, Russia developed such weapons, but never tested them in space. The reason for the ban was that there was (and still is) a very real concern that the debris field created by the destruction of a single satellite could cause a cascading effect. Such an effect could destroy many orbiting satellites and severely damage worldwide communications for years. Such devastation is called "collisional cascading" or the "Kessler effect," named after NASA scientist Donald Kessler, who theorized it in 1978. This effect was the subject of a 2013 Hollywood movie called *Gravity*.

Despite the theoretical risk, Space Command believed that they could safely destroy the two North Korean satellites, provided a tight window of time was respected. The first satellite was to be destroyed by a low-yield RIM-161 missile fired by one of the destroyers (the other ship was a back-up). The second satellite was to be destroyed by an old ASM-135 multi-stage missile launched from one of the two Super Eagles, with the other serving as back-up. The two old ASM-135 (two of the fifteen built in mid-1980s) were brought out of the Air Force's reserves and revamped to substantially *lower* the warhead yield. Guidance systems were far better in 2033 than they had been in the 1980s, so larger yields of yesteryear were no longer required. Space Command predicted that the two debris fields would be minimal because kinetic energy hitting the satellites was considerably reduced from the tests undertaken decades before.

At Space Command headquarters in Colorado, General David Whitechurch stood at the back of the operations center and listened to the mission control officer, Lieutenant Colonel Eduardo Marla, talk to the technicians at their desks. Whitechurch remembered the moment:

I stood there listening to Colonel Marla. He was asking various technicians for a status check. I glanced at the wall clock. It was 06:59 [in Colorado]. Another clock displayed that it was 21:59 in North Korea. Marla shouted out the one-minute warning. My gut tightened up. If this wasn't done right, I could be responsible for destroying the world's communications network. I had visions of me seated before a Senate committee with my grim-faced lawyer sitting beside me and television lights nearly blinding me. They [the senators] would be howling for blood—my blood. And rightly so. It was upon my recommendation to the Joint Chiefs that, if done right, the collateral damage from this mission would be minimal to non-existent. If I was wrong, I deserved what was coming. Others were risking much more than their career on that night.

I remember watching the seconds tick by. Time moved so slowly that night. Every second seemed like an eternity. I was brought back from my melancholy reflections of my impending disgrace by Colonel Marla. Satisfied with the responses from his technicians, he shouted "The board is green. Stand by. Launch order imminent. Stand by…"

I prayed to God that I was right.

Chapter 12

Night of the Bats

Strategic air attack is wasted if it is dissipated piecemeal in sporadic attacks between which the enemy has an opportunity to readjust defenses or recuperate.

General Henry H. Arnold,
U.S. Army Air Force, World War II.

Officially, it was called Operation Cyclone, part of the larger Operation Retribution, but that name never caught the public's imagination. The *New York Times* called it "The Night of the Bats," after the silhouette of many of the stealth bombers involved, and that name stuck.

Strikes on WMD Sites

August 4

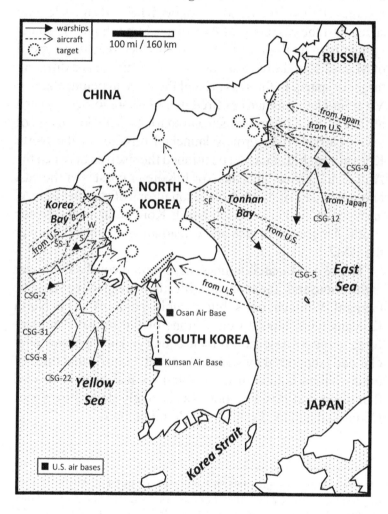

At H-hour on August 4, 22:00 Korean time, a great many events, separated by great distances, all happened at once. Orders were extremely clear about the timing of events. In the Indian Ocean, an Arleigh-Burke class destroyer, the USS *Quentin Walsh*, launched a single RIM-161 missile into space. Off the east coast of America, a Super Eagle flew near vertically to its flight ceiling of 60,000 feet, reaching a speed of Mach 2.5, and fired a single AST-135 missile at a different target in space. In the seas around the Korean peninsula, five Virginia-class submarines fired two Mark 48 torpedoes each at five North Korean ballistic submarines. The destroyers of seven carrier strike groups launched missiles at the North Korean warships that had positioned themselves between the American carriers and the North Korean coast. On the east and west coast of North Korea, squadrons of stealth bombers and stealth fighters entered North Korean airspace. To the south, American, British and Canadian warplanes flew over the DMZ.[1]

The two anti-satellite missiles, simultaneously fired over eight thousand miles apart, hit their respective targets. General Whitechurch's big gamble paid off. The North Koreans were blind to the actions of the massive military force about to descend on their country. The Russians later claimed (supported by widely disputed "proof") that three of their civilian communication satellites had been destroyed that night, but this assertion was strongly denied by Space Command and by the Anders Administration.

---

[1] Unpacking the complex military action of the night of August 4/5 is a daunting task for any historian. For readers interested in a more detailed account of this night, the scholarly article *A detailed timeline of U.S. aerial and naval operations on August 4 and 5, 2033*, by retired Air Force Major John Gilshaw, provides a comprehensive timeline of events. His many charts and maps were carefully, and enthusiastically, scrutinized by this author.

Underwater, the five North Korean ballistic submarines that were at sea were destroyed by U.S. attack submarines. Commander Anton Zeligs, the captain of the USS *Vermont*, remembered it as being like "an exercise":

We had been tracking the enemy boomer [ballistic submarine] for twenty-five days straight. In that entire time, we only lost it once. We reacquired it eighteen hours later, but that was a tense eighteen hours. If it were not for the fact that the [North Korean] subs had to recharge their batteries on the surface, we might not have reacquired—at least not in time. I suspected that the [North Korean] captain sensed we were out there, but I was confident in my sub's [lack of] noise profile. There was no way he could hear us—not with the crappy Russian or Chinese sonar equipment that he likely had on board. At 22:00, we fired two Mark 48s [torpedoes]. The enemy sub never had a chance. He [the captain] made a sharp turn starboard and launched some countermeasures, but it was futile. My torpedoes had him. Both impacted. There were obvious break-up sounds. It was a textbook attack.

With my mission successfully completed, we began our search for the enemy attack subs. Those old boats [submarines] would be easy to find, because they were noisy as hell. There were a lot of them, but even then, I knew that we'd eventually sink them all.

Commander Bain Williston, the captain of the USS *Hawaii*, had a different experience:

I watched the clock get closer to H-hour. I had the sub in my sights. There was no way it could escape. Then, two [North Korean] attack subs arrived at 21:40. The noise from those bastards drowned out the boomer's signature [the ballistic submarine's noise profile]. The two attack subs were escorting my target. Weird for them to do, but effective. I had just twenty minutes to penetrate the noise of those subs and reacquire my target. Fortunately, my acoustics [sonar] team knew their stuff. I had trained them and trained them until they could do their tasks in their sleep. At 21:58, we reacquired, and two minutes later, I blew the fucker to hell. Tight, but mission completed.

The two attack subs fired [launched torpedoes] on me, and I fired back. I had a torpedo in the tube locked on to each of them. As soon as my torpedoes were away, I ordered a full spread of countermeasures and dove to the bottom. The Yellow Sea was really shallow and a difficult environment for my sub to work in. Two of the [enemy] torpedoes got confused by the seabed reflections and ran off harmlessly, but the other two exploded on the decoys [countermeasures]. The explosions were close and the shockwaves took out a few systems [on the *Hawaii*]. Our acoustic equipment [sonar] was temporarily disabled, so I didn't know if the two [enemy attack] subs were destroyed or not. I assumed that we got the bastards, but I couldn't be sure. We sat motionless on the sea bottom and remained on silent [mode] until we fixed our systems. Just after zero-hundred [00:00, midnight], my acoustics team got their equipment working. There was nothing out there. I eased out of the mission area, and then starting looking for more enemy subs to sink.

On board the USS *Spruance* (an Arleigh-Burke destroyer escorting the aircraft carrier USS *Gerald R. Ford* in the East Sea), the ship's weapons officer, Lieutenant Greg Miller, prepared to attack. One hundred miles away, a line of torpedo boats and missile boats had taken up position thirty miles out from the naval base at T'oejo Dong. A frigate was some five miles behind the line, accompanied by a corvette. Under normal circumstances, a squadron of fighters from the *Ford* would have destroyed the small attack boats, but the fighters had other tasks that night. It was up to the destroyers of CSG-11 to neutralize the threat.

Miller recalled the action of that night:

The boats were just sitting there in a line in the sea. They were clearly waiting for something. Behind them, a solitary frigate was steaming in slow circles, with a corvette trailing behind. The intel [intelligence] was that this frigate was the enemy's only modern one and the flagship of the enemy's East Fleet. I had a Six [Standard Missile 6, or RIM-174] locked on to the frigate, and another one on to the corvette. The [USS] *Howard* had done the same. Overkill, but everyone wanted to make sure. I had four Twos [Standard Missile 2s, or RIM-156s] locked on to the line of attack boats. The range was well within the capabilities of the Sixes, but it was at max [maximum] range for the Twos. It wasn't mission-critical to destroy all the [enemy] boats, just scare them off.

At H-hour [22:00], I launched. The Sixes went first, then the Twos. At over Mach 3 [the speed of the missiles], the [North] Koreans had barely two minutes to react. We sunk the frigate and corvette, and a couple of the attack boats. They were mighty small targets, so some misses were inevitable. The rest of the boats retreated, back to their base. We let them go. As long as they weren't a threat to the [U.S.] task force, we didn't bother with them that night. There was simply too much else to do.

To the east, the destroyers escorting the USS *George Washington* (CSG-5) undertook a similar mission to neutralize the small attack boats offshore of the naval base at Wŏnsan. The engagement was equally one sided. On the west coast, the warships of the North Korean West Fleet remained in port, except for a few patrol boats loitering offshore of Ch'o Island. Missiles from the USS *Farragut* and USS *Thomas Hudner* of CSG-2 (the USS *Enterprise*'s strike group) destroyed two patrol boats and sent the rest retreating back to their base.

Concurrent with the naval actions, the main event—and the reason for the massive attack that night—got underway. The destruction of North Korea's stockpile of weapons of mass destruction was the night's primary mission. Even if just one such weapon was used, the dimensions and consequences of the war would change out of all recognition—and no one wanted that!

Forty Lancers of the 28th Bomb Squadron (from Dyess Air Force Base in Texas) and the 37th Bomb Squadron (from Ellsworth Air Force Base in South Dakota) arrived at the DMZ. They were only two minutes behind schedule—a remarkable achievement considering that they had flown over six thousand miles, and had to be refueled several times. The operation had flexibility built into it in the form of speed, particularly on the last leg of the Lancers' flight. Delays that the bombers had experienced when refueling had been made up by increasing speed. During the last leg of the flight, the old bombers had swept in their wings and gone supersonic. The first Lancer crossed the DMZ at 22:02.

The targets for the Lancers were the long-range artillery shelters that the North Koreans had constructed along the western half of the DMZ. The artillery's primary mission would have been to bombard the population centers of northern South Korea, including the capital of Seoul. Such an act would have created political mayhem in South Korea. It was widely suspected that some or even many of the shelters had small stocks of chemical artillery shells. Nineteen of these shelters had been identified, with many of them dug into the southern foothills of Mount Taedun.

Alongside the Lancers, Lightnings and Raptors from U.S. bases in South Korea flew in stealth mode. These included eight CF-35A Lightnings from the Canadian 401st Fighter Squadron, which took off from Osan Air Base. The CF-35A was the Canadian variant of the F-35A. It had improved cold-weather performance, reinforced landing gear, and a longer range, but this came at the cost of a smaller weapons load capacity. Visually, the planes were identical. At the same time, six F-35B Lightnings from the HMS *Prince of Wales*'s 809th Naval Air Squadron attacked the artillery shelters located at the extreme west end of the DMZ.

Lieutenant Lise Swarbrick of the 401st recalled the night mission:

We took off from Osan [Air Base] first. The Bulldogs' F-22s [Raptors of the American 525th Fighter Squadron] took off after us. We had further to go, and they were faster. Only half our squadron was going on this mission. The other half was in reserve, along with all the Fiends [the American 36th Fighter Squadron]. Our targets were on the extreme right of the line of artillery shelters, around a village called Ch'olwŏn. We had ten B-1s [Lancers] flying just behind us. Our CO [commanding officer, Lieutenant Colonel Russell Notay] described it as we were the surgeons, precisely opening up the skin, and the B-1s were boxers who would pummel the gaping wound.

I crossed the DMZ in stealth mode and immediately launched all my missiles [four AGM-154s] and turned for home. The range to target was barely fifteen kilometers [nine miles]. We had been ordered that under no circumstances could we launch from South Korean airspace. The political situation in South Korea was already tense enough. The North Koreans belatedly fired some SAMs [surface-to-air missiles] at us, but I just put the balls to the wall [flew as fast as possible] and got out of there. As I turned, I saw the B-1s unload their [guided] bombs. Tons of ordnance was heading to the [artillery] shelters. I pitied the poor bastards inside them.

Technical Sergeant Lee Beyer, who had been on board a Lancer that attacked artillery shelters in the Mount Taedun area, recalled:

A squadron of Raptors had hit the targets first with some guided penetrating missiles [AGM-154s], and then we unloaded with a combination of Twenty-fours and Twenty-eights [2,000-pound GBU-24 and 4,000-pound GBU-28 guided bombs]. Major overkill! As soon as I called that we were bomb-free, the captain [pilot] turned sharply away, and we headed to Andersen [Air Force base on Guam] to refuel for our flight back home [to Ellsworth Air Force Base]. Although the old plane was not as stealthy as the fighters that accompanied us or the newer bombers, it was good enough for this mission. The [North] Koreans had very little time to react and fired only a couple of missiles at our flight, and none at all at my plane. We had no losses that night. All of us on our plane were really pumped. We were eager to get to Andersen to hear how successful we had been in destroying those shelters.

The attack on the artillery shelters to north of the DMZ was a resounding success. The word *obliterated* was frequently heard throughout the headquarters of the squadrons involved. All nineteen shelters were confirmed destroyed, without a single aircraft being lost. Elsewhere, however, events did not go quite as well.

Off the west coast of North Korea, four carrier strike groups (two American, one British, and one French) sailed eastward and launched their aircraft. The French Rafale M fighters were not stealthy, so they did not attack; instead, they provided combat air patrols over all four carriers. In the northwest, the newly commissioned *Enterprise* launched against the rocket-launching facility at Sŏhae. The aircrews of this new carrier were green and untested, so they were assigned an "easy" coastal target. Their attack was a success, but they lost two Lightnings to North Korea's air defenses near the target. Lieutenants Robert Warner and Nasir Abbar were America's first known casualties in the war.

Commander Dillion Trautman, the commander of the *Enterprise*'s 83rd Strike Fighter Squadron, remembered the action that took their lives:

We flew in low, barely above the waves. The Air Force's bombers were up there somewhere, but nothing showed on my radar—which was good for them and for us. Stealth was our only real protection on this mission. We were all in stealth mode and were careful about our maneuvers. No tight turns. No showing our belly to the enemy. There was no need. It was a straight flight to our target, the rocket-launching facility at Sŏhae. We got within twenty [nautical] miles, and then increased our altitude to one thousand feet and launched our [AGM-154] missiles. All thirty-six missiles ran hot and true.

I ordered us out of there, we banked sharply left, and that was when my missile warning alarm sounded. A volley of eight surface-to-air missiles were heading our way. The North Korean's were not as unprepared as our briefing had suggested. We trailed our decoys [AN/ALE-50 towed decoys, affectionately known as Little Buddies]. Warman and Lion [the callsigns of Lieutenants Warner and Abbar] were the last to turn. Both were hit by one missile and possibly two. One of my aviators reported that she had seen Lion eject, but Lion was never heard from or found. It might have just been debris from his aircraft as it disintegrated. ... They were good men. ...

The rest of us escaped the incoming missiles and returned to the *Big E* [the *Enterprise*]. The loss of two of us just gutted the squadron. The mission was successful, but I felt no satisfaction. I felt responsible for their deaths, because I was in command. I had trouble meeting the eyes of the others [aviators in the squadron]. What could I have done differently? From that moment onward, the war was no longer an exciting adventure, just a grim dark struggle to keep everyone alive.

Elsewhere in the northwest, fourteen Spirits and eight Raiders attacked various targets further inland. One spirit (the *Spirit of Pennsylvania*) developed a serious fuel leak and had to turn back. It made an emergency landing at Andersen Air Force Base on Guam. With the runway in sight, the fuel tanks ran dry and the bomber had to glide on its final approach. It landed hard and collapsed its landing gear. The aircraft was damaged beyond repair, but its pilot and co-pilot walked away unharmed.

The rest of the bombers continued on to their targets. The target furthest inland was a probable nuclear weapons storage facility near Taegwan. After the fuel-leaking Spirit departed, the other three of the 13th Bomb Squadron unloaded their ordnance, mostly 2,000-pound GBU-24s with one large 10,000-pound advanced penetrating GBU-79. They completed their mission without any losses. The attacks on the probably nuclear storage facilities at Kusŏng, Taech'ŏn and Yŏngbyŏn also met with success.

Nearer the capital, however, the air defense network of fixed and mobile missile batteries was denser and more alert. The attacks on facilities near Sukch'ŏn and Phyŏngsŏng were costly. Four of the eight attacking bombers were destroyed. Two before they unloaded their guided bombs and two shortly afterwards. The density of the air defenses around the capital were not unexpected by U.S. planners; nevertheless, the high losses came as an unwelcomed shock.

Offshore in Korea Bay, three Block V submarines from Submarine Squadron 7 (the USS *Barb*, the USS *Wahoo*, and the USS *Silverside*) launched a combined total of seventy-three 1,000-pound Tomahawk cruise missiles (fifty of which were the new UGM-109G JMEM penetrating variant). These missiles were a supplement to the bombing raids; they were intended to destroy whatever the bombs had not. Forty-nine of the cruise missiles were intercepted, but the remaining twenty-four hit their targets.

In addition, the Navy sent in two strange-looking destroyers to fire off a volley of Tomahawk missiles at various targets near the capital. The destroyers of Special Squadron 1 were the USS *Michael Monsoor* and the USS *Lyndon B. Johnson*, two of only three controversial Zumwalt-class stealth destroyers ever made. The prototype, USS *Zumwalt*, was the other ship in the class, but it did not participate in the war because it was undergoing a ten-month refit at San Diego Naval Base.

Each of the three stealth destroyers cost an eye-opening eight billion dollars—almost as much as an aircraft carrier. These technologically experimental warships had a unique hull design and eighty oversized vertical launch cells (each containing a land-attack or naval-attack Tomahawk, a submarine-attack RUM-139, an air-intercept RIM-174, or four air-intercept RIM-162s). The missile cells on board the Zumwalt class were one of only a few designs that could accommodate the new and larger supersonic Tomahawks.

Of all surface warships involved in the attack that night, the two stealth destroyers approached the closest to the North Korean coast. Each launched ten Tomahawks synchronized with the launches from the submarines. The Tomahawks were all of the new supersonic variant. Only four of the twenty missiles were intercepted. The stealth ships also acted as a screen for CSG-2 (the *Enterprise*'s group), which was the carrier strike group furthest north.

Commander Christopher Schoelrok, the captain of the USS *Lyndon B. Johnson*, recalled that night's action:

I took the *LBJ* [the *Johnson*] in to within thirty [nautical] miles of the coast. This was what my ship was designed to do. Get in close and let loose a volley of destruction. We arrived at our assigned launch position and launched our ten cruise missiles [supersonic RGM-109S Tomahawks]. We launched just before the *Monsoor* [USS *Michael Monsoor*]. Soon twenty missiles were speeding towards their targets. The missiles were of the new supersonic variant, so the North Koreans didn't have much time to react. Two or three minutes at most. As it turned out, sixteen of our combined twenty hit their targets. The Air Force had already destroyed much of the targets, but we made sure that nothing remained.

As we turned to head back to CSG-2, I was informed that we had spotted some enemy naval activity. Three patrol boats were heading towards the *Enterprise*. Clearly, they were hoping to get within missile range. Although the *Enterprise*'s escorts could have handled them, I decided to launch three marine Tomahawks [RGM-109F MSTs], one at each target. They never stood a chance. Brave men though. Three patrol boats against an entire carrier strike group, plus two stealth destroyers, which they didn't even know were there. A useless sacrifice, but then if my country was being attacked, would I have done anything different? That display of courageous determination made me wonder just how difficult this war would become. I kept my doubts to myself. To my crew, I just congratulated them on a job well done.

South of the capital, the air defenses were even more formidable. The three targets, all suspected chemical weapons storage facilities, were well defended. All four squadrons of Lightnings from the *Truman* attacked in a coordinated attack with four Raiders and four Spirits. One attack was almost a disaster. Four Raiders from the 34th Bomb Squadron and eight Lightnings from the *Truman*'s 32nd Strike Fighter Squadron attacked a probable chemical weapons storage facility near Kangsŏ, barely twenty miles from the capital. Three Lightnings were destroyed before they reached the target and two Raiders and two more Lightnings were destroyed afterwards. Seven of the twelve aircraft lost. Two guided bombs were also intercepted. However, the target was destroyed. Two of the six Tomahawks from the USS *Silverside* also hit the target. In the end, there was little left of the chemicals manufacturing plant or the underground storage facility.

The attack on the probable chemical weapons storage facility near Sariwŏn saw three wartime "firsts": the first combat use of the massive 30,000-pound deep-penetration GBU-57 bomb, the first combat use of the advanced 10,000-pound GBU-79 very-deep-penetration bomb, and the first combat use of the new 2,000-pound CBU-112 unguided cluster bomb. Each CBU-112 bomb, nicknamed the Hammer, contains thirty-six incendiaries. The bomb was specifically designed to destroy chemical weapons. All these specialized bombs worked perfectly.

Captain Williamina Brown, pilot of the *Spirit of New York*, remembered watching the visually stunning effect of the bombs exploding:

My Raider carried the MOP [Massive Ordnance Penetrator, the GBU-57]. It was all I carried. The three other Spirits in my flight carried a mix of Twenty-eights and the next-gen Seventy-nines [next generation penetrator bombs]. The brass [top command] really wanted this target destroyed. Some of the Lightnings from the *Truman* carried the new 112s, a nasty unit designed to fry chem weapons. It promised to be quite a show, and it didn't disappoint!

The *Alaska* [the *Spirit of Alaska*] was the first to unload. It sent a Seventy-nine [GBU-79] into the target. Before the bomb had even hit, the *Florida* [the *Spirit of Florida*] did the same. With the target already smoking, I dropped my big bomb into it. My aircraft really bucked [jolted upwards] when I dropped that unit. I'd never experienced anything like that, but then no one but some test jockey [test pilots] had ever done so either. I banked the *New York* to the left so that I could get a good look at the target. The ground erupted like a God-damn volcano! After most of the debris had settled, the *Georgia* [the *Spirit of Georgia*] dumped a full-load of Twenty-eights [twenty GBU-28 guided bombs] into the crater. The *Alaska* and the *Florida* did the same. The Lightnings dropped their Hammers [CBU-112 incendiary cluster bombs]. It was real fireworks down there. What a fucking light show!

After we unloaded, we bugged out [left the target area]. Our flight got out okay, but three of the Navy's Lightnings were shot down. That was bad, but otherwise, it was a really successful mission.

Mission Targets and Allocation of Aircraft

Region	Location	Sqn.	Aircraft type	Deployed	Lost
East	Ch'aho (n)	F-14	Lightning A	18	-
		N-31	Lightning C	10	-
	Ch'ŏngjin (c)	F-13	Lightning A	17	-
	Kanggye (n)	B-9	Raider	4	3
	Kilchu (n)	B-9	Raider	4	-
		N-154	Lightning C	10	2
		N-213	Lightning C	10	-
	Pup'yŏng (n)	N-25	Lightning C	10	4
	Tonghae (n)	B-9	Raider	4	-
		N-37	Lightning C	10	-
	Wŏnsan (c)	N-27	Lightning C	10	-
		N-195	Lightning C	10	-
Northwest	Kusŏng (n)	B-13	Spirit	4	-
	Phyŏngsŏng (n)	B-34	Raider	4	2
	Sŏhae (n)	N-83	Lightning C	9	2
		N-105	Lightning C	10	-
	Sukch'ŏn (c)	B-393	Spirit	4	2
	Taech'ŏn (n)	B-34	Raider	4	-
	Taegwan (n)	B-13	Spirit	4	1
	Yŏngbyŏn (n)	B-13	Spirit	2	-
Southwest	Kangsŏ (c)	B-34	Raider	4	2
		N-32	Lightning C	8	5
	Namp'o (c)	N-11	Lightning C	10	2
		N-81	Lightning C	10	1
	Sariwŏn (c)	B-393	Spirit	4	-
		N-143	Lightning C	10	3
DMZ	19 artillery	B-28	Lancer	20	-
	shelters (c)	B-37	Lancer	20	-
		F-80	Lightning A	18	-
		F-525	Raptor	22	-
		CF-401	Lightning A	8	-
		RN-809	Lightning B	6	-
			TOTAL	298	29

Notes:
- One Lancer and four Lightnings had to turn back due to mechanical issues, and two Spirits were undergoing extensive maintenance. They are excluded from the above totals, but the one Spirit that crash-landed is included.
- Abbreviations: n – possible nuclear site; c – possible chemical site; B – bomb squadron; F – fighter squadron; N – naval strike squadron; RN – Royal Navy air squadron; CF – RCAF fighter squadron.

Launches of Cruise Missiles

August 4

Submarine or Destroyer	Target	Number of Tomahawks launched
Arizona	Ch'aho (n)	7
	Wŏnsan (c)	12
Barb	Kusŏng (n)	7
	Taech'ŏn (n)	7
	Taegwan (n)	6
San Francisco	Kanggye (n)	20
Silverside	Kangsŏ (c)	6
	Namp'o (c)	7
	Sariwŏn (c)	14
Wahoo	Phyŏngsŏng (n)	7
	Sukch'ŏn (c)	12
	Yŏngbyŏn (n)	7
L.B. Johnson	Phyŏngsŏng (n)	10
M. Monsoor	Kangsŏ (c)	10
	TOTAL	**132**

Notes:
- The five submarines were all Block V Virginia-class nuclear-powered attack submarines with the Virginia Payload Module. They could launch forty-four Tomahawks: twenty-eight vertically from aft, twelve vertically from forward, and four horizontally from the forward torpedo tubes.
- The two destroyers were both Zumwalt-class stealth destroyers.
- Abbreviations: n – possible nuclear site; c – possible chemical site.

On the east coast, there were seven targets. Most were located on the coast or near to it, and so relatively easy to get to, but two were not. A possible nuclear weapons storage site at Pup'yŏng was eighty miles inland, and the weapons research facility and suspected nuclear weapons storage site at Kanggye was 160 miles inland. Twelve Raiders and 105 Lightnings from three carrier air wings (CAW-5, 8 and 11) entered North Korean airspace on schedule. Six of the attacks were successful, but the attack on research facility in Kanggye, deep inside North Korea, was a nightmare and nearly a disaster.

Four Raiders from the 9th Bomb Squadron, flying out of Dyess Air Force Base in Texas, entered North Korean airspace promptly at 22:00. No Lightnings accompanied them. They relied entirely on their stealth; their radar signature was that of a bird. They flew at 530 miles per hour and at an altitude of 45,000 feet (slightly more than their usual cruising altitude of 40,000 feet). It would take eighteen minutes to get to the target and another eighteen minutes to escape North Korean airspace. Thirty-six minutes of flying through hostile territory—and territory that would be on high alert after the bombs started to fall on the coastal targets.

Captain Eric Mendez remembered that long flight and the harrowing mission:

Ken [Captain Kenneth Connety, the co-pilot] and I had been in the air for nearly fourteen hours, with two refueling evolutions [operations]. We had taken turns having naps in the cot behind us, but we were both in our seats when we entered hostile airspace. We crossed the coastline well away from any obvious target. Shortly after we did, we turned and headed directly towards our target. It must have been the turn, because we lost one bomber moments after we completed it. A solitary [surface-to-air] battery opened up with a full spread [of four missiles]. It must have been a mobile battery, because our flight plan avoided all known fixed batteries. None were locked on to my aircraft, so I maintained a level course. The rear Raider took evasive action. It avoided two missiles, but the other two hit.

We were approaching the target when a pair of batteries fired on us. The lead aircraft was destroyed, and the commander [of the mission, Major Max Zaborowski] died. I became the new mission commander. We were only two minutes from our launch point. More missiles were heading our way. I accelerated to 600 [miles per hour, the Raider's top speed] and headed up to 50,000 [feet, the Raider's maximum ceiling]. We shook off the missiles and began to unload our bombs. I carried two Seventy-twos and two Twenty-eights [5,000-pound GBU-72 advanced deep-penetration guided bombs and 4,000-pound GBU-28 penetrating guided bombs]. I was near max load [maximum weapons load capacity]. Ken opened the [bomb bay] doors and we dropped all four bombs]. The other surviving bomber did the same.

When the doors opened our [stealthy radar] profile was shot [ruined]. Eight more missiles headed our way. I took the aircraft into a near vertical descent. The other Raider tried to do the same thing, but it didn't make it. I was the only one left—and angry North Koreans were looking for me.

I took the Raider down to treetop level. A missile impacted on a hill beside me. I dropped my speed to 280 [miles per hour] and started contouring [flying low and following the terrain. I don't think that my aircraft flew in a straight line for more than five seconds at a time. We were twisting this way and that. More missiles were fired at us. I dropped even lower and followed a valley. I was below treetop level. Two more missiles impacted the hills beside me. Ken was glued to the screen calling out contacts and obstacles. I banked hard to avoid a hill and just as I did, a missile hit that same hill. That was way too close!

Finally, and looking back, miraculously, we reached the coast, not far from where we crossed it coming in. I skimmed the waves for five minutes and then climbed to 35,000 [feet]. Ken kept his eyes glued to the screen for another five minutes. Only then could we relax. We two had survived, but six from our squadron did not.

Our relief didn't last. Both the engines started to overheat. I suspected at the time that we may have picked up debris from flying so low. I didn't think I could make it to Andersen [Air Force Base on Guam], so I decided to head to Misawa [Air Base in Japan]. A fire developed in the left engine. I ordered Ken to cut the fuel [supply to the engine]. The right engine continued to work, but it was making strange noises and a disturbing vibration ran through the aircraft. It seemed a long flight to Misawa.

I managed to land [at Misawa], and I was guided to a hanger with a Spirit parked nearby. Ken and I both kissed the ground when we got out, and then we went over and kissed our Raider's landing gear. The beautiful lady had brought us home. One of the keepers [maintenance technicians] at Misawa later told me that he had to pull pine needles out of the [engine rotor] blades. That must be a first for a Raider!

Captains Mendez and Connety were awarded the Air Force Cross for their extraordinary achievement that night. They were the first two medals awarded in the war.

In support of the attack on Kanggye, the newly commissioned USS *San Francisco*, hidden in the relatively shallow waters of Tonhan Bay, launched a volley of twenty "bunker-busting" UGM-109G JMEM Tomahawk missiles. Fifteen were intercepted, but five made it through the air defenses and completed the destruction of the weapons research facility that Captain Mendez and the others in the 9th Bomb Squadron began. To the southeast, the USS *Arizona* launched a volley of Tomahawk missiles at two coastal WMD sites: the submarine base at Ch'aho and an underground air force base near Wŏnsan.

The Night of the Bats was a resounding success. It had been planned brilliantly and executed superbly with professionalism and bravery. It has, rightly, been touted as one of the greatest military planning achievements for a one-day operation since the D-Day landing in Normandy in 1944. The commanders and planners at Indo-Pacific Command and Global Strike Command basked in universal praise, and the pilots and aviators who flew in the operation were all hailed as heroes. Nevertheless, of the 298 aircraft involved, twenty-nine were lost and thirty-nine airmen were dead or missing. A loss rate of ten percent was high for any mission, and such a rate could not be sustained for long. However, for that high cost, all seventeen WMD sites and all nineteen long-range artillery shelters had been destroyed. With the specter of nuclear warfare gone and the threat of chemical attack on South Korean civilians removed, the U.S. military could now turn its attention to winning the war.

Chapter 13

Battle for Supremacy

Air battle is not decided in a few great clashes, but over a long period of time when attrition and discouragement eventually cause one side to avoid the invading air force.

Major General Dale O. Smith,
U.S. Air Force, Cold War.

On the morning after the big operation, many in Indo-Pacific Command and Global Strike command were figuratively—and in many cases literally—hung over. The sense of relief was overwhelming. Once the results of Operation Cyclone (or the Night of the Bats as it was soon to be known) were announced by President Anders, the same sense of relief swept through America and around the world. There would be no nuclear war. For South Koreans, the horror of chemical attacks on their cities evaporated. Huge celebrations took place across Seoul and in the other northern cities. On August 5, the possibility that North Korea might surrender or collapse, or both, was a whispered hope. Supreme Leader Kim soon quashed that hope. He appeared on North Korean television giving a vitriolic speech about the "warmongering imperialists" and vowed to "destroy them utterly." The assembled crowds before him cheered to the point of hysteria. Scenes of aircraft wreckage with American insignia prominently in view were shown after the speech. The next day, a captured American pilot, Lieutenant Vernon Ferrill of the Navy's 32nd Strike Fighter Squadron, was paraded before television cameras for the world to see, and publicly berated for his "cowardly attack on a peaceful people."

Late on August 5, President Yeon of South Korea made a stern speech informing Koreans on both sides of the border that South Korean forces did not participate in the attack, but that would change if North Korean forces attacked any part of South Korea. This warning had the desired effect. Supreme Leader Kim, who had his hands full dealing with the American forces attacking his country, did not want to have more forces arrayed against him. Although bombardments of South Korean cities and military instillations using conventional munitions were feared, none occurred.

The Eighth Air Force was temporarily a spent force. Its entire fleet of operational stealth bombers had been involved in the Operation Cyclone. Its bombers had no bombs left and they were scattered across the Pacific: some were at air bases in Guam or Japan, more were in flight back to their U.S. bases, and ten bombers never returned. Eighteen of its pilots were missing in action. Its fleet of Stratofortresses were ready for missions, but until air supremacy was won, the old bombers would be far too vulnerable. Their huge weapons load capacities remained unutilized.

The battle for air supremacy started at dawn on August 5. Several fighter squadrons of the Fifth and Seventh air forces did not participate in the Night of the Bats. It was for them to make the initial blows on the antiquated North Korean air force. In South Korea, Lieutenant General Dunn, the commander of the Seventh Air Force, had held back three-and-a-half squadrons of Lightnings from the initial attack: the 35th, the 36th, the 355th and half of the Canadian 401st. In Japan, the Super Eagles of the 44th and 68th squadrons were available. These aircraft were superb "dogfighters," and with a maximum speed of Mach 2.5, they were the fastest fighters that the U.S. Air Force had.

For the upcoming air war, General Dunn decided to start with the enemy air bases located near the coast, which were most of them. They were easier targets, because they could be approached from the sea, and thus avoid most of the anti-air missile batteries. The heavy air defenses around the capital were to be avoided. There were two objectives with these attacks: destroy the air bases and force the North Korean air force to respond. General Dunn recalled:

> Their aircraft were terribly obsolete. At the time, I thought that they would be reluctant to engage us. It would be suicide for them to take on a modern F-35 [Lightning] with a fifty-year-old plane. I expected them to disperse their aircraft at small airfields and keep their fleet [of fighters] hidden and "in being" as best they could. I had to make it painful enough so they would have to respond. Only then, could my fighters shoot them down. I confess that I was surprised at the tenacity of their pilots. Eighty years of indoctrination can really motive people.

The attacks on the morning of August 5 started with the coastal air bases of the North Korean Second Air Division on the east side of the country and its Third Air Division in the southwest. The bases of the First Air Division around P'yŏngyang, with its relatively modern fighters, were avoided in those early days. The weak and strategically irrelevant bases of the Eighth Air Division in the remote far northeast of the country were only infrequently attacked.

A Boeing E-7 Wedgetail from the 961st Airborne Control Squadron took off from Kadena Air Base in Japan at dawn (04:30). It stationed itself over the East Sea. This command-and-control aircraft was relatively new to the U.S. Air Force in Asia. The modified Boeing 737 replaced the long-serving Boeing E-3 Sentry (a modified Boeing 707) in 2027, although it had been in service for over twenty years in some other countries (Australia, Britain, South Korea and Turkey). All eighteen Super Eagles from the 44th Fighter Squadron also took off from the same air base.

A second Wedgetail, from the 16th Airborne Command Squadron, took off from Osan Air Base. It stationed itself over the Yellow Sea. Lightnings from the 36th Fighter Squadron, also from Osan, followed it out over the sea. They were all in "beast" mode, with four times the ordnance but at the cost of a loss of stealth. Two General Atomics MQ-9 Reaper drones from the 11th Attack Squadron departed after the last fighter took off. The Reapers headed straight north. To the south, Lightnings from the 35th Fighter Squadron took off from Kunsan Air Base, also in "beast" mode.

There were two separate attacks that day. The first was on two coastal air bases in the southwest region of North Korea: Kwail to the north and T'aet'an to the south. The second attack was on two coastal air bases on the east coast: Tŏkran'gwan to the north and Sŏndok to the south. Of them all, the attack on Tŏkran'gwan was the most important, because the base also served as the headquarters for the Second Air Division. These four bases had MiG-21s, F-6s and F-7s, all 1960s-vintage fighters, and some even older F-5s. The more modern fighters, MiG-29s and MiG-23s, were stationed near the capital.

North Korean Air Bases

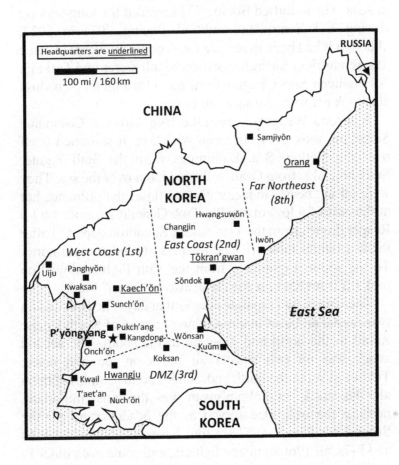

146

The attack in the southwest began first at 05:30. After the devastating attack the previous night, North Korean air defense forces were on full alert. The sixteen Lightnings of 36th Fighter Squadron approached the coast from the west. Ten MiG-21s and ten 1950s-vintage F-5s flew out over the Yellow Sea to meet them. The North Korean pilots were expecting a dogfight, where luck might play a role, but the Lightnings were at their core a standoff aerial weapon platforms with superb onboard sensors. It was a slaughter.

When the two forces were eighty miles apart, each of the Lightnings launched an AIM-120 air-to-air missile or a newer AIM-260. At Mach 4, it took ninety-four seconds to reach the North Korean fighters. Sixteen missiles resulted in fifteen kills. The five surviving enemy fighters fled north to the safety of the air defense network around P'yŏngyang. They never had a chance to launch their own missiles. The Lightnings then closed to fifty miles from the two bases and launched four AGM-88 anti-radar missiles and four 1000-pound AGM-154 precision missiles. After that, the squadron split up. Eight headed towards Kwail and the other eight towards T'aet'an. When the fighters got to within fifteen miles of their respective targets, they dropped sixteen 500-pound GBU-12 laser-guided bombs and departed.

Captain Mitchell Sutton of the 36th recalled the lopsided engagement:

Everyone in our squadron was disappointed that we hadn't participated in the big attack the night before, so we were pumped for this mission. After reaching our rally point over the Yellow Sea, we linked our onboard sensors with the AWAC [the E-7 Wedgetail] and data started flowing in both directions. We flew in two triangle formations [of eight Lightnings each] and headed towards the coast.

The AWAC informed us that twenty bogies were heading our way. We knew that the North Koreans were flying some really old stuff, but I was still surprised when the AWAC informed us that some of the bogies were F-5s.

They were seventy years older than my plane! It was like a World War I biplane taking on an F-4 Phantom [a Vietnam War jet]. Unbelievable! It took me a moment to get my head around that. We each launched an air-intercept missile. Our volley destroyed most of them. The survivors fled away to the north. We ignored them. The rest of the mission was just like an exercise. We launched our missiles and bombs and then returned to base. Mission complete. We were back in time for a late breakfast.

After the attack, the two Reaper drones arrived over the targets and surveyed the extensive damage to the two air bases. They then each dropped a wind-corrected CBU-103 cluster bomb on the runways. The explosions from 202 bomblets in each bomb made the runways unusable. One Reaper was destroyed by a surface-to-air missile on its return journey. It was the missions only casualty.

On the east coast, again a mix of old fighters took off to intercept the incoming Lightnings and Eagles. The result was the same. The few surviving enemy fighters retreated inland. The small air base at Sŏndok was destroyed in the same manner as the air bases on the west coast. At Tŏkran'gwan, the larger air base and the divisional headquarters were destroyed with a combination of larger bombs and more missiles. This time luck was against the American fighters. Two anti-air batteries guarding the headquarters sent eight surface-to-air missiles at the attacking squadrons. A Lightning was destroyed, killing Lieutenant Jane Fleck, and an Eagle was severely damaged. Its pilot, Lieutenant Mojam Sireg, managed to fly his aircraft almost a third of the way back to Japan before his luck ran out. The Eagle suddenly lost power and rapidly descended towards the sea. Sireg safely ejected and was later picked up by a Seahawk helicopter sent from the *George Washington*.

After the initial attacks on their air bases and the rapid destruction of their fighters, the North Korean generals pulled back their fighters to less-exposed inland bases, just as General Dunn expected they would. American fighters would have to run the gauntlet of anti-air missile batteries before reaching the bases, and another gauntlet on their return journey. The Second Air Division never recovered from the destruction of its headquarters. In the east, the U.S. Air Force had effectively swept the skies of enemy fighters on the first full day of the war. On rare occasions, solitary fighters or pairs of them, usually MiG-21 or F-7s, attacked the American fighters, but they were quickly dealt with.

Achieving air superiority in the western half of the country was more difficult and time-consuming. The air defenses around the capital region were extensive, and the North Korean air force generals took advantage of that. The well-protected air bases in that region were packed with aircraft, and more planes were dispersed to nearby airstrips. The generals made sure that their thirty-five precious MiG-29 were carefully dispersed and well protected.

In the northwest and far northeast of the country, the empty runways of the denuded air bases were attacked with cluster bombs to make sure that they could not be used again. Lieutenant Shane Neilson of the 355th Fighter Squadron (flying out of Kunsan Air Base) remembered the attack by six Lightnings on the air base at Uiju in the extreme northwest of the country:

We came low over the Yellow Sea. Twenty miles out, we climbed to 5,000 feet and fired off our HARMs [AGM-88 anti-radar missiles]. Me and the others then climbed to 10,000 feet and approached the base. No [enemy] fighter came out to greet us. We dumped our loads [a combination of 500-pound GBU-12s and CBU-103 cluster bombs], and we shacked it [achieved direct hits on the target runway].

Off to my left I could see the Yalu River and China on the other side. That gave me a chill. The CO [the commanding officer of the 355th, Lieutenant Colonel Anthony Campanelli] was crystal clear that we were not to hit anything on the Chinese side of the river under any circumstances. No excuses. No forgiveness. That was gofo [grasp of the fucking obvious]. I half expected the Chinese to fire on us, but nada [nothing]. One NK SAM [North Korean surface-to-air missile battery] did fired at us, but we'd bugged out of there before its missiles got anywhere close.

By August 9, four days into the aerial campaign, coastal air bases in the east, southwest, and far northwest were all destroyed and their runways cratered and inoperable. The fighters of North Korea's Second and Eighth Air Divisions had been effectively wiped out. The eastern squadron of forty antiquated 1950s-vintage H-5 bombers (a Chinese variant of the Russian Il-28 bomber) had been destroyed on the ground. The North Koreans had never attempted to use them or effectively defend them.

General Dunn took stock of the situation:

The North Korean fighters were now entirely limited to five inland air bases in the capital region [Kaech'ŏn, Sunch'ŏn, Pukch'ang, Kangdong and Hwangju] or dispersed on nearby airstrips. There was a ring of air defenses around each one, which were supported by the capital's air defense network. I wasn't worried about the older MiGs [Russian and Chinese F variants], but I wanted to destroy the newer MiGs [MiG-29s]. There were thirty-five of them at or near Sunch'ŏn and Pukch'ang [air bases]. The North Koreans had not committed them yet, preferring to sacrifice their older fighters than lose their newer ones. On August 8, I decided it was time to take them out. I put my planning staff on to it.

The attack on Sunch'ŏn and Pukch'ang took place on August 10. Unlike previous attacks on air bases, which had taken place at night or just after dawn, this one took place in the afternoon. Skies were clear, just as they had been all week. The fighter squadrons that had taken part in the Night of the Bats had by now returned to operational status. In addition, four Raiders from the 9th Bomb Squadron had been temporarily rebased to Guam and transferred to the Seventh Air Force while they were stationed there. They were thus under Dunn's direct command for the attack.

The attack started by six fighters from the 35th Fighter Squadron each launching an AGM-158 stealth cruise missile. After that, eight fighters from the 36th and another eight from the Canadian 401st attacked with precision AGM-154 missiles. The former squadron attacked the air base at Pukch'ang, while the latter attacked the one at Sunch'ŏn. While this was going on, and the air defenses were fully occupied, the two Raiders flew over each air base and dropped a deluge of cluster bombs. The available stocks of the wind-correction devices had been temporarily exhausted, so the bombs were dropped without any adjustment for the wind, which reduced accuracy. The twenty bombs in the first bomber were CGB-97s, each containing forty target-seeking "skeets" (a type of bomblet). These were intended to destroy the fighters on the ground. The twenty bombs in the second bomber were CBU-87s, each containing 202 bomblets. These cluster bombs were intended to destroy the runways, so that any surviving North Korean fighters could not take off. In total, 4,840 bomblets dropped on each air base.

Lieutenant Jason Halmahera of the 36th recalled his harrowing mission:

We approached our target [Pukch'ang Air Base] from the Yellow Sea. Our route was predictable, but thirty miles over flat coastal land is preferable to 130 miles over mountainous terrain with a missile battery on every peak. The cruise missiles went in first, and took the brunt of the air defenses. I have no idea if any of them got through [seven of the eight were intercepted].

With the enemy occupied, we came in low and fired our [AGM-154] missiles as soon as we reached the coast. The defenses only had seconds to react. As soon as my missiles were away, me and BeeBee [the callsign of his wingman, Lieutenant Robert "Bob" Bickerton] turned to leave. My missile warning alarm sounded inside my helmet. Beside me, BeeBee's plane exploded. Bob didn't get out, but I had no time to think about that. My radar picked up a flight of four bogies high above me. I turned on them. I put my nose [of the plane] vertical, fired both my 120s [AIM-120 air-intercept missiles] at them, and then closed to engage with my two Sidewinders [AIM-9Xs]. By now, I had lost track of where the rest of my squadron had gone. One of my 120s found its target. The three surviving bogies split up. Two came from my ten [ten o'clock or left] and one from my two [two o'clock or right]. They were still above me. They fired and I had three missiles coming at me. I went to full blower [on afterburners] and dived and turned, really banging off the stops [aggressively moving the joystick].

I deployed my [towed] decoy. It took out one of the missiles. I've no idea where the other two went, but they didn't hit me and that was what was important. I went vertical again. Three miles from the bogies, I launched one of my Sidewinders. I got one of the bastards and another bugged out, but the last one was really determined. He launched a missile at the same time that I launched my last Sidewinder. I had no idea if I got him, as I was fully concentrating on the missile on my tail. I twisted [the plane], headed up, turned over, and then nosedived. A real rollercoaster ride. I was pulling some really serious g's [gravitational forces]. I pulled up barely a hundred feet from the ground. I could see people below watching me fly by. It was surreal. The missile impacted the ground. I went to full blowers again, and got the hell out of there. I could see the sea in the distance. It just sparkled out there.

I busted the number [exceeded Mach 1] as I flew over the coast, and headed out at wavetop level. It wasn't until I was a hundred miles out that I took her up [gained altitude], turned south, and headed back to base. Only then did I remember Bob. Karen [his wife] and his kids were devastated when I called to tell them the news. I wasn't supposed to, but it was something I really had to do. Bob

and I had known each other since we were five [years old].
He was a really good friend, and I miss him terribly.

Lieutenant Halmahera's aerial battle against four MiG-29s was the only real dogfight during the war. His three independently confirmed "kills" was the highest number of any fighter pilot during the war and of any pilot of a Lightning ever. For his "outstanding aerial achievement" on that day, he was awarded the Air Force's Air Medal.

After August 10, the North Korean air force effectively ceased to exist as an organized force. On rare occasions, lone fighters took off, but they either fled or were destroyed. A few North Korean pilots escaped to China where the pilots and their aircraft were interned. Some who tried to escape were shot down by their own anti-air missile batteries. The Seventh Air Force, with help from the Fifth Air Force in Japan, had achieved complete air superiority over North Korea. There was, however, still the extensive network of anti-air batteries to deal with. It was to that problem that General Dunn now turned his attention. This longer and more costly battle is the subject of the next chapter.

Concurrently, the U.S. Navy was engaged in achieving naval supremacy over the North Korean navy. On the Night of the Bats, the enemy navy had lost its only modern frigate, several patrol boats, all its ballistic submarine fleet, and a third of its attack submarines. Its submarine base at Ch'aho had been turned to rubble.

North Korean Naval Bases

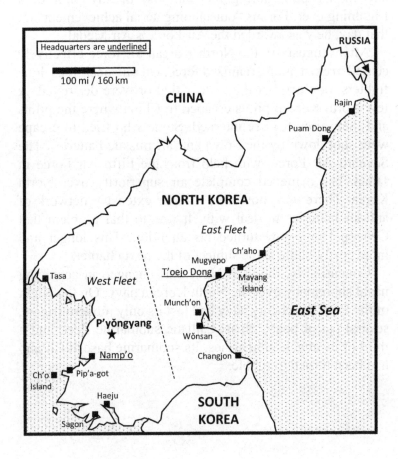

The North Korean navy was divided into two fleets. The destruction of its East Fleet was the mission of Task Force 70, which consisted of three carrier strike groups in the East Sea, plus five attack submarines. Task Force 20 was tasked with destroying the West Fleet. That task force consisted of two American carrier strike groups, two allied carrier strike groups, seven attack submarines, and two Zumwalt-class stealth destroyers.

On the west coast, a large raid by naval strike fighters flying off the *Truman* and the French carrier *Charles de Gaulle* destroyed the last remaining frigate (an obsolete 1970s-vintage Najin-class frigate) in Namp'o harbor. Three corvettes were also sunk there. The small warships (missile boats, torpedo boats and patrol boats) hid in bays and estuaries along the coast. They never ventured out and were systematically found and destroyed. North Korea's West Fleet was handled timidly and did not achieve much.

It was an entirely different situation on the east coast, where the fleet's commander, identified as General Khang Sang-hoon, handled his fleet of small warships far more aggressively.[1] A force of five missile boats sailed out into the East Sea and launched their missiles at the *George Washington*. All incoming missiles were successfully intercepted by a combination of RIM-156s and RIM-162s, and the last one was destroyed by the USS *John Finn*'s Phalanx close-in weapons system (a radar-controlled automatic six-barrel 20-mm rotary gun that fires fifty rounds per second). The missile boats were subsequently destroyed by fighters from the *George Washington*. The next day, a second force of five missile boats came south from Puam Dong to attack the *Ford*. The results were the same.

---

[1] The ranks in North Korea are the same across all armed forces (that is, no special naval ranks). They range from *wonsu* (marshal) down to *chŏnsa* (private). Herein, the ranks have been Anglicized and adjusted to conform with U.S. ranks.

The attack submarines of the U.S. Pacific Fleet tracked down and sank the surviving North Korean attack submarines. Most were thirty to seventy years old, with a few newer ones launched in the early 2010s. Many of the older ones had been destroyed in their berths in Ch'aho Submarine Base. Those at sea on August 4 had sought shelter in bays and estuaries along the coast or bravely attempted to close on the American carriers. When they did, there were invariably pounced on by one of the patrolling MH-60R Seahawk anti-submarine helicopters.

There was one stark—and nationally embarrassing—exception to this string of successes. At 12:04 on August 8, after a morning of launching and recovering aircraft, the USS *Theodore Roosevelt* and the escorting destroyers of CSG-9 were 155 nautical miles (178 miles) southeast of Musu Point (a coastal promontory near Kilchu). All seemed normal. Suddenly, alarms rang in the combat information center on the *Roosevelt*. Sonar center had detected a spread of four torpedoes heading towards the carrier. Captain Tyden Webber ordered an emergency turn to port, away from the torpedoes, but it was too late. Two torpedoes missed, but two hit the carrier. One hit the bow and did minor damage, but the other one hit midship and ripped open a large hole just below the waterline. The *Roosevelt* started to take on water. Bulkhead doors were closed and well-practiced damage control procedures were implemented. No one was killed, although there were some injuries, two serious. The carrier quickly developed a list of five degrees. Webber ordered counter-flooding to retrim the ship. The *Roosevelt* and two escorting destroyers changed course and limped back to Yokosuka Naval Base. The other two destroyers of the escort, the USS *Daniel Inouye* and the USS *Carl. M. Leven*, and two Seahawks from the *Roosevelt* began their search for the submarine. It was quickly found and just as quickly sunk. The *Inouye* and a Seahawk both claimed the kill.

Somehow, a North Korean Sang-O-class submarine had slipped inside the protective ring of destroyers surrounding the carrier. Submarines of the Sang-O ("Shark") class were first launched in 1991, and improved versions were launched in the late 1990s and again in the early 2010s. The improved versions were the newest attack submarines that North Korea had. It has never been established whether the submarine that successfully attacked the *Roosevelt* was a newer improved version or an older obsolete version.

Since the 1980s, in wargames with allied navies, American carriers had been "sunk" at an uncomfortable frequency by the quiet diesel-electric attack submarines of allied nations. The Navy had learned a lot from these encounters, and it had done much to eliminate the threat that such submarines posed. By the late 2010s, the incidents of wargame "sinkings" of carriers was much lower, and during the 2020s, only one such incident was reported.[1]

After the *Roosevelt* arrived at Yokosuka Naval Base, repair teams worked on the ship, but it no longer played a role in the war. Its carrier air wing, CAW-11, was transferred to Marine Corps' Air Station Futenma on Okinawa and

---

[1] Between 1981 and 2026, there were a total of ten reported incidences of allied diesel-electric submarines "sinking" aircraft carriers during wargames: the USS *Eisenhower* by a Canadian submarine in 1981, the USS *Forrestal* by a British submarine in the same exercise, the USS *America* by a Dutch submarine in 1989, the USS *Independence* by a Chilean submarine in 1996, the USS *Theodore Roosevelt* by a Dutch submarine in 1999, an unidentified U.S. carrier by two Australian submarines in 2003, the USS *Ronald Reagan* by a Swedish submarine in 2005, the HMS *Illustrious* by a Canadian submarine in 2013, the USS *Theodore Roosevelt* by a French submarine in 2015, and the USS *George H.W. Bush* by a Canadian submarine in 2026. In the 2026 wargame "attack," the Canadian submarine HMCS *Chicoutimi* (originally the HMS *Upholder*) was five years *older* than the oldest Sang-O-class submarine. It was not all notional wargame issues. In 2006, there was a real-world incident of a Chinese diesel-electric attack submarine being discovered only five miles from the USS *Kitty Hawk* and well within the submarine's attack range.

continued its wartime operations. The four escorting destroyers of Destroyer Squadron 9 returned to the East Sea and joined the escorts of the remaining two carriers. The incident was not reported by the Navy until after the war had ended. At the time, the unexpected appearance of the aircraft carrier in Yokosuka harbor was explained away as being caused by "a serious mechanical issue."

Captain Webber and CSG-9's commander, Rear Admiral James Rubino, were relieved of their commands pending an inquiry. To date, the Navy has not released the results of this internal investigation, possibly because the investigation highlighted a weakness in the carrier strike group's defenses. Although there was an inquiry, neither Admiral Rubino nor Captain Webber was court-martialed, but neither of them ever again held a sea command. Rubino retired from the Navy in 2035, and Webber followed a year later.

The successful attack on the *Roosevelt* marked the zenith of the North Korean navy's efforts and the nadir of America's naval war. Afterwards, North Korea's few surviving warships withdrew to harbors protected by air defenses. Repeated attacks on these harbors by navy fighters and drones sank most of the remaining warships. No confirmed enemy submarines were detected at sea after the attack on the *Roosevelt*, although there were many false alarms. By August 11, the operations staff at Indo-Pacific Command felt confident that the U.S. Navy had firmly established naval supremacy in the seas around the Korean peninsula.

Chapter 14

"I'm just off hunting for SAMs"

Our warfighting concept has to take account of the fact that almost nothing ever works right. As with the game of golf, our only real hope is to make smaller mistakes.

General Merrill A. McPeak,
U.S. Air Force, Gulf War.

With the one exception of a Lightning from the 36th Fighter Squadron, all American aircraft losses were from surface-to-air missiles. The North Korean air defense network of anti-air batteries was extensive, particularly around the capital. Units of mobile vehicle-mounted batteries, or even individual squads of soldiers carrying small man-portable anti-air missiles, were lethal to U.S. and allied pilots. Whereas U.S. aircraft could conduct stand-off attacks on coastal targets with relative impunity, venturing inland was a scary prospect. Until the North Korean air defense network had been neutralized, the Air Force was unwilling to further risk its bomber fleet, particularly the vulnerable Stratofortresses. Lieutenant General Dunn, the commander of the Seventh Air Force, was tasked with finding a solution. The fixed air defenses were identified and then systematically destroyed, but the mobile batteries were far more difficult to counter as they could be quickly moved to a different location.

At a meeting on the morning of August 9, via video-conference with General Alexander Sweeny, the commander of U.S. Forces Korea, Lieutenant General Carlos Mofettas, the commander of the Fifth Air Force in Japan, and Lieutenant General Catherine Guney, the commander of the Sixteenth Air Force (electronic warfare and reconnaissance), Dunn outlined his radical approach to counter the mobile air defenses. The Dunn tactic, as it later became known (or "Dunn-to-death" as some pilots dubbed it), was four-aircraft teams that would flush out, locate and destroy mobile anti-air batteries. Two fighters would fly over a target area and act as bait. The enemy mobile battery would launch its missiles at the first fighters, and from a distance the other two fighters would then destroy the battery. The "bait" aircraft would be the faster, more agile Raptors of the 525th Fighter Squadron based in South Korea and the Super Eagles of the 44th and the 67th based in Japan. The Lightnings of the other fighter squadrons based in South Korea and Japan, with their superb sensors, would then locate and destroy the battery. The four-aircraft teams would be supported at a distance by the electronic-warfare and reconnaissance aircraft of the Sixteenth Air Force's assets in South Korea. On August 12, the risky tactic was put into practice.

Captain Frank Schott of the 80th Fighter Squadron recalled the very first air defense suppression mission, universally known as a "Dunn" mission:

Me and Jolly [the callsign of Lieutenant Jeff Lonigan, Schott's wingman] took off from Kunsan [Air Base in South Korea] and headed west over the Yellow Sea. The sun was just rising behind us. We were joined by two Raptors [from the 525th] out of Osan [Air Base in South Korea]. I was in contact with a Wedgetail and a Compass Call [an EA-37B, a military version of the Gulfstream 550 modified for electronic warfare]. Our target was the area around Sariwŏn, on the southern edge of the ring of air defenses surrounding P'yŏngyang. The chemical weapons depot there had been pounded on 8/4 [August 4], but the local air defenses had not been touched. Command thought this was the best place to start the new missions—no idea why.

The Raptors accelerated away from us and headed to the coast. We followed twenty miles behind. The Raptors never even got close to the target area before the enemy fired missiles at them. The Raptors took off at high speed. I reversed tracked the missiles and identified the likely battery. I launched a pair of anti-radar missiles and dropped a Ninety-seven [CBU-97, a cluster bomb with forty target-seeking "skeets"]. We then bugged out and headed back out over the Yellow Sea. The Raptors, who thankfully had evaded the enemy missiles, joined us, and we all headed home.

General Dunn, himself, stood in the back of the briefing room and listened to our report. Everyone came back safely, and recon images confirmed that we had destroyed an anti-air battery. General Dunn's experiment was successful. He looked pleased. One down. Hundreds more to go.

With the first test mission successfully completed, the Air Force started in earnest that afternoon. Three days later, on August 15, the Navy also began to copy this tactic, but much less frequently than the Air Force. On the west coast, the French Rafales flying from the *Charles du Gaulle* acted as the bait, with the Lightnings from the other carriers destroying the air defense batteries. On the east coast, Lightnings were both the bait and the destroyers, or occasionally EA-18G Growlers (F/A-18F Super Hornets modified for electronic warfare) acted as the bait.

It took several days for the North Koreans to adapt to this new tactic. They paired up their mobile batteries. The nearest one held off launching its missiles at the first pair of fighters and instead waited for the second pair; the battery further back then launched at the first pair. Losses mounted on both sides in this rapid war of attrition. Two weeks into the Dunn missions, North Korea's air defense on the east coast and in the southwest were noticeably diminished. The price, however was high, particularly among the "bait" fighters. The newer and faster Super Eagles fared better than the older Raptors and Rafales. For the Raptors, their primary defense—stealth—was deliberately negated in order to attract the attention of anti-air batteries.

Captain Schott noticed the difference from his first air defense suppression mission:

The never-ending tension was getting to me. On almost every mission, at least one of our [four-plane] team was shot down, damaged, or had a really close call. On one mission, a Raptor bought it [got shot down]. One minute I had him on my radar, then next, nothing. I could see the explosion in the distance. He didn't get out [eject]. Morale in our squadron was shaky, but I can't imagine what it was like with the Bulldogs [525th Fighter Squadron]. Their losses were high. However, no matter how bad it got and how tense I got, Jolly [Lieutenant Lonigan] was always cheerful and pumped for the next mission. I don't know how he did. He was the best pilot I ever knew. A really jet jockey. He was born to it.

By the third week in August, I began to notice a slacking off [of enemy attacks], and we had to hunt for the batteries. I didn't know if we were thinning the defenses, or if the enemy was saving his resources for later. On 8/21 [August 21], we got our next mission. I had a bad feeling about this one, but Jolly was pumped as always. I remember him telling one of his load toads [loaders of his plane's ordnance] "I'm just off hunting for SAMs." He made it sound like he was just going to get a bite to eat at the canteen.

We left late, just after 15:00. It was severely clear [excellent weather conditions, virtually no clouds]. It had been that way for most of August. We headed out into the Yellow Sea and then turned and headed to the North Korean coast. Me and Jolly were the bait this time, and two other Lightnings from our squadron [the 80th] were supporting us. As I said, losses among the Raptors had been high, so the brass [top officers] had been forced to use Lightnings in their place. In the latter half of August, being the bait was only slightly more dangerous than being the destroyers. The enemy had adapted to our tactics.

Our mission target was the hills south of Kaech'ŏn [in northwest North Korea]. It was fairly deep inland. The 411 [intelligence] was that there were several mobile launchers in that area. We came in from the southwest, which was too close to P'yŏngyang for my comfort. We arrived over the target, but we received no attention. I remember hoping that maybe the North Koreans were finally running out of mobile batteries. No sooner had I thought that when my missile alarms went off. I counted eight missiles coming at us. One of the destroyer planes was hit and the other bugged out. Beside me, Jolly fired off both his HARMs [AIM-88 anti-radar missiles] at some target that he must have spotted. We turned to get out of there, deploying our decoys as we turned. A missile took out Jolly's decoy and another one hit his tail. He punched out [ejected], and I saw a chute—thank God—but I had no time to note his location. I had a pair of missiles heading towards me. I dove low and headed back out to sea on full blowers [afterburners]. Somehow, I got back to base safely.

My mood, already sour, turned positively grim after losing Jolly. I was teamed up with another pilot who had lost his wingman. He was frequently drunk when off duty, but I didn't say anything to him. Maybe I should have. We did three missions together before he was shot down. There was no chute that time.

By the last week in August, the number of losses to anti-air batteries dropped markedly. With the exception of the region near the capital, U.S. and allied fighters were now flying across North Korean countryside without being fired upon. On August 29, General Sweeny, the commander of U.S. Forces Korea, informed Admiral Sentsey, the commander of Indo-Pacific Command, that most of North Korea's airspace was now safe enough for the bombers of the Eighth Air Force to return. They had been absent from the war for twenty-five days. In that time, the Seventh Air Force, with the assistance of the Fifth Air Force and seven carrier air wings, had destroyed the North Korean air force and its extensive air defense network. The generals of the U.S. Air Force were ready to move to the next phase of the war.

Weekly U.S. and Allied Fighter Strength

August 7 to September 10

| | USAF | | | USN | British | French | |
Fighter:	35A	22	15EX	35C	35B	Rafaele	TOTAL
August							
7-13	95	22	36	205	24	30	**412**
14-20	91	19	30	202	23	27	**392**
21-27	82	14	26	192	18	18	**350**
28-3	81	13	25	190	17	18	**344**
September							
4-10	82	13	25	188	18	18	**344**

Notes:
- The air campaign against North Korea's air defenses commenced on August 12 and escalated quickly thereafter.
- Losses include those aircraft taken out of service for repairs or maintenance. Increases in totals indicate aircraft returning to service.
- Totals do not include the reinforcements of thirty Lightnings from two fighter squadrons (the 4th and the 34th) out of Hill Air Force Base, Utah, at the end of August. These fighters did not see action until mid-September.

Chapter 15

Beyond the DMZ

Our sensors show that the preponderance of the Republican Guard divisions that were outside of Baghdad are now dead. I find it interesting that folks say we're "softening them up." We're not softening them up. We're killing them.

Lieutenant General T. Michael Moseley,
U.S. Air Force, Iraq War.

The war in North Korea had many unique aspects, but one was particularly odd in our modern world. There was a complete lack of media coverage from the battlefront. The media in North Korea was little more than a propaganda tool for the government. It saw its role as keeping morale high and exhorting its people to make greater and greater sacrifices. After the initial defiant reports on the bombing during the Night of the Bats, it never again reported defeats, showed damaged buildings, or interviewed distraught relatives of the dead. Its repeated claim that "the imperialists are reeling from the glorious defense of the Korean People's Army" was unbelievable to Western viewers, but such a message was not intended for them.

As for the Western Media, it was shut out of on-location reporting. North Korea was a secretive place where foreigners were not allowed. American army and air bases in South Korea and Japan were strictly off-limits. There were a few embedded reporters on two of the American aircraft carriers (the *Ford* and the *Truman*), but their stories were limited to a few carefully scripted interviews with pilots and repetitive scenes of aircraft taking off or landing. North Korea in 2033 was not Ukraine in 2022 or Gaza in 2024; there were no disturbing images of destroyed buildings, bleeding casualties, or dead children to trouble Western consciences. The U.S. military enjoyed a surprising lack of public scrutiny during the war in North Korea—something which it had not had to such an extent since before its war in Vietnam.

Up until the end of August, the Air Force had limited its attacks to precision strikes on military targets, but that changed on August 31 when the bombers of the Eighth Air Force rejoined the war. Bombing became more widespread and destructive when the Air Force began to attack army bases and key infrastructure. There was an "unspoken understanding," as one unidentified senior American officer called it, at every level of American command that North Koreans were "different" than the citizens of other nations. In that country, nearly one-third of the entire population belonged to various military or paramilitary organizations (the highest participation level in the world), and so as combatants, the U.S. military considered them to be legitimate military targets. This sentiment was exacerbated by the deep outrage over the nuclear attack on Seattle that permeated the U.S. military (and indeed American society in general). The U.S. military did not offer media access, and the mainstream media did not press too hard for it. Everyone was happy with the status quo. News reports generally followed the military's media releases, interviewed generals and admirals from the Pentagon or high-ranking officers who were recently retired from service, and then openly debated a myriad of strategies to win the war.

Winning the war was precisely what was on the minds of those in Global Strike Command and the Eighth Air Force. The new bombing campaign started with a massive strike on the ground defenses just north of the DMZ. On August 31, for the first time in the war, the large weapons load capacity of the Stratofortress was unleashed. The old bombers flew directly from their bases in the U.S., refueling in the air along the way. Three bomb squadrons were involved in this first of many strikes on the DMZ: the 11th and 96th flying out of Barksdale Air Force Base in Louisiana, and the 23rd flying out Minot Air Force Base in North Dakota. There were thirty Stratofortresses in all. The 11th and 96th struck at the North Korean defenses on the west side of the DMZ, while the 23rd hit those in the center.

Technical Sergeant Noah Rathwell of the 11th Bomb Squadron recalled the bombing:

> The flight over the Pacific was uneventful. Nothing that we hadn't done in training a hundred times before. Once we reached the South Korean coast, near Busan, the tension on our Buff [Big Ugly Fat Fucker, the sentimental nickname for the Stratofortress] rose sharply. We were actually going to do this. When we reached the northern part of South Korea, we could see the DMZ in the distance. It was like an ugly scar running across the landscape. We reached our assigned target and dropped our entire load. A really nice combo pack [a mix of bomb sizes and types]. The Buffs in front of us were doing the same. I could see the bombs fall.

Deployment of North Korean Ground Forces

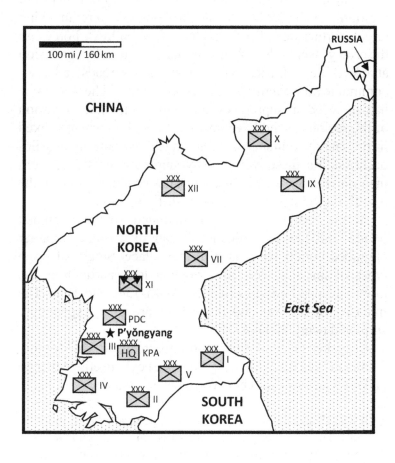

Once we were Winchester [out of bombs], the captain turned us around and we headed home. We were inside enemy airspace for maybe fifteen minutes, but it sure was an exciting fifteen minutes. We were finally doing our part against the bastards who nuked Seattle.

While the Stratofortresses pounded military targets just to the north of the DMZ, the stealth bombers were attacking targets further inland. The fighters of Seventh Air Force and the Navy were also attacking targets, usually precision attacks on key infrastructure such as bridges, roads, railways, communication facilities, and power plants. The Air Force had achieved air supremacy, and with the notable exception of the region around P'yŏngyang, it could go where it liked in the enemy's airspace. Some attacks by anti-air missiles occurred, but these were mostly single missiles fired from man-portable weapons. These missiles generally targeted the low-flying fighters and not the high-flying bombers.

As the bombing campaign continued, stocks of guided bombs and heavier ordnance began to dwindle. Smaller unguided bombs were used in their place. Stocks of some types of missiles were also running low, particularly the more advanced missiles like the AGM-154s and 158s. The intensity of the war and the rate of ordnance expenditure surprised many in the Air Force.

Brigadier General Benjamin Crossman of Air Mobility Command recalled the many "emergency" meetings that he had with generals in other Air Force commands:

It was always the same from the other generals. More, more, more. Faster, faster, faster. There was only so much that my boys [staff in Air Mobility Command] could do. Getting the ordnance to the bombers and fighters was only one part of the problem—a small part. The bigger issue was that our prewar stocks [of ordnance] were simply being used up too fast. I had one of my staff project the exhaustion dates for each type of guided and unguided units [bombs] assuming that we kept up at the same rate we were using them in August. I shared the analysis with the other generals. That gave them pause for thought. A deafening silence filled the room. I believe that the analysis was eventually shown to the President by SECDEF [Secretary of Defense Woodtke].

Crossman's disturbing analysis did not change the Air Force's overall strategy. In fact, the bombing intensity increased as August turned into September. The generals were gambling on a short, intense war. No one wanted a long, drawn-out war of attrition.

On September 6, the Air Force unleashed one of its most destructive non-nuclear bombs: the 20,000-pound GBU-43/B MOAB. This massive airburst bomb was intended to destroy large-area surface targets. Only five of these bombs were dropped during the war. They were carried in custom-designed cradles on airdrop platforms. On all five occasions, the bombs were carried by a MC-130J Commando II (a modified Hercules) from the 1st Special Operations Squadron. The planes flew to Guam to pick up the bomb and then continued on to their target. The first one was dropped on the headquarters of North Korea's II Corps, which defended the western part of the DMZ. One day later, a second bomb was dropped on the headquarters of IV Corps, which was assigned to defend the southwest coast of North Korea. Both attacks were on the prewar locations of the headquarters involved, despite the likelihood that the two headquarters would have moved to more secure locations once the war started. Results were less effective than hoped for, but the actual results of the attacks were less important than the attacks took place in the locations that they did. These two attacks were a vital element of a deception plan called Operation Windmill. The last three deployments of MOAB bombs will be discussed in a later chapter.

Colonel Cole of Indo-Pacific Command explained:

There was one terrible inescapable fact from which we [the U.S. military] couldn't get around: the North Korean army was huge. Whereas its air force and navy were small and obsolete, its army was massive and well-supplied with weapons. In addition, paramilitary forces were everywhere. We were looking at a third of the population armed and rising up against us. We simply couldn't land a small invasion force and expect a walkover. It would be a horrible slog. Our beachhead would be vulnerable for days, even weeks. And the idea of us being pushed back into the sea was too horrible to contemplate. It was imperative that we kept the enemy off-balanced and out of position.

Operation Windmill was the brainchild of Marine Lieutenant General Emiliano Rodriguez, deputy commander of Indo-Pacific Command. It was his task to select a suitable landing site for the invasion force. He concluded that a direct attack on the west coast, either north or south of the capital, would face strong opposition right from the start. The majority of the North Korean army was based there, as were its best units. The likelihood of the invasion failing was unacceptably high. Instead, he chose to land on the less-defended east coast at Wŏnsan. This landing, coupled with an attack on the eastern end of the DMZ, would give American forces control of a large part of the eastern side country. Once U.S. forces had built up, they would then break out and move west across the mountains to attack P'yŏngyang.

The forces on the southeast coast near Wŏnsan amounted to two corps: the VII Corps protecting the city of Hamhŭng and the I Corps guarding the eastern end of the DMZ. In Wŏnsan itself, there was the 425th Independent Mechanized Division, one of North Korea's better equipped units. One division, even a good one, was manageable (or so planners at Indo-Pacific Command hoped). It was vital to the landing that the two eastern corps remained where they were, and even more critical that they not be reinforced by units from the west side of North Korea.

The bombing campaign of early September was designed to attack four times more targets on the west coast than on the east coast. The area north of the capital around the mouths of the Ch'ŏngch'ŏn and Taenyong rivers was particularly hard hit. In addition, the Navy kept four carrier strike groups in the Yellow Sea, whereas after the withdrawal of the *Roosevelt*, it had only two in the East Sea. All this was to give the North Koreans the strong impression that American forces would land north of P'yŏngyang while simultaneously attacking the western end of the DMZ. Such an attack played on the North Koreans' ingrained memory of a previous American amphibious landing on the peninsula's west coast, which took place in 1950 at Incheon. That landing, which was at the time considered a strategic masterpiece, had placed a large force in the rear of the North Korean army and necessitated its humiliating retreat.[1]

Postwar analyses of Operation Windmill's effectiveness have shown that no reinforcements were moved to the east coast. In fact, there were very little movement of North Korean ground units at all during early September. Some military analysts have considered this evidence of the

---

[1] In 1950, after an agonizing retreat from the Yalu River on the border with China, the American Eighth Army was trapped in the southeastern part of the Korean peninsula in what became known as the Pusan Perimeter. To relieve the army, on September 15, X Corps landed on two beaches near Incheon, just west of Seoul. The surprise was complete and casualties were very light. The amphibious landings were (and still are) considered a brilliant success and a strategic masterpiece. However, the subsequent advance to Seoul was slow and tentative, and this reduced the impact of the decisive victory at Incheon. Nevertheless, by September 28, Seoul was liberated after a bloody battle. In an attack coordinated with the Incheon landings, the Eighth Army began its breakout from the Pusan Perimeter on September 16. By September 23, the North Korean army was in full retreat. The landings at Incheon saved South Korea and destroyed North Korea's hope for a sweeping victory.

deception's effectiveness, while others consider it proof of a breakdown of North Korea's command structure. Yet others note that with the Air Force's command of North Korean airspace, any movement of troops was extremely hazardous. More likely, the lack of reinforcements to the east coast was a combination of all three factors.

The Air Force continued its bombing campaign against military and infrastructure targets throughout the first part of September. There was some hope that the intense bombing might force North Korea to surrender, but that did not happen. After the first week of September, it became clear that North Korea had to be invaded. The Army and the Marine Corps prepared to land at Wŏnsan. The American Eighth Army was about to return to the towns and villages of southeastern North Korea from which it had retreated eighty-three years before.

Chapter 16

Special Forces

Any general who's worth his salt cares very much for his troops. Any general who's worth his salt knows that war is not a Nintendo game, war is not something that's fought by robots. He knows that war is fought by soldiers, by people. That liberty is bought by the blood of soldiers, and the sacrifices of these people.

General H. Norman Schwarzkopf, Jr.,
U.S. Army, Gulf War.

Before the ground war is discussed, it is appropriate here to discuss the overlooked role of American special forces.

The secretive world of special forces is a difficult one to penetrate, but some facts about their wartime operations have come to light. During the war, the primary mission of special forces was that of reconnaissance. This was particularly true for identifying nuclear and chemical weapons storage facilities. The success of the Air Force's strikes on the Night of the Bats was due in large part to the intelligence that special forces discovered.

This was one area where the South Korea armed forces contributed significantly to the war effort. After the war, the government of South Korea wanted to dispel the lingering resentment the American public had over South Korea's lack of action in the early phases of the war. Because of this, it permitted a slight "official openness" into the missions of its special forces.

Throughout July, the South Korean 9th Special Forces Brigade, called the Ghost Brigade, undertook clandestine reconnaissance of various installations in North Korea. The brigade had approximately six hundred soldiers distributed in four battalions: the 51st, 52nd, 53rd and 55th. The commander of this brigade, Brigadier General Son Min-hyuk, took advantage of this policy of official openness and permitted access to a brigade spokesman and to a not-to-be-named officer who infiltrated into North Korea, a lieutenant in the 51st Battalion. In a carefully scripted and sanitized (and unverifiable) interview, the lieutenant recalled one of his missions:

My squad of twelve men guided a team of four American chemical warfare experts [believed to be soldiers in the 23rd Chemical Battalion] across the DMZ. Two of the four Americans were of Asian descent, so they could physically fit in if needed, but it was my job to make sure such a situation never arose. If it did, I would have failed in my mission.

We humped [American slang for a long march with full packs] across the mountains of South Hwanghae [a province in southwest North Korea]. We crossed the Chaenyong [River] at night, two soldiers at a time. Most of our travel was at night. Daytime movement was too risky. It was also much cooler at night, which helped to conserve our water rations and our strength.

Our destination was just to the east of Sariwŏn. Photographic intelligence suggested that the Bukhans [those who live in North Han, that is North Koreans] had built an underground facility there. A defector had suggested that a shipment of chemical weapons might have been moved to that facility some months ago. Our mission was to confirm this intelligence by infiltrating the facility and allowing the Americans to make certain tests. The mission was made more difficult because our presence could not be detected under any circumstances. If it was, the Bukhans might move the chemical weapons to another location, and whatever intelligence we gathered would be useless.

For three days and nights, we closely observed the activity around the facility's gate. Some trucks entered or departed from time to time. We took photographs of their markings. The entrance to the underground facility was large enough that the trucks could drive in without having to be unloaded outside. The guards inspected every load before the trucks drove in. They were diligent and very thorough, which gave us time to carefully observe the trucks.

On the last night, we slipped through the perimeter fence and avoided the guards. The entrance to the underground facility was too heavily guarded to make a covert entrance, so we found a good hiding place and waited while the Americans took air and soil samples. After that, we created a small disturbance to distract the guards. The Americans entered the guardhouse and took photographs of documents that they found inside. When they returned to us, they seemed pleased, but they did not tell us what they had found.

We slipped back out through the perimeter fence and headed to our extraction point. It took two nights to reach it. I felt confident that the Bukhans did not discover our presence. I was later informed that our mission was successful, which I assumed meant that we had confirmed the presence of chemical weapons at that facility.

Other South Korean special forces may have also been active in North Korea. It has been rumored that the 13th Special Mission Brigade, called the Black Panthers or occasionally the Decapitation Unit, was active and that its losses were high. It is not known if the brigade was successful in assassinating any of North Korea's top government or military leaders. Some of the paralysis that seemed evident within the North Korean General Staff might be due to the work of this highly secretive unit.

In addition to on-the-ground reconnaissance, American and South Korean special forces were tasked with rescuing American or allied pilot who had ejected from their aircraft. It was called Operation Shepherd, and it was started by the commander of Indo-Pacific Command, Admiral Sentsey. The experience of Lieutenant Davis Kozelek, a Super Eagle pilot from the 44th Fighter Squadron, provides a rare example of the work of U.S. special forces after the air war began. Kozelek remembered his "wild adventure":

During an afternoon raid on the air base at Kuŭm, a SAM [surface-to-air missile] got me and I had to punch out [eject] at 10,000 feet. There were no clouds below me, so I could see that I was coming down somewhere in the mountains southeast of Wŏnsan. It looked rugged and remote, but also picturesque. As I descended, I calmed down and accepted that I would be captured. I'd heard horror stories about North Korean prisons, but there was nothing that I could do about it.

I hit the ground and collected my chute [parachute]. The ground was dry and rock-hard, so I couldn't bury it. I hid it behind a boulder. I stayed put for a while, hoping that someone would send a SAR helo [search-and-rescue helicopter]. When it got dark, I found a nearby boulder and slept behind it. I expected to be captured by the North Koreans the next morning. When morning came, I was still alone. I was hungry and thirsty, so I decided that I had to hike down the mountain. I headed east because that was where the coast was. I didn't think that there was any chance of me making it, but where else could I go?

I reached a pine forest and started hiking through the trees. It was brutally hot and my thirst grew. I found a trickle of water coming out of a boggy mat of vegetation. I bent down and started to fill my canteen. Suddenly, a voice behind me said in English, "Don't drink that." I span around and saw an American soldier standing there in full camo [camouflage gear]. I was stunned—overjoyed, but stunned. He told me that his team were here to rescue me. That sounded outstanding to me. Three other soldiers came out of the undergrowth and approach me. I didn't know what to do, so I offered my hand to shake. It seemed comical and pathetic at the same time. They just laughed. I asked who they were and how they found me. The leader, a sergeant, said with a definite tone, "It's best you don't know." I stopped asking questions after that. I later found out that they were from the 1st Special Forces Group out of Fort Lewis, Washington.

They led me down the mountain. We rarely moved during the day, so I had to learn to sleep in daylight, which was tough. After two nights, we reached a river and they told me to swim across. They did not come with me. On the other side, I was met by another team, and they took me up into another mountain range. Two nights later, I was handed off to a third team. These guys were Navy SEALs [from Team 5]. I took that to mean we were near the coast. I remember feeling very excited about that.

The SEALs took me to their boat, which was concealed and camouflaged. One of the SEALs got in, and I was told to join him. The two of us quietly motored away. I think the motor was electric, because it barely made any noise. We reached an empty spot in the sea and waited there for ten minutes or so. A submarine broke the surface not far away, and we motored over to it. I was taken on board the *Vermont*, and the SEAL motored back to his team. I was shown to my berth. There were two other pilots already there: a pilot from the 13th and an aviator from the *GW* [the *George Washington*]. The submarine went back under. The next night we picked up another pilot, also from the 13th. Then, I guess that the submarine went and did some other missions. We weren't told very much. I didn't see land or sky again until mid-September. The *Vermont* surfaced and a SAR helo [a Sikorsky HH-60 Pave Hawk] from the 33rd [Rescue Squadron] came to collect the four of us. It took us back to Kadena [Air Base in Japan], which was the helo's base, and mine. That was convenient. As soon as I arrived, I walked over to my CO's office and reported for duty. I must have looked like shit. He was relieved to see me and congratulated me on my escape. We were short of planes, so I spent the rest of the war doing nothing but queep [bureaucratic paperwork] and briefing other pilots on what to expect if they got shot down.

Not all pilots who were shot down were as lucky as Lieutenant Kozelek. Lieutenant Lonigan (Captain Schott's wingman, Jolly) was shot down near Hwangju just south of P'yŏngyang. After he ejected, he landed safely in a river valley. He had just removed his parachute harness when he was captured. He was released after the end of the war. Lonigan recalled his awful experience:

I was surrounded by a dozen soldiers, and all of them had their rifles pointed at me. I put my hands high in the air and waited. One came up to me, the squad leader, I suppose. Without warning, he smashed his rifle butt into my gut. I doubled over. They took my helmet. It was something of a marvel to them.[1] They wanted to make it work, but that

---

[1] The F-35 Generation III Helmet Mounted Display System was an integral part of the plane's advanced systems. The helmet was an information-display device, showing targeting data, status of the aircraft systems, and visual and infrared views of the world outside the airplane. It combined a sensor suite, night-vision technology, an information-packed display system, line-of-sight tracking based on head movement, and targeting software. Each custom-made helmet costed $400,000, and because of wear-and-tear, each pilot went through two, three or four helmets during his time flying a Lightning.

wasn't happening because it was keyed off of my biometrics. Happily, they didn't know that, because something bad might have happened to me if they did.

I was marched off to a town and put on a truck. I was driving into P'yŏngyang, right into the heart of the enemy capital. I was put in a room with two other pilots, but we weren't allowed to talk to each other. It was a rifle butt in the gut if you did. We stayed in that room for a day and a night. One small bowl of rice was all we got during our stay time, and some water. It smelt strange, but tasted okay—not that we had a choice. It was terribly hot, and we needed water badly.

The next day we were marched through the streets. Crowds glared and shouted at us, but no one approached the ring of guards around us. It was the only time that I was thankful for the guards being around. A television crew filmed us. When they finished with us, they interviewed a high-ranking officer, by the looks of his uniform. A truck came to collect us, and we were taken away. After an hour or so, we arrived at a building surrounded by a high wall topped with barbwire. We were separated. In a room with five guards watching, I had to strip and put on some rough clothing and poorly fitted slippers. I was hosed down after I got dress, not before. They did it deliberately so I'd be sitting around in wet clothes. I think that they meant it as a punishment, but it was sweltering in the prison, so I welcomed the cold shower. I was then taken to a tiny cell, with a concrete block for a bed and a hole in the floor for a toilet. I was left there in my wet clothes.

A few hours later, a man in a suit came in with two guards. The man asked, in perfect English, my name, rank and unit, all of which I gave freely. He then asked for details about our bombing campaign and its future targets. I didn't know any such information, and I told him so. The two guards then beat me—badly. The man asked again, and again I got beat up. When he asked for the third time, I was in pretty bad shape. I simply made stuff up, stuff that even my wing commander wouldn't know. He listened to all my crap, and then left without a word. The guards left with him.

I remained in that cell for days. In the morning, I got a bowl of rice, a bowl of a brown soupy liquid, and a big mug of cloudy water, and the same again in the evening—all shoved through a small opening at the bottom of the door. I never saw anyone for a week. On the third day of my captivity, I was violently ill all day, but the next day, I felt better—weak but better. No one came to see how I was doing.

One day, I was taken to an open yard and allowed to walk about. Twenty other Americans were already there. We looked at each other, but we weren't allowed to talk on pain of a severe beating. Five more Americans arrived during my stay there. They looked pale and gaunt. I suppose I did too.

That was my routine until I was released. Eat, shit, go to the yard, eat, sleep, repeat. Never any talking. I almost forgot how to. It was hell. It really was.

The brave work of American and South Korean special forces saved many pilots from a similar fate.

Special forces also took part in the invasion of North Korea, most notably rangers from the 75th Ranger Regiment. Their actions were not secret and were, in fact, well documented. Their story will be described in later chapters.

With air and naval supremacy secured, and with North Korea's infrastructure smashed, American soldiers prepared to invade North Korea—a land with nearly two million enemy soldiers waiting for them. By now, it was clear that North Korea would never surrender from bombing alone (in fact, no country has ever done that). An invasion had to happen first—that much was clear to those at Indo-Pacific Command, at the Pentagon, and in the White House. The risks, however, were enormous.

Part III

The Army's War

Chapter 17

Invasion!

Two kinds of people are staying on this beach! The dead and those who are going to die! Now, let's get the hell out of here!

Colonel George A. Taylor
on Omaha Beach, France, 1944,
U.S. Army, World War II.

Wŏnsan, a port city on North Korea's east coast, is due east from P'yŏngyang across the central mountains. In 2033, it had a population of 386,000. It was a center for shipbuilding, textiles manufacturing, and chemical production. It was also a seaside resort for domestic tourism; foreigners were rarely allowed to go there. The previous Supreme Leader, Kim Jong-un, had built a palace complex on a spit of land to the east of the city, complete with a racehorse track, a walk-through aquarium, a boathouse, and a private beach. Kim Ji-ho, however, was never known to have visited the palace after becoming Supreme Leader; he rarely left P'yŏngyang. Wŏnsan had an international airport, an air force base, and a naval base. It was also home to the 425th Independent Mechanized Division, the best equipped army unit on the east coast. During the First Korean War, American forces had destroyed the city of Wŏnsan, and eight decades later, they were to do so again.[1]

The invasion of North Korea began with a parachute drop just before sunrise, just like invasions had started in other wars. As the pre-dawn glow of September 10 illuminated the eastern sky, thirty-two Globemasters from four airlift squadrons (the 3rd, the 14th, the 15th and the 16th) arrived over the coast just north of Wŏnsan. They had flown directly from Pope Air Force Base in North Carolina, which was close to Fort Liberty, home of the Eighty-second Airborne Division. Each transport plane carried between 95 and 102 paratroopers. The Globemasters had been built with the capability of dropping paratroopers, and that was what they did. The bulk of the Eighty-second's 2nd Infantry Brigade Combat Team (three battalions plus artillery and engineer support) descended just to the south of Kowŏn. The first paratrooper jumped at 05:50. The combat team's mission was to create a defensive line to stop enemy units coming south along National Highway 7 from Hamhŭng.

To the south, twenty-nine Globemasters from three other airlift squadrons (the 4th, the 8th, and the 21st) dropped paratroopers from the 2nd Infantry Brigade Combat Team from the Eleventh Airborne Division (two battalions with

---

[1] From February 1951 to the end of the First Korean War in July 1953, the U.S. Navy and its allies blockaded Wŏnsan and frequently bombarded the city. The 861-day blockade remains the longest naval blockade in modern history. By the end of the war, the city was in ruins, and it remained that way for many years. Due to its strategic location, it was eventually rebuilt by the North Korean government.

artillery and engineer support). They had flown directly from Elmendorf Air Force Base in Alaska, which was near Fort Richardson, home of the Eleventh. Its paratroopers were experts in arctic and cold-weather warfare, but they had no need for such expertise on that sweltering day.

A heatwave had blanketed the Korean peninsula for over a week, and there were no signs of it breaking. A stable mass of high-pressure air had settled over the peninsula. The warm weather and clear blue skies of August had changed to sweltering temperatures and hazy skies. The temperature in downtown Seoul hit 107.1°F on September 9, shattering the previous record of 105.6°F set on August 15, 2031.[1] The high at Wŏnsan on September 10 was over 103°F, cooled slightly by a sea breeze. In the nearby inland valleys, temperatures soared to nearly 110°F. The highs for Wŏnsan for the next seven days were predicted to remain in the high nineties. The heatwave of the second and third week of September became a significant factor in the battle for the city.

Corporal Hector Galanis of the 1st Battalion of the 501st Infantry Regiment (hereafter abbreviated as the 1/501st Infantry Battalion) recalled the jump:[2]

---

[1] From the 1990s onwards, daily record-high temperatures were reported in Seoul at an increasing frequency. The record high of 101.1°F set on July 24, 1994 lasted for twenty-four years, while the record high of 103.3°F set on August 1, 2018 lasted for only seven years. Thereafter, the record was broken more frequently: 103.9°F on August 23, 2025, 105.6°F on August 15, 2031, and 107.1°F on September 9, 2033.

[2] In the U.S. Army, battalions from different regiments are often combined into brigade-size combat teams, depending on the mission. Regiments are frequently administrative in nature, while battalions are the combat units. The battalions in a U.S. Army regiment rarely fight together. To avoid lengthy descriptions of battalions, hereafter the nomenclature for battalions has been simplified from, for example, the 1st Battalion of the 501st Infantry Regiment to the 1/501st Infantry Battalion.

186

It had been a long flight from Elmendorf [Air Force Base], and I think we were all eager to get off the plane. We'd trained for this, so I really didn't give the reality of the moment much thought, although it did feel odd to jump without wearing our heavy arctic gear. It felt as though I had forgotten something. The descent was uneventful, and I landed without any issues. I unclipped my harness and ran over to the rally point. I collected together my team [of four] and ensured that they were okay and focused. I then reported to Sergeant Jukes that all were present and ready for action.

Captain Mitchell [Alpha Company's commander] had found us some good [defensive] ground, and we started to dig in. As we were doing so, some engineers came by and talked things over with Sergeant Jukes. As a result, we moved our position some fifty yards further forward. The sun came up. You could already tell that it was going to be another scorcher [of a day]. It felt like the mid-eighties already. I did a check of my team's water rations. Not enough, in my opinion. I went back to company command post to ask for more. I was told that they were looking into it. That didn't sound good to me. I went back to my team and told them to be really fucking careful with their water rations.

To the south, airmobile troops of the 101st Airborne Division flew in by Black Hawk and Chinook helicopters of the Second Infantry Division's 2nd Combat Aviation Brigade. They were supported by the brigade's Apache attack helicopters. The two infantry brigade combat teams of the 101st (the 1st and the 3rd) had left their own helicopters behind in the U.S. to lessen the burden on Transportation Command and the Eighteenth Air Force. The troops had billeted at Camp Humphreys in South Korea, which was (and still is) the largest U.S. overseas base in the world. In the early hours of September 10, the first of ten groups climbed on board the 2nd's helicopters and flew east across South Korea and then out to sea, turned, and then flew west to landing zones south of Wŏnsan. It was their mission to stop any reinforcements coming north from the DMZ. The 3/75th Ranger Battalion landed by boats to support them. Private Ralph Beute of the Rangers remembered the scene:

> We came in fast in a flotilla of small speedboats launched from the [USS] *Philadelphia*. We landed [on the shore] just as a fleet of helicopters flew overhead. It was the 101st [the first elements of its 3rd Infantry Brigade]. They landed just north of our position. Between us and them was the town of T'ongch'on. Together, we had to take and hold it. We were told to expect North Koreans to come north along the highway [Highway 7]. The town fell without a fight. I think the locals were stunned by the airshow.

To the north at Kowŏn, the paratroopers of the Eighty-second Airborne Division captured the town without a fight and began to fortify a line along the Tokchi River. Twelve miles to the north of Kowŏn, Bravo Company from the 2/1st Special Forces Battalion flew in MV-22 Ospreys from the USS *America* and landed in a rural area at the south end of Hamhŭng Bay. The company's mission was to delay any reinforcements coming south from Hamhŭng, likely mobile elements of the 34th Infantry Division. The company reached Highway 7 and set up an ambush near the village of Ch'owŏn. The highway bridge over a small river had been destroyed earlier by a missile strike from Navy fighters, so reinforcements would have to bridge the river with bridging equipment, or dismount their vehicles and march the rest of the way.

Lieutenant Francis Eddy recalled the mayhem that Bravo Company "happily created":

> We set up east of the highway and south of the river. The bridge lay in pieces in the river. We waited there well into the afternoon. It wasn't until just after 14:00 that the first North Koreans showed up. They took up positions by the

bridge and waited. An hour or so later, more vehicles arrived. It was not until 17:30 that bridging equipment arrived. This was what we had been waiting for. As soon as they deployed their bridging equipment, we called in an airstrike from the *Ford*. Twenty minutes later, the ground erupted with explosions. The bridging equipment was blown to hell. We opened fire on the survivors. We hit them hard, but more kept coming from the north. Our single company was facing two battalions at least.

As soon as the enemy was over the river in force, we retreated. That was when everything went fubar [fucked up beyond all recognition]. Our extraction flight had been fired upon by a SAM battery that we must have missed. They had to bug out, which left us hanging and royally fucked. The captain had no choice but to order us to hump [march] south. The Eighty-second [2nd Infantry Brigade of the Eighty-second Airborne Division] was at Kowŏn, and we were ordered to link up with them. We humped south with an enemy battalion close on our six [behind]. I can tell you that no one asked to take a knee [rest] during that hump.

Far to the north of the invasion beaches, Alpha Company from the 1st Marine Raiders Battalion landed near Ragwŏn. Their mission was the same as that of the special forces at Ch'owŏn: delay reinforcements from moving south and act as a diversion. It was a hazardous mission, as the marines would be unsupported and risked being cut off and surrounded. The marines were soon attacked by elements of the 37th Infantry Division, which moved out of its bases near Hongwŏn with unexpected vigor. Overwhelmed by ten times their number and not wanting to be cut off from their only line of retreat, the marines hastily returned to their boats. The marines experienced only a few casualties and no deaths, and no marines were left behind during the evacuation. The decision to launch this remote, and ultimately futile, mission has been hotly debated ever since.

Meanwhile, an armada of warships sailed closer to the coastline near Wŏnsan. Elements of four brigades had been squeezed on to two assault ships (the USS *America* and the USS *Tripoli*) and ten landing ships. To achieve this impressive logistics feat, the tightly packed troops had to land with no artillery support and with very limited armor and engineer support. The decision to leave the invasion troops without their own "organic" artillery units was controversial at the time and remains much debated. It was necessitated by the shortage of landing ships. Even without artillery and barely any armor, the landing ships exceeded their "surge" capacities (built-in additional capacities beyond their normal ones). Planners at Indo-Pacific Command believed at the time it was crucial to have more "boots on the ground" than heavy equipment. Even with the advantage of hindsight, it is still impossible to say whether fewer soldiers with more equipment would have made the battle for Wŏnsan easier or would have resulted in a disaster.

The eight air wings from two carrier strike groups and the fighters of the Seventh Air Force provided "flying artillery" support. The Seventh Air Force also sent in its 25th Fighter Squadron, which had remained unemployed up until this moment. The 25th was equipped with A-10C Thunderbolt IIs, the last squadron in the Air Force to have the 1970s-vintage aircraft. The odd-looking fighter, affectionately nicknamed the Warthog (because it looked so ugly), was specifically designed as a close-support ground-attack plane. Besides missiles and bombs, it had a 30-mm rotary autocannon that caused havoc among enemy ground troops. The aircraft also had a huge morale-boosting effect on any friendly troops who saw it in action.

Landing at Wŏnsan

September 10

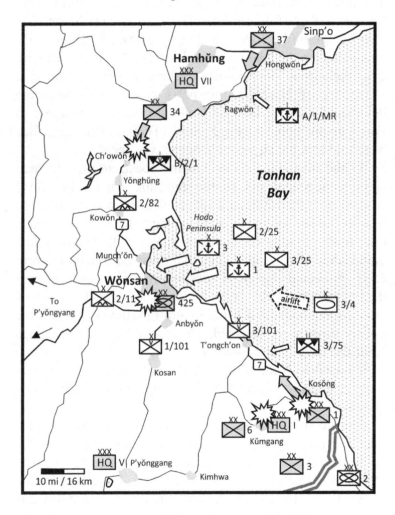

The most important first-day objective for the invasion was to secure the Wŏnsan-Kalma International Airport. Once secure, reinforcements would arrive in the form of an airlift of the 3rd Armored Brigade Combat Team of the Fourth Infantry Division. It consisted of two armored battalions with infantry, reconnaissance and engineering support, and one full battalion of much-needed field artillery. This battalion (the 3/29th) had eighteen M109 Paladin 155-mm self-propelled howitzers, all of the latest A7 variant. Two squadrons of the giant Galaxy transports and five squadrons of Hercules transports stood ready to leave Peterson Air Force Base in Colorado (which was close to Fort Carson, home of the Fourth). They waited until they were told that the airport at Wŏnsan was open.

As the invasion fleet neared the coast, an unwelcomed surprise appeared out of the morning haze. The North Korean navy had hidden away among the nearby offshore islands the last survivors of its modern stealth attack boats. Four boats got into within missile range of the invasion fleet before they were spotted. The two invasion squadrons were each protected by four destroyers. The two nearest destroyers (the USS *Daniel Inouye* and the USS *Lenah Sutcliffe Higbee*) fired off anti-ship missiles as soon as the enemy boats were detected, and a squadron of Lightnings from the *George Washington*'s combat air patrol also fired their missiles. None of the attack boats survived, but they each managed to launch an anti-ship missile before they were sunk.

One incoming missile was intercepted by a RIM-162 anti-missile missile fired by the *Higbee*. A second missile hit the landing ship USS *Fort Lauderdale*, but failed to explode. Debris was scattered across the foredeck, but otherwise the ship was unaffected. The last two missiles headed towards the assault ship USS *America*. One was destroyed by the ship's Phalanx close-in weapons system, but the other hit the ship. The missile struck the *America*'s island (its command tower) and did significant damage. Captain Glen Horaine and most of the others in the combat information center were killed. Rear Admiral Lilianne Borkman was severely wounded and had to relinquish her command. Rear Admiral Jacob Merryweather, the commander of Amphibious Squadron 7, temporarily took over command of Amphibious Squadron 11 as well. Fortunately, the ship's hull, internal docks, and flight deck were not damaged by the attack, other than debris and two wrecked Ospreys strewn across the central third of the fight deck. The *America* maintained its position in the invasion fleet and remained on course for the North Korean coast. None of the marines on board were injured.

At 06:09, the first of the marines landed on Kalma beach. It had been eighty-three years since Americans were last in Wŏnsan.[1] They had now returned in force, but the North Koreans were waiting for them. The flat, open beach was a terrible place to land troops. It was overlooked by dozens of apartment blocks and resort hotels, and every room might have a sniper in it. The beach's only redeeming feature was that it was only a few hundred yards from the shore to the airport. Capturing the airport was absolutely necessary for the invasion to succeed. It was the only immediate access route for reinforcements and supplies to come to the landing forces. The airport simply had to be taken. Just prior to the marines landing, two submarines (the USS *Arizona* and USS *San Francisco*) launched a volley of fourteen Tomahawk missions at the row of buildings that overlooked the beach.

---

[1] After the successful invasion at Incheon during the first year of the First Korean War, General Douglas MacArthur, the commander of the United Nations's forces in Korea, considered repeating his success at Wŏnsan. The invasion was called Operation Tailboard, but it never took place. The North Korean army withdrew from the city in October 1950, and allied ground forces moved in unopposed and secured the city before the invasion could be mounted. American and allied forces did not remain for long. They had to evacuate from Wŏnsan on December 9, 1950, as a part of the general retreat to the Pusan Perimeter.

Naval aviators from the *George Washington* dropped dozens of guided bombs (mostly smaller 500-pound GBU-12s, but a few larger 2000-pound GBU-24). The bombs were all guided and generally small because it was vital that the nearby airport not be damaged (also the larger bombs were becoming increasingly scarce as stocks dwindled).

Private Willis Nagle of Bravo Company, the 1/1st Marine Battalion, later remembered the horrors of Kalma beach:

My company came ashore on board the *155* [*LCAC-155*, a Class 100 hovercraft ferry].[1] There were 133 of us, not counting the crew. It was a rough ride and incredibly noisy, but the enemy already knew that we were coming anyway. Just before we hit the beach, the Navy laid waste to the row of apartment buildings with a massive missile strike. Boom, boom, boom! The row of buildings exploded, and several buildings collapsed. Smoke was everywhere, and debris dropped all over the beach.

We drove [hovered] ashore and popped some smoke [the hovercraft launched smoke grenades]. The pilots [drivers] went high up the beach, almost to the row of buildings. We were getting some small-arms fire, but nothing big. We charged out and made our way towards the nearest building, mostly rubble after the missile strike. Suddenly, we were getting a lot more fire coming from every direction. The [platoon] sergeant bought it [was killed]. Kale [Private Fred Kalanick], a buddy of mine, got one in the head. He had been running right beside me. I hit the deck [fell to the ground] and started to crawl towards some cover. A lieutenant ordered me to get up and run, but he was shot dead before I had a chance to tell him "No fucking way!"

I glanced back and saw the hovercrafts bug out [depart]. They were heading back to the ship [USS *Tripoli*] to get the second wave. I remember thinking that they had better

---

[1] The Class 100 was a landing craft air cushion, the Navy's term for a military hovercraft ferry. It was also known as a ship-to-shore connector, or SSC. It could carry up to 70 tons or up to 145 marines. It could travel over the water at speeds exceeding 35 knots (40 miles per hour).

hurry, because we were getting murdered. In the distance, I noticed Captain T [Captain Ulysses Tannehill] and the company's signals [radio] man hunkering down behind some rubble. Suddenly, they both lay flat and put their hands over their ears. I took my cue from them and did the same. Seconds later, missiles hit the building in front of the captain. It fucking imploded! No shit! The captain and some other got up and started running forward. I decided that the captain seemed to know what he was doing, so I got up and followed him.

We entered what was left of one of the buildings and went room to room. It was fish [fighting in someone's home] all the way. Most rooms were empty, but some had a three or four [enemy] soldiers in them. Usually, we just threw in a grenade, but in one [of the rooms], me and two other jarheads [marine privates] got into a real firefight. We got them all, but not before a bullet grazed my leg. Jesus, it hurt! After we had done with them, I looked out the window at the beach below. I could see the second wave coming in, and about time too!

Further up the beach, the eight-wheeled amphibious combat vehicles (ACVs) of the 3rd Assault Amphibian Battalion (nicknamed the Gators) came ashore. The Marine Corps decided to use four different variants of the vehicles for the invasion: the ACV-P, which could carry thirteen marines plus a crew of three, the new ACV-2.0, which had better operational capabilities at sea, the ACV-30, which was armed with a Mk44 Bushmaster 30-mm chain gun, and the ACV-C, the command-and-control variant used for the battalion's headquarters.

Private Janie Chen, a driver of an ACV-P, recalled her mission and the bizarre sights of that morning:

My amtrac [the generic name that marines give to all types of ACVs] landed at the far north end of the beach. The buildings before us had been pounded by the flyboys [Naval aviators], so it was fairly quiet, other than some small-arms fire, which didn't affect us. Me and two other amtracs headed north to the tip of the cape. One of the others was armed with a Bushmaster, in case things got hot. It was our mission to secure some government buildings at the far end. They called the place the "Palace." It was where the Supreme Leader came to hang out. His summer cottage, I guess.

We got off the beach and on to the beach road. We headed north. It wasn't far. I could see our objective ahead. I made a tight left turn, then smashed through some metal gates. The four-story building inside was painted a pastel pink, like what you'd see in Miami Beach. The place was deserted. I drove across the courtyard to the front door. Very ornate, it was. My squad [of thirteen marines] egressed [got out] and made their way into the building. We hung around for a while and then Sarge [Sergeant Mario Fratelli, the vehicle's commander] ordered me to drive around to the back. I smashed through a small brick wall. Imagine my surprise to see horses running around in a field [these were racehorses that ran on the palace's private racetrack]. Good looking horses too. I used to ride when I was girl. Thoroughbreds, for sure.

The other squad was ordered back into their amtrac and headed south. The Bushmaster [amtrac] went with them. My squad searched the Palace, the stables, and the other outbuildings. It was all abandoned. While they did so, the three of us sat in our amtrac and waited for orders. I nibbled on some Mystery-E (a ready-to-eat meal) and watched the horses run about. I hope that nothing happened to them. We sat there guarding horses and empty buildings until nearly 11:00. Four amtracs arrived. The colonel [the battalion's commanding officer, Lieutenant Colonel Reid Inayah] came out of one of them, and the Old Man (the commander of the 1st Marine Expeditionary Brigade, Brigadier General Max Gemmill) came out another. He had a blood-and-guts rep [reputation], so no way was he not going to be on the beach with us. He and the colonel and their staff headed into the Palace, and we were ordered south to reform with our battalion.

Corporal Luke Waters of Alpha Company, the 1/1st Marine Battalion, remembered seeing the airport for the first time:

> We had fought our way through the row of buildings. Nasty work! I prayed to Jesus Christ to watch over me. My squad arrived at the edge of the airport. We could see the terminal on the far side of the runways. That was our OB [objective]. There was a lot of open ground between us and the terminal. A killing zone for sure. I prayed again. It helped calm me down. I remember thinking that if God decided that it was my day to die, there was nothing that I could do about it.
>
> There was nothing for it but to run across that killing field. I left the safety of the rubble and ran flat out across the runways. Thinking back now, it was real John Wayne of me [a brave but unsound act]. Others followed me. It was not until we neared the terminal that we were fired upon. Some good friends died, but most of us made it into the terminal. As soon as I got into the terminal building, I kneeled and thanked Jesus for my safe deliverance. It just wasn't my time.

Alpha company had been stuck at the edge of the runways for some time before Corporal Water's sprint. His courageous act inspired others to follow and moved the company forward at a critical moment. He was the first marine to enter the airport terminal. Waters was later awarded a Bronze Star.

A second landing took place to the north of Wŏnsan. Elements of the 3rd Marine Expeditionary Brigade entered Yŏnghŭng Bay and landed on the shore between Wŏnsan and the village of Bumpyo to the north. The landing was intended as both a diversion and as a back-up. It was hoped that the second landing would divert the attention of the general in command of the defenses of Wŏnsan (later identified as Major General Yun Sung-ho, the commander of the 425th Independent Mechanized Division). In addition, if the landings on Kalma Beach became stalled—or worse, failed—the marines from the northern landing could fight their way through the city of Wŏnsan and eventually capture the airport.

Elements of two marine regiments from the 3rd Expeditionary Brigade landed on a marshy shore. Their hovercrafts moved to more solid ground before the marines disembarked. The hovercrafts returned to the landing ships waiting offshore to collect the second wave. Meanwhile, the marines already onshore were receiving intermittent fire from hidden positions in Bumpyo, a village of just over one hundred terrified inhabitants. Bravo Company of the 1/4th Marine Battalion, was tasked to clear the village.

Private Pedro Beyea of that company remembered the action:

We headed north towards a collection of houses. We stayed on either side of the highway [Highway 7]. No one was stupid enough to march down the center of the road. There was no one around, just lots of chickens and some cows. It was a poor place, but remarkably clean. No litter or graffiti anywhere.

Sergeant Baker motioned for us to hit the deck [go to ground]. He'd seen something. He pointed to a Tango [target building] and motioned that we should unzip [continual automatic fire]. I aimed my [XM7] rifle at one of the Tango's windows. The marine beside me dropped to prone [laid down] and let loose with his [XM250] machine gun. That ripped through the Tango. Someone fired off a grenade. Boom! No more problem. We continued forward. Stopping every now and then to unzip at another Tango.[1]

---

[1] The XM7 assault rifle and the XM250 belt-fed machine gun had been the standard infantryman's weapons since the mid-2020s. These new weapons were phased into Army and Marine Corps units between 2022 to 2027. They replaced the M4 carbine, the M249 light machine gun, and the M240 machine gun, which had cartridges of different calibers and

Me and three others entered one building to flush out the enemy. They were likely on the second floor. Me and Joyce [Private Harold Joyce] headed up there, while the other two swept the ground floor. We surprised them and quickly neutralized the threat. Only then did I realize that we had killed some kids. Fourteen years old, maybe less [Private Beyea was eighteen]. It was not the regular army that we had engaged, but some kind of paramilitary unit. We had been briefed on the likelihood of encountering such units. I didn't feel bad about killing them. They were the enemy, and they had guns. Even dropping [killing] the girl soldier didn't bother me. She'd have dropped me, if I hadn't done her first. We left the building and rejoined our squad.

Bumpyo was quickly cleared. The rest of 1/4th Battalion, along with the 2/4th Battalion, headed south and set up defensive positions along the banks of a stream. Ahead lay a city of nearly 400,000 people. The city was surrounded by American airborne forces and cut off from help. The battle for Wŏnsan was about to begin.

---

were designed in the late 1970s and early 1980s. The new weapons used standardized 6.8-mm-caliber cartridges, which considerably simplified supply logistics. They were manufactured in New Hampshire by SIG Sauer, Inc., the American subsidiary of the German company, SIG Sauer GmbH & Co. KG.

Chapter 18

Battle of Wŏnsan

The infantry soldier, well-trained in stealthy approach and in the art of taking cover, makes a small target, and if he is an expert rifleman, there is nothing that can take his place on the battlefield.

General John J. Pershing,
U.S. Army, World War I.

By 13:00 on September 10, the marines of 1st brigade had captured the airport, pushed out of the Kalma beach area, and reached the eastern edge Wŏnsan. To the north, the marines of 3rd brigade had cleared the village of Bumpyo and set up a defensive line just north of the city. Follow-up troops from elements of the Twenty-fifth Light Infantry Division had begun to land on the beachheads: the 2nd Brigade Combat Team to the north and the 3rd Brigade Combat Team to the south. For political reasons, a Canadian battalion had been attached to the 3rd. The Canadian light infantry battalion had trained frequently with the light infantry battalions of the Twenty-fifth, and its officers were well known to the American officers. The Canadians landed on the extreme southern end of Kalma beach and made their way south to the campus of Wŏnsan Agricultural University.

Lieutenant Colonel Brent MacFarlane, the commander of the 3rd Battalion of Princess Patricia's Canadian Light Infantry Regiment (nicknamed the Pats), recalled his arrival:

The American hovercraft landed us on the beach at Kalma. The fighting for the beach was over, but the cleanup was not. A hovercraft high on the beach was still burning; another one had sunk in shallow water and waves were breaking over its hull. Bodies were everywhere. Medical teams moved from one to another to check if the soldier was still alive. When they found someone, they [the medical teams] burst into action. Equipment was littered all across the beach. The long row of apartments facing the beach was mostly just rubble. Several buildings were on fire.

The engineers had marked out a path off the beach and on to the beach road. My 2IC [second-in-command, Major Philip Ushant] and I followed C Company off the beach and towards our objective. We were ordered to secure the university campus. A marine recon unit [the 1st Light Armored Reconnaissance Battalion] was already heavily engaged there, and I was told that there was some urgency in us supporting them.

I located Major Nilsson, the [acting] commander of the marines, and received a briefing from him on what we were facing and what needed to be done. Our enemy was a company-strength unit from the regular army, supported by an unknown strength of paramilitary forces, probably from a university-based organization. That was worrying, because they would certainly know the terrain well and be highly motivated to defend it. It would be close-fighting in a built-up area—and that was always messy.

Battle of Wŏnsan

September 10 to 17

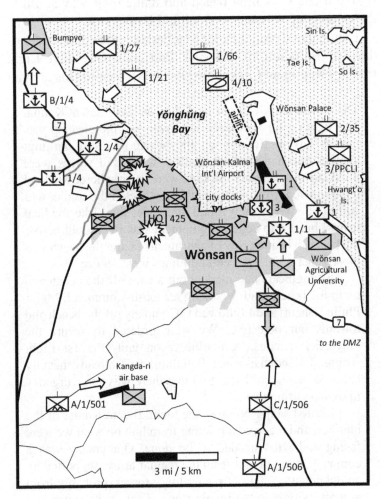

The university had been frequently favored by visits from North Korea's second Supreme Leader, Kim Jong-il. It had two main teaching buildings, several practice farms, a large greenhouse, dormitories, and administration buildings. The two teaching buildings were originally the monastery and the seminary of a German Benedictine abbey (completed in 1932). The attractive university grounds had many pine trees, including a "state natural treasure": a pine tree planted in 1890. The 143-year-old tree did not survive the battle.

While the Canadians attacked from the north directly into the university grounds, the marines worked their way around the east side of the university buildings, alongside a channel built for the university's flotilla of training fishing boats. Eventually, the two battalions managed to gain access to both teaching buildings. It was then a room-to-room firefight, occasionally resorting to hand-to-hand combat. It was grim and bloody struggle, and it was not until 04:00 on September 11 that the last of the enemy resistance was crushed. The Canadians suffered twenty percent casualties, while the 1st Marine Light Armored Reconnaissance Battalion lost forty percent of its initial strength, including both its commander and deputy commander.

Just to the north of the university, other marines were facing a spirited counterattack by a mix of mechanized and infantry troops supported by armor. The armor was in the form of eight P'okp'ung-ho tanks (T-62/72-type tanks).

Private Willis Nagle of Bravo Company of the 1/1st Marine Battalion, recalled the North Korean counterattack:

We had been fighting hard all day, with only a brief rest after we captured the airport. Jesus, I was tired! About a mile or so from the beach, we crossed some open ground, heading towards a row of apartments about a thousand yards ahead. It was after 17:00 and still furnace-hot. I'd already gone through my water. One guy passed out from the heat and was casevacked back to the beach. Lucky bastard!

The enemy knew just when to hit us. We were completely exposed. Some small-arms fire coming from the south pinned us down. We returned fire, and that was when the tanks rolled into view. They were at the edge of the [row of] apartments. I only saw two of them, but I later learned that there were more. Mostly they strafed us with machine-gun fire, but every now and then they let loose with their main [125-mm] gun. That caused us a lot of grief. One shell took out our CP [Bravo Company's command post]. The captain bought it [died]. Oh yes, we were in a ton of shit!

To the right of the 1/1st Battalion, the amphibious combat vehicles of the 3rd Assault Amphibian Battalion were receiving the brunt of the tanks' fire. Private Janie Chen remembered the one-sided fight:

Things really heated up in the late afternoon. We were advancing across an open area. The amtracs were in the rear, empty because all our squads were out in front. Only the Bushmasters [ACVs armed with Bushmaster chain guns] were supporting them. Suddenly, we were receiving shell fire. The Bushmaster [amtrac] in front of me was hit and the amtrac to my left blew up. I turned quickly to the right and hightailed it out of there. A shell landed near me and blew me on to my side [the vehicle's side]. I scrambled out. The Sarge and Kevin [Sergeant Mario Fratelli and Private Kevin Gul of the ACV's crew] climbed out too. The Sarge had a bad head wound and was bleeding into his eyes. Otherwise, he seemed okay. Kevin and I led him back to the med station [a first-aid post run by marine corpsmen]. We were still there when the Army finally showed up.

The soldiers of the 2/35th Battalion of the Twenty-fifth Light Infantry Division arrived on Kalma beach at the same time as the Canadian battalion. While the Canadians headed south to the university, the 2/35th moved west to support the marines and stop the counterattack. The combined weight of the three American battalions forced the North Korean's back into the city. Four of the enemy's eight tanks were destroyed. By 22:00, both sides were exhausted and badly needed to regroup. The open land between the two forces remained a deadly no-man's land.

Meanwhile to the north, the 1/4th Marine Battalion left its defensive position behind a stream and attacked. Lieutenant Colonel Ronald Kirkwood, the commander of that battalion, believed that he saw an opening in the North Korean lines. However, just after the battalion's attack began, five Ch'ŏnma tanks (older T-62-type tanks), with their 115-mm main guns, arrived to bolster the North Korean line. Kirkwood quickly pulled his men back to their start line. Two battalions of the Twenty-fifth Light Infantry Division arrived to support the marines.

The night of September 10/11 and all the following day was a time of regrouping and resupplying for both sides. Supplies of water were particularly worrisome. Pre-invasion estimates of water consumption was dramatically out of step with the reality of combat operations during a heatwave. Major Ryan Lowry of the 1st Marine Expeditionary Brigade was the beachmaster and in charge of organizing troops and supplies when they arrived on Kalma beach. He recalled the desperate situation:

> We were bringing in adequate food rations, but medical supplies were low, and we were burning through small-caliber ammunition at a staggering rate. However, of all the shortages, it was water that worried me the most. The heat was brutal. There was no supply [of water] in the airport area at all. All the mains had been smashed, and there was no electricity for pumps or anything else.
>
> There was no shade on the beach, and inland, there was no ocean breeze. All of my men were going shirtless, and the women were down to their bras. No one who wasn't on that beach that afternoon can imagine the heat. It was like working inside a furnace. I ordered a rotation of quick plunges into the sea to keep my men cool and able to work.

No such relief was available to the poor bastards inland. The corpsmen commandeered two amtracs to use their a/c's [air-conditioning units] to keep the seriously injured cool before they were medevacked out.

I put in repeated calls to the task force [the Navy's invasion fleet] for more supplies of water. It was always the same reply, "We are aware of the situation." Oh, that wasn't good. That was Navy code for "No one has a fucking clue how to fix your problem." Yes, it was a complete snafu [situation normal, all fucked up].

By midday on September 11, things improved for the American forces in Wŏnsan. The first of the transport aircraft landed at the airport. First, it was three Hercules transport aircraft from 36th Airlift Squadron out of Yokota, Japan, carrying medical supplies, ammunition, food rations, and most importantly, water. With the airport open, more Hercules landed. With the Air Force providing supplies to the troops in the Kalma area and dropping supplies to the airborne forces surrounding Wŏnsan, the Navy focused its attention on supplying the troops north of Wŏnsan. Hovercrafts loaded with supplies landed on the northern beachhead. The Navy crews dashed in, unloaded the supplies while under intermittent fire, and then dashed out.

At 21:11 on September 11, the first of the huge Galaxy transport aircraft landed at the airport. It had been a fifteen-hour trip from Peterson Air Force Base in Colorado. The Galaxies from two airlift squadrons (the 9th and the 22nd) arrived and unloaded the armored vehicles from the 3rd Armored Brigade Combat Team from the Fourth Infantry Division, plus a battalion of engineers and a battalion of much needed field artillery.

The first to land were the lead elements of the 4/10th Cavalry Squadron. The 10th Cavalry Regiment was formed in 1866 as one of the original post-Civil War African-American "Buffalo Soldier" regiments, which served in the western United States from 1867 to 1896. The squadron was equipped with the long-serving M3 Bradley cavalry fighting vehicles. After the Bradleys were unloaded, the Abrams main battle tanks of the 1/66th Armor Battalion began to arrive.[1] The 66th was the oldest armor regiment in the U.S. army, tracing its lineage back to 1918 and the killing fields of France during World War I. Neither of these two units were ready for action until the afternoon of September 12.

Although fighting was relatively light on September 11, American forces struggled with the heat. They experienced more casualties due to heat exhaustion and heatstroke than they did from combat. The North Koreans fared no better. Whereas September 11 was a day of regrouping, resupplying and reinforcements, September 12 was a day of movement and action. The attack was planned by Major General Blair Brownlee, the overall commander of the ground forces in and around Wŏnsan. It involved coordinated attacks by the northern and southern forces, with a large airstrike in the north. However, before those attacks could get underway, other events unfolded.

Airborne troops held the approaches to Wŏnsan. To the north at Kowŏn, the 2nd brigade of the Eighty-second Airborne Division had a desperate battle with elements of the North Korean 34th Infantry Regiment. More on this battle will be discussed in the next chapter. To the west and south, elements of two airborne divisions, the Eleventh and the 101st, held the approaches to the city. All remained quiet in their sectors. No enemy units had so far traveled east from the capital, and the North Korean commanders of the units

---

[1] The Army had intended to replace its 1980s-vintage M3 Bradleys for some time, but various programs to replace it were cancelled in 2009, in 2014, and in 2026. The Army currently foresees the Bradley remaining in service until the mid-2040s. Funding for a replacement for the 1970s-vintage M1 Abrams was cancelled in 2023. Work on a new variant, the E3, was cancelled in 2028. The A2 variant was the one that saw action during the Second Korean War. It will likely remain in service until at least 2050—a remarkable longevity for a tank design.

to the south were evidently reluctant to leave the DMZ less defended.

Because their sectors were quiet, Colonels Andrew Shifnal and James Wong, the respective commanders of the 2nd brigade from the Eleventh and the 1st brigade from the 101st, independently decided to send probing forces towards the city to see what lay in that direction. Wong sent two companies along the road from Anbyŏn. Upon reaching the outskirts of the city, they were engaged by a company of mechanized troops. Both sides were content to dig in and await developments. To the west, Shifnal sent a company along a winding road through the hills. Their objective was the Kangda-ri underground facility, a runway that the North Korean air force had built into the slope of a hill. The facility had been hit hard by the fighters from the *George Washington* and a volley of Tomahawk missiles from the *Arizona*. Shifnal believed that it was important to confirm that this facility was no longer functioning.

Captain Peter Goreau, the commander of Alpha Company of the 1/501st Battalion recalled what his men found:

> We came down the mountain road and could see the damage that the Navy had inflicted. The outside runway was torn up, and the entrance to the underground hangers had partially collapsed. We entered and were immediately under fire. We faced an undersized mixed company of [North Korean] army and air force personnel. It took my men about twenty minutes to neutralize the resistance. The facility was not so destroyed as the intel reports had suggested. When I entered the long and narrow facility, I noticed an ancient jet fighter standing in a carved-out shelter. It looked like something from the fifties [1950s]. I doubt that it had flown in decades.
>
> While I was admiring the antique, Lieutenant [Erin] Rost reported to me that her men had found something interesting. She took me to a room at the very back of the facility. There was a dozen or so boxes stacked along the wall. One was open. Rost's men had opened it. There were

two medium-caliber artillery shells inside. Probably 115s or 125s [115-mm or 125-mm shells]. Nothing unusual there, but the boxes themselves were covered with numbers and a lot of Korean writing—much more than you would expect. I called for Corporal Park, who spoke fluent Korean. He translated the writing on one of the boxes. My heart stopped when he read what some of it said: "Danger. Handle with care. Organophosphorus compound VX. Chemical nerve agent." Good God, it was GA nerve gas! We hadn't got all the WMDs, and that news was absolutely huge!

I had everyone back off, and I ordered a squad to guard the boxes and not under any circumstances to touch anything. I left the facility, found my signals [radio] man, and immediately called it in.

GA is NATO's designation for VX (Venomous agent X) nerve agent. VX is a sulfur-containing organophosphorus compound with a chemical formula of $C_{11}H_{26}NO_2PS$. It is not a gas, but an odorless aerosol of lethal droplets. VX attacks the nervous system, which paralyses the body's muscles. Death is caused by paralysis of the diaphragm muscle, which causes asphyxiation. Death usually occurs one to ten minutes after contact with the skin or inhalation. VX is far more potent than Sarin gas (or GB nerve agent). It is slow to evaporate, and it can last in the environment for days or weeks depending on the circumstances. VX was banned under the U.N.'s Chemical Weapons Convention of 1992, which North Korea never signed.

The news that a stockpile of chemical weapons had been found was kept a tightly guarded secret. Very few in United States Forces Korea or Indo-Pacific Command knew of the discovery. Even Lieutenant General Dunn, the commander of the Seventh Air Force, was never told, and neither was Vice Admiral Floyd Trudel, the commander of Seventh Fleet and in overall charge of the invasion's naval forces. Lieutenant General John Yates, the commander of the Eighth Army in South Korea, and overall commander of all ground forces in North and South Korea was told, because it was his forces that could potentially face a chemical attack.

At a hearing of the House Armed Services Committee after the war, Admiral Sentsey, the commander of Indo-Pacific Command, described the impact of the discovery on the war: "None. It had no strategic impact at all on the prosecution of the war." When pressed to explain his curt response, and after a long discussion with his military legal counsel, he stated:

At that time, we were committed to a ground war. Unless a diplomatic option presented itself, no one [in the military] could see any alternative but to continue the prosecution of the war as planned. North Korea had not surrendered, and there was no indication that it would. The fact that North Korea still had some chemical weapons was, of course, alarming, but up to that date, they had not used them—not on the invasion force and not on civilian targets in South Korea. We believed that this lack of use was indicative of the North Korean leadership's reluctance to escalate the war. We believed at the time that it was because they feared our retaliatory response to a chemical attack—and rightly so.

One person who knew of the discovery was Major Carlos De Silva, a response team leader from the 2nd Chemical Battalion. The battalion had arrived in South Korea on July 28 to reinforce the 23rd Chemical Battalion. The major described his involvement in dealing with the troubling discovery:

I reported directly to General Sweeny. There was no one else in his office but him and me when he briefed me on my mission. I left to assemble my company. A Chinook [a medium-lift helicopter from the 501st Aviation Regiment] flew to the east side of South Korea, where we picked up an escort of four Cobras [attack helicopters]. We crossed the coast, flew north and swung west across Wŏnsan. I could see the battle raging below. Smoke was everywhere.

Our Chinook landed at Kangda-ri. The paratroopers guarding the underground facility backed away from us when we approached in our full protective gear. A frightening sight, I imagine. We entered the facility and got to work. We were looking at twelve boxes of shells containing GA nerve agent. Two shells per box, twenty-four in total. They were stable and contained, so they posed no immediate threat. We neutralized the shells on location and helicoptered them to the *Pinckney*, a destroyer that had been assigned to us, because we were not permitted to take them into South Korea. The captain [Captain Timothy Thorne] knew nothing of our cargo. I was under orders not to discuss it with him, and he knew enough not to ask. The *Pinckney* sailed to Guam to deliver the shells for proper disposal. I flew back to Kangda-ri to search for more WMDs hidden at the site.

Meanwhile, the war continued. By the afternoon of September 12, Abrams tanks and Bradley combat vehicles, which had been airlifted to Kalma airport, were ready to strike at the North Koreans. The attack started at 14:30. The Abrams quickly destroyed the few P'okp'ung-ho tanks that remained. Supported by marines of the 1/1st Marine Battalion, six Abrams and twelve Bradleys entered Wŏnsan. The North Koreans launched a barrage of anti-tank missiles. Two Abrams were destroyed and one was damaged. The Bradleys were initially ignored, as all the enemy fire was directed at the tanks. Another Abrams was damaged and the surviving tanks retreated. The advance of the tanks did, however, allow the marines to penetrate the North Korean lines. "Urban operations," as one unidentified officer called it, began. It was a grim house-to-house battle. Casualties on both sides were high.

Meanwhile a four-battalion attack started in the north, involving two marine battalions and two battalions from the Twenty-fifth Light Infantry Division. It was preceded by a three-squadron airstrike from the *Ford*. The airstrike hit the enemy's front lines, and more importantly, the headquarters of the 425th Independent Mechanized Division. The headquarters had been precisely located in the northeastern suburbs by RQ-170 Sentinel drones of the 44th Reconnaissance Squadron flying out of Japan, but controlled from Cheech Air Force Base in Nevada. The fresher troops of the Twenty-five broke through the shattered North Korean lines and entered the northern suburbs of Wŏnsan. Like the soldiers to the south, they now faced a grim urban battle with a desperate but unyielding enemy.

In the south, the city docks were captured during the night of September 12/13. In the north, the Kangwŏn Provincial People's Hospital was captured later that morning after fierce fighting. The North Koreans had fought ferociously inside the hospital, even with helpless patients still trapped inside. Private Beverley Van Dusen of the 1/21st Battalion described the grisly scene inside:

> It was horrific, absolutely horrific. Patients lay dead in their beds, riddled with bullets. The floors were covered in blood. Rivers of it. Blood and body parts. I don't think that I'll ever be able to forget what I saw that day. I can't close my eyes at night without seeing it.

Once the fighting had ceased in the hospital, two teams of naval doctors were flown in from the *Ford*. Lieutenant Commander Jeremy Hunt, a Navy surgeon, recalled how he became "hardened" to the gruesome sights, and his patients were "just pieces of meat for me to patch up and send away as quickly as possible. I stopped identifying them as human beings."

The headquarters of the 425th were captured late on September 15. The division's commander, Major General Yun (who had been wounded during the airstrike on his headquarters), surrendered his forces to Marine Brigadier

General Eric Ilma, the commander of all ground forces in northern Wŏnsan. All resistance in the city ceased at 19:00 on September 15, except for sporadic attacks by fanatical units, which continued fighting until September 17. The last stronghold, the Sinhŭng Market in central Wŏnsan, fell on that day at 15:10, and when it did, an eerie silence fell upon the ruined city.[1]

---

[1] Ironically, the Sinhŭng Market was a bastion of capitalism in the communist country. It, along with other local markets for food and homemade goods (called *jangmadang*), had been tolerated by the North Korean government ever since the disastrous famine of the late 1990s. Combined, these markets (and a thriving black market) formed an informal, but vital, segment of the North Korean economy. The majority of North Koreans were dependent on these private markets for their daily survival.

Chapter 19

Big Left Turn

If officers understand each other, operations succeed. This is the only "must" principle in the issue of orders.

Major General Robert W. Grow,
U.S. Army, World War II.

The American strategy after the fall of Wŏnsan had been decided upon, and committed to, long before the first marine landed on Kalma beach. There had been two broad options available to planners: move west and drive directly on P'yŏngyang, hoping for a quick surrender, or swing south and open up the DMZ for reinforcements from South Korea.

Colonel Cole, at Indo-Pacific Command, recalled the debate:

Immediately moving west was favored by some planners, because it would keep the North Koreans off balance and held the promise of a swift victory—something that we all wanted. If events unfolded as they hoped, we could quickly force a surrender and our casualties would be light. However, that option risked being trapped in the central mountains with roadblocks in front and enemy forces attacking from both sides, both on a tactical level and on an operational level. Our forces in North Korea wouldn't be able to hold the enemy back everywhere. It was a high-risk option, either winning big or losing everything.

The other option, and the one that I favored, was to hold in the west [and the north] and turn south towards the DMZ. If we could open up the eastern end of the DMZ, particularly Highway 7, we could get all—or even just some—of the Second [Infantry] Division through the gap. And maybe some South Korean forces too, if we could show them that victory was within reach. Everyone knew that would be a gamechanger.

The planners ultimately decided on the slower, less risky option, and Admiral Sentsey approved what came to be known as Operation Pivot. With two brigades of airborne forces holding the northern and western fronts, the rest of the ground forces headed south towards the Demilitarize Zone. The operation required that the northern and western approaches to Wŏnsan held; the western approach was quiet, but the northern approach was in jeopardy.

On September 10, special forces and an airstrike had delayed the North Korean 34th Infantry Division in its march south from Hamhŭng. However, by the next day, the enemy division was approaching Wŏnsan in force. All that stood in its way was the 2nd Brigade of the Eighty-second Airborne Division, which had set up a defensive line at the northern edge of the town of Kowŏn. The 2nd comprised of three infantry battalions, an engineering battalion, and a battalion of field artillery.

At the same, Bravo Company of the 1/1st Special Forces Battalion, which had not been able to evacuate after it completed its mission, was marching south with enemy forces close behind it. The company planned to link up with the airborne troops at Kowŏn. Every now and then, Bravo Company stopped and pinned the approaching North Koreans. When the enemy deployed for battle, Bravo Company departed. Lieutenant Francis Eddy recalled that the march was "utterly exhausting" and that the North Koreans were "constantly trying to flank us, because if they got behind us, we would be trapped." The presence of the special forces had an unfortunate impact on the battle at Kowŏn, a battle which started during the night of September 11/12.

At a military hearing on the battle, Colonel Rubin Deskin, the commander of the 2nd, described the battle and the confusion of that night:

We had set up a strong defensive line along the northern edge of the town facing the Tokchi River. The highway and railway bridges had both been destroyed by the Air Force, but due to the ongoing drought, the river was running very shallow. It could be easily forded at many points. It was particularly shallow to the west, which was where much of my concern lay prior to the battle. I placed my artillery so that my westernmost unit [the 2/508th battalion] would be more easily supported. We were in contact with the CAW-5 [Carrier Air Wing 5 on board the *George Washington*], which had been assigned to provide us air support if we needed it. We were also in contact with an isolated unit of special forces that was making its way south to our lines. They were expected to reach us by midnight [00:00 on September 12].

At 22:33 [on September 11], I received drone intel that a force of at least three, possibly four, regiments were making their way south along Highway 7. I contact CAW-5 and requested an airstrike on the highway. Four Lightnings were dispatched, and the airstrike occurred at 23:28. I was subsequently informed that the aircraft had attacked what they believed were two regiment-size columns making their way south to us.

At the time, our analysis of the situation and the estimated speed of the approaching columns led us to believe that the aircraft had attacked the forward enemy units. This turned out not to be so. The aircraft had in fact attacked rear units. The North Koreans had moved far faster than we projected. Their forward units had already reached the [Tokchi] river and swung far to our right in an attempt to outflank us. They crossed the shallow river and attacked the 1st [the 1/325th battalion], our easternmost unit, just after midnight. The commander of that battalion had been told to expect a friendly unit to be approaching his position at that time. As a consequent, he delayed opening fire on the enemy forces until too late. North Korean soldiers had already crossed the river and the intervening flat farmlands. The 1st was outnumbered by at least five to one, and it was quickly overwhelmed. Survivors retreated southwest into the town.

Colonel Deskin's carefully worded summary downplayed the chaos of that night. Sergeant Gilford Freeman of the 1/325th Battalion recalled the confusion:

My squad was in the center of our line. We were told to expect some friendlies coming down from the north around midnight. About that time, we saw figures moving towards us through the farmers' fields. They were walking slowly, nothing suspicious. It was dark and I couldn't make out their uniforms clearly with my night-goggles. I assumed that these were the friendlies and I held my fire. We all did. The figures were walking in the open and looked relaxed. There were a lot more of them than I thought were coming. We had been told company strength, this was more like battalion strength or more. When more kept appearing, I grew concerned.

Defensive Line at Kowŏn

September 11 to 14

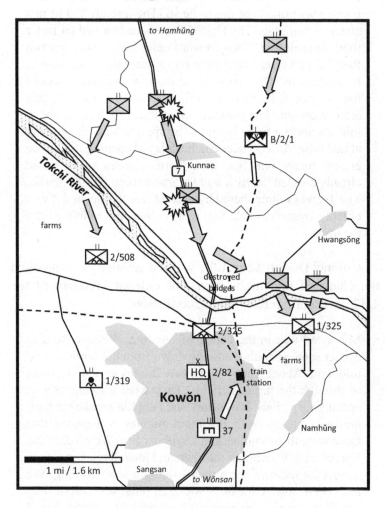

Suddenly, bullets were flying around my head, and I dived for cover. I ordered my squad to open fire, and the other squads on either side did the same. The enemy charged. They really didn't have a choice. For them, to retreat over the open terrain would have been a slaughter. We killed many, but we were overwhelmed and found ourselves in close combat—really close. I lost three of my squad in that initial charge, three that I know of. Most of the others in my squad disappeared into the darkness. I had with me only four from my original squad and one from another squad. No idea where he came from. We couldn't hold the line, so we retreated. I call it a retreat, but it was really a rout. We ran as fast as we could back to the town. We didn't stop until be found ourselves safely among our engineers.

When his right flank collapsed, Colonel Deskin ordered his only reserves available at that time, the 37th Engineer Battalion, to protect the open flank. Major Matthew Franks, the battalion's commander, quickly moved his men to the train station on the eastern edge of the town. It was a sturdy building and defensible, with a flat, open killing zone to the east. Within ten minutes, the engineers had turned the train station into a fortress bristling with heavy weapons. Survivors from the 1st Battalion rallied when they found the engineers holding a fortified location. Two North Korean regiments repeatedly attacked the train station. Despite being heavily outnumbered, the engineers held, but with many casualties. Major Franks was subsequently awarded the Silver Star for his heroic stand that night and a Purple Heart for a bullet wound he received to his hand (two fingers had to be amputated). The 37th Engineer Battalion received a Valorous Unit Award.

Exhausted, the North Koreans withdrew to the south bank of the river just before dawn. They attacked again the following night, including a battalion-size diversionary attack to the American left flank. The paratroopers were ready for them this time. The company of special forces, which had been delayed, had by this time reached the safety of the American lines; they added their firepower to the defenders of Kowŏn. Navy fighters from the *George Washington* stuck the North Korean regiments northeast of Kowŏn repeated on September 12 and 13, as did the brigade's own artillery (the 1/319th Field Artillery Battalion). The attack on the night of September 13/14 was modest in comparison to the previous two. By 05:00 on September 14, the third and final attack petered, and the North Koreans waded back over the river and began to dig in along its northern bank. The northern approach to Wŏnsan had held.

Once Wŏnsan and its northern and western approaches were secure, the invasion forces started their move south toward the DMZ. The ground forces available to Lieutenant General Yates, the commander of the Eighth Army, were seven brigade-size combat teams, one of which was armored, plus some units of special forces. He also had two brigades of marines, but these had been decimated by the fighting in Wŏnsan, and they required rest and reinforcements. He also had the two fresh brigades of the Second Infantry Division, along with its powerful artillery and aviation support, waiting in their bases in South Korea.

On September 14, Yates ordered the division to move to the east coast and take up position on the DMZ north of Ganseong. Its units were ordered not to advance into North Korea or even to fire into the country. Their orders were to "visibly demonstrate their presence to pin" the enemy, and nothing more. There could be no firing over the DMZ. South Korean government still feared retaliatory strikes by North Korean artillery, and the political sensibilities of America's South Korean hosts had to be respected.

The logistical staff of the Second had practiced such a move and were fully ready to implement the transfer of the division from one side of South Korea to the other—a road distance of two hundred miles. Two mechanized brigades and a brigade of artillery were moved during the night of September 15/16. They did not go through the South Korean capital, but used the motorways to the south and east of the metropolis. The division's aviation brigade flew to empty fields north of Sokcho.

In North Korea, early on September 17, even before the fighting in Wŏnsan had completely stopped, two units started moving south on Highway 7 to meet up with the airmobile troops holding positions around T'ongch'on. These units were the 4/10th Cavalry Squadron, with its Bradley cavalry fighting vehicles, and the newly arrived by airlift 1/8th Infantry Battalion. During the battle for Wŏnsan, the Bradleys had made less-tempting targets for North Korean anti-tank weapons than the Abrams tanks. Consequently, the battalion had lost only fifteen percent of its initial strength.

The airmobile troops, finding no enemy before them, began to move south even before the reinforcements had reached them. The 2/506th Infantry Battalion joined with rangers from the 3/75th Ranger Battalion to attack the town of Kosŏng, which was the headquarters of the North Korean First Infantry Division. At the same time, the troops of the 3/187th Infantry Battalion took to their helicopters and flew to the Mount Kŭmgang area to cut off any reinforcements going to Kosŏng from the west.

Meanwhile, the 1/187th Infantry Battalion turned inland and headed along a secondary road that went from Kuŭm to the deserted village of Kasen. Its inhabitants had fled before the American soldiers arrived. The 1/187th reached Kasen just as the Bradleys of the 4/10th caught up to it. Both battalions rested for the night of September 17/18 before continuing on to the big prize: the town of Kŭmgang, headquarters to both the Sixth Infantry Division and I Corps—the corps that commanded the entire eastern third of the DMZ.

The two American units intended to leave Kasen at dawn.
They did not.

Order to Move East

September 14

EIGHTH ARMY HEADQUARTERS
Camp Humphreys, ROK
Office of Commanding General

Classification: TOP SECRET
Transmission: 09-14-33 16:35KT
Confirmation: ███████

>> MOVEMENT ORDER <<

To: MG BRUM, COMSECONDDIV

From: LTG YATES, COMEIGHTHARMY √

Info: GEN SWEENY, COMUSFK
      ADM SENTSEY, COMINDOPAC

1.   Move all combat elements of SECONDINFDIV to northeastern ROK north of Ganseong.
2.   ████████████████████████████████
3.   Do not use routes through Seoul. ██████████
    ████████████████
4.   After arrival, combat units are to visibly demonstrate their presence to pin the KPA forces along the DMZ.
5.   Units are not repeat not permitted to move into or fire into DPRK territory from ROK territory even if fired upon.
6.   The move must be completed before 09-16-33 06:00KT.

Chapter 20

Kasen

When things go wrong in your command, start wading for the reason in increasing larger concentric circles around your own desk.

General Bruce D. Clark,
U.S. Army, First Korean War.

On September 18, a waning crescent moon rose over the village of Kasen at 01:07. The night was clear, dark and hot. A brilliant display of stars twinkled overhead. The moon and the rest of the celestial sky were entirely indifferent to the plight of North Korean commanders on that night. The situation facing them was dire in the extreme. Wŏnsan had fallen; their air force and navy had effectively ceased to exist; reinforcements were being constantly interdicted by the American air force, which flew unimpeded across most of the country; the American invasion forces were moving south to trap the 40,000 soldiers of I Corps; and the American division in South Korea had moved to the eastern end of the DMZ and could attempt to force its way across at any moment.

It was within this dire situation that, at 01:32, artillery shells fell on Kasen. The village was tiny, just a few homes at a road junction. Although the village was strategically irrelevant, the road junction was not. North Korean troops who wanted to retreat from the impending encirclement had to travel along the east-west road that went through Kasen— a place that two Americans battalions now held. The American troops in Kasen were used to being shelled by North Korean artillery. The 4/10th Cavalry Squadron had survived through the fierce battle for Wŏnsan, and the 1/187th Infantry Battalion had been shelled on and off since it arrived by helicopter on September 10, eight eventful days ago. This particular barrage was not even a heavy one.

The shells exploded in the air and the explosions themselves did no damage. An invisible, odorless mist came from the exploding shells and descended on to the village. Those soldiers outside started twitching and gasping for breath. They doubled over, vomited, and collapsed. Within two or three minutes, they were dead. Those inside buildings or tents lasted ten minutes or more, and a few survived for an hour before they too died. Those outside of the contaminated area rushed in to help those in need. They too died. All were conscious to the end—mutely panicking as their immobile bodies screamed for air.

One of the survivors of the attack, Private Louis Burgos of the 4/10th, described the awful scene:

Corporal [Amanda] Hume and I were working late inside our Bradley. The comms unit [radio] had been acting up, and we'd been ordered to fix it. We heard some screaming from outside. Our first thought was that the North Koreans were attacking. Amanda popped open the turret hatch and looked about. "Someone's in trouble," she shouted to me, and then she jumped out. I looked out of the hatch and watched her run. She hadn't gone fifty yards before she dropped to her knees and puked. I panicked.

Before landing [at the airport in Wŏnsan], we had been warned about what to expect if we were under chemical attack. Something in the back of my mind must have remembered that briefing. I hastily shut the hatch, started the Bradley's engine, and turned on the life support system.[1] Now that I was sealed in tight, I began to calm down. A part of me wanted to go out there and save Amanda, but I told myself that I would be dead before I reached her. I was right, of course, but that didn't help. I still wonder …

I had to tell someone. I reached for the comms unit, but it was in pieces. We'd been working on it. I tried to fix it, but my hands were shaking too badly. Instead, I used the scope [the vehicle commander's pericope] to look about. It was dark outside, so I turned on the turret's spotlight and did a three-sixty [turned through 360°]. There were bodies everywhere. No one was moving. Eventually, I returned to the broken comms unit. If nothing else, it kept me busy and stopped me thinking about what was outside.

Burgos never managed to fix the radio. He was rescued after being trapped inside his Bradley for seven hours. Wisely, Burgos never drove the Bradley away from the contamination site; the exterior of the Bradley was heavily contaminated with VX droplets covering its surface.[2] A team

---

[1] The M3 Bradley cavalry fighting vehicle had been designed for a high-intensity Cold War conflict in Europe, where it was likely that nuclear and chemical weapons would have been used. Its crew were protected from both nuclear fallout and chemical contamination.

[2] North Korea had used VX nerve agent before. On February 13, 2017 at Kuala Lumpur International Airport in Malaysia, two female North Korean agents used a spray of VX to assassinate Kim Jong-nam, the eldest brother of the Supreme Leader Kim Jong-un. He died fifteen minutes after exposure.

from the 2nd Chemical Battalion provided him with a chemical-protection suit so he could safely climb out of the vehicle. Burgos was one of the lucky ones. The 1/187th took the worse of it, losing 526 men and women, while the 4/10th lost 385. Another eighteen died later that day, and 472 were injured, many severely so.

Forty-five minutes after the attack, news reached the headquarters of the 3rd Brigade of the 101st Airborne Division that there had been a chemical attack on the units in Kasen. After getting confirmation, the brigade's commander, Colonel Arden Bruckheimer, directly contacted the Eighth Army's headquarters at Camp Humphreys in South Korea, as per his standing orders in such a situation. General Yates was immediately informed. The general ordered the team at Kangda-ri (near Wŏnsan) to immediately travel to Kasen. He also dispatched, by four Chinook helicopters, four teams from the 23rd Chemical Battalion and four medical teams from the 168th Multifunctional Medical Battalion of the 65th Medical Brigade.

Major Carlos De Silva, a response team leader from the 2nd Chemical Battalion, was one of the first experts on the scene. He later described the gruesome sights:

Bodies were lying everywhere. Most had time to roll on to their backs before they died, so they were all looking up at me. It was the look of fear in their staring eyes that I remember the most. It had been frozen there in the moment of their death. Vomit was everywhere—a pool of it by each body—but very little blood, just speckles in the vomit.

After surveying the scene, I headed back to our command post to confer with my team and develop a plan of action, both for ourselves and the medical teams that were heading our way. On my way back [to the command post], one of my team called me over to a Bradley. A soldier was trapped inside [this was Private Burgos]. I'd given up on finding anyone alive this close to the epicenter. We cleaned up the Bradley around the hatch as best we could. We found a spare chem suit, carefully opened the hatch, and dropped the suit inside without it touching any of the exterior. Once he had dressed himself in the chem suit, we pulled him out.

You could see droplets covering the steel [armor] of the Bradley. They were my first indication that we were dealing with GA [VX nerve agent]. That was a bitch, because GA was very deadly and very persistent. The hot temperatures would help to disperse it faster than normal, but this area would be contaminated and off-limits for a week or more.

After dispatching the teams by helicopters from Camp Humphreys, General Yates notified Admiral Sentsey at Indo-Pacific Command in Hawaii. Admiral Sentsey in turn called Secretary of Defense Woodtke. At 15:16 on September 17, Washington Time (04:16 Korean time on September 18), Woodtke briefed President Anders on the details of the attack (as they were known at the time) and offered three reasons for it. The chemical attack could have been ordered at a high level within the North Korean government; it could have been ordered by a panicking local commander who had exceeded his authority; or it could have been an accident, such as a mix-up of munitions or mislabeled containers. However, politically, the reason did not matter. The President had publicly committed himself to retaliate if North Korea used nuclear or chemical weapons. He had to act on his threat, or he would face an emboldened North Korea which may then escalate to a full chemical or nuclear war (if it still had such weapons). The political posturing was over, and now President Anders had to face the stark reality that the United States had no chemical weapons in its arsenal with which to retaliate. The last of its stocks of VX weapons had been destroyed in 2012, and its last chemical weapon of any type (a Sarin-filled M55 rocket) had been destroyed in 2023.

President Anders had to decide on two grave questions: should the American retaliation use conventional or nuclear weapons, and what should be the target? The debate on these questions within the Anders Administration continues to be shrouded in secrecy, as does its discussions with the Joint Chiefs. Nevertheless, there are indications that some (most notably National Security Advisor Alan Martin) pressed for a nuclear attack on P'yŏngyang to give the North Korean's an unambiguous message and prompt them to surrender. The majority of his advisors, however, preferred a massive conventional attack on some other target. President Anders followed the advice of the majority and did not select the nuclear option. The President had already decided that no public announcement of the chemical attack on American soldiers would happen until after the retaliation was completed.

As to the target, he sought advice from the theater commanders, with the provisos that the target would not be the capital or any of the larger population center, and that there should be some military justification for selecting the target. Admiral Sentsey, in consultation with Generals Sweeny and Yates, recommended to the President that the town of Kŭmgang would be ideal for operational purposes. It could be militarily justified by being the dual headquarters of North Korea's I Corps and its Sixth Infantry Division. It was almost certain that an officer in I Corps gave the order to bombard Kasen—whether or not the officer knew that the shells were filled with VX nerve agent. Their joint recommendation was accepted by the President. Global Strike Command was given the order to undertake "maximum-effect area bombing of the target" using the largest conventional bombs in the U.S. arsenal—a message that the command passed on to the Eighth Air Force to implement.

Major General Ronald Stoltman, the commander of Eighth Air Force, had been ordered to use two of the largest types of bombs in the Air Force's arsenal, and that added complications to the mission. He could not just assign one squadron to make the attack; he needed to use different types of bombers from different squadrons. Such a multi-squadron mission needed careful coordination, and there was no time for that. He decided that the mission would take place in five waves by bombers from three different squadrons. The precise timing of the waves was not mission-critical, but the sequence was.

Technical Sergeant Vincent Craig, a munitions loader with the 1st Special Operations Squadron, recalled the rush:

> We [the ground crew] flew in the [MC-130J] Commandos down to Guam [from Kadena Air Base in Japan]. The big Mothers [GBU-43/B MOABs] were ready there waiting for us, already in their [airdrop] cradles. Three of them! That was a quarter of the entire stocks that the Air Force had left.[1] Whatever the target was, someone wanted it wiped out. We put the three cradles inside the Commandos as quickly as we could. The bombs had been designed to be carried in this way, so the task was straightforward enough. We had them loaded in twenty minutes flat. The planes refueled as soon as we finished. They took off ten minutes later. It was a really quick prep [preparation for a mission].

Three Spirits preceded the Commandos, the *Spirit of Washington*, the *Spirit of Alaska*, and the *Spirit of New York*, all from the 393rd Bomb Squadron. The first two each carried a single 30,000-pound GBU-57 MOP deep-penetration bomb. The last one carried four thermobaric (or "vacuum") bombs. This type of bomb disperses an aerosol of fuel which then explodes. The fireball and blast wave are larger and last longer than conventional explosives. The

---

[1] Only fifteen of the GBU-43/B MOAB (Massive Ordnance Air Blast, or popularly, Mother of All Bombs) were ever made. The bomb was designed to be most effective in deep valleys and mountainous terrain. Prior to the Second Korean War, it had only been used once, and that was in Afghanistan in 2017. Two bombs had been used earlier in the Second Korean War to attack two headquarters, but met with only limited success due to the flatness of the terrain.

United Nations had attempted to ban thermobaric bombs in 1980 and again in 2010, but both attempts failed.

The final squadron involved in this mission was the 23rd Bomb Squadron. Eight Stratofortresses took off from Minot Air Force Base in North Dakota, but one had to turn back shortly after leaving U.S. airspace due to an engine issue. The planes were refueled in the air while crossing the Pacific Ocean. Five of the bombers carried twenty-five 2,000-pound unguided ("dumb") bombs each. The stocks of guided bombs had dwindled as the war consumed them at an alarming rate. However, the Air Force had considerable quantities of unguided bombs remaining. The last two bombers carried a mix of cluster bombs and incendiaries (as did the bomber that turned back). Over two hundred *tons* of bombs were heading to a small town in southeastern North Korea.

The town of Kŭmgang was nestled in deep valleys of the western foothills of Mount Kŭmgang, a 5,374-foot-high mountain and a national park. The park had some of the most dramatic and spectacular scenery in all of North Korea. Between 1998 and 2008, during a thaw in relations between the two Koreas, the park opened to tourists from South Korea.[1] The Kŭmgang River flows down from the mountain, through the town, and south to the Bukhan River, which flows into South Korea. The river bisected the town into the larger western sector and the smaller eastern sector.

Kŭmgang served as the local government center for the region, as well as the army's regional command center, with both I Corps and the Sixth Infantry Division having headquarters in the town. The town had a prewar population

---

[1] Guided group tours to the Mount Kŭmgang Tourist Region from South Korea were permitted starting in 1998. However, in 2008, while watching a sunrise from a beach, a woman tourist was shot dead by a guard. After that, South Korea stopped its tours. Tourism in the region dwindled to nothing by the late 2010s, and in 2024, the North Korean government finally closed the region's tourist administration.

of 23,000 (about the same as Watertown, New York, or Vicksburg, Mississippi). By mid-September 2033, some of its citizens had been called up to fight and others had fled the warzone. It is uncertain how many remained. Because of the deception strategy of Operation Windmill, the town had been attacked only once. On September 11, the two military headquarters had been heavily attacked by Navy fighters from the *Ford*. It was believed that some of the town's inhabitants fled after that attack.

Just after dawn on September 20, thirteen bombers from the U.S. Eighth Air Force approached the town from the west, over Mount Kŭmgang. Flying at 20,000 feet, they would have been barely noticed by those below. They were escorted by ten Lightnings from the 80th Fighter Squadron, but the escort proved unnecessary as the bombers were not attacked. The Spirits arrived first. At 07:11, the first two dropped their massive penetrating bombs, one each on the prewar site of the headquarters of I Corps and of the Sixth Infantry Division. It was suspected that the two headquarters had deep bunkers built beneath the surface buildings—buildings that were already in ruins.

Captain Williamina Brown, pilot of the trailing bomber, the *Spirit of New York*, recalled the raid:

> In the distance, I could see the two MOPs [massive penetrating bombs] drop. I watched them fall through the air. It was surreal in a way. They disappeared into a deep valley. I didn't see them explode, because the surrounding mountains obscured my view, and I was too busy completing my own mission.
>
> Unlike the two MOPs, my payload was unguided. I dropped the four 118s [thermobaric bombs], one at a time. They were intended to walk [traverse] across the target from west to east. The 118s were nasty, but that was my mission and those were my orders. I had turned and was already heading east by the time my bombs hit. I assume that they

hit their targets. I caught up to the other two Spirits, and we all headed home to the States.

After the three Spirits departed, the three Commandos arrived and released their massive airburst bombs. These bombs were GPS-guided and each had an explosive yield of eleven tons of TNT and a blast radius of one mile. (For comparison, the atomic bomb that destroyed Seattle had a yield of twenty-five *thousand* tons of TNT and a blast radius of nearly four miles.) Their targets were spread across the town—one in the east, one in the northwest, and one in the southwest. These bombs were designed to work in deep valleys, such as the one Kŭmgang was located in, where the valley walls would magnify the blast effect.

The Stratofortresses came next. The target was now marked by a thick column of black smoke rising into the clear morning sky. The first five bombers dropped over one hundred 2000-pound bombs on to what remained of the town; the last two dropped a combination of cluster bombs and incendiaries. As they turned for home, photographs and videos were taken as required by the mission, but nothing could be seen of the town beneath the layer of black smoke, which completely filled the valley.

Four hours later, a RQ-170 Sentinel reconnaissance drone from the 44th Reconnaissance Squadron flew over Kŭmgang, but smoke still obscured the target. More drone missions were ordered. It was not until 18:30, some eleven hours after the attack, that the first clear images of the target could be seen. Somehow, the bridge across the Kŭmgang River remained intact, but little else did. It was a moonscape of rubble.

Order to Bomb Kŭmgang

September 18

AIR FORCE GLOBAL STRIKE COMMAND

Classification: TOP SECRET
Transmission: 09-18-33 00:53Z
Confirmation: ▮▮▮▮▮

AF REC. OFF.
AFSTRAT 33/1311/TAO
Rec. 12-06-33

DECLASSIFIED
04 23 2034
AF REC. OFF.

Appr: LTC WN

>> TARGET ATTACK ORDER <<

To: MG STOLTMAN, COM8AF

From: GEN VERCH, COMAFSTRAT

Info: RESTRICTED. No distribution.

1. Priority A1 target: Town of Kumgang, PDRK. Grid ▮▮▮▮▮ 38.4857N 128.0201E. Authorized by POTUS.
2. Maximum-effect area bombing of target using multiple 43MOAB and 57MOP and other ordnance as required. Nuclear ordnance is not repeat not to be used.
3. Prioritize military command facilities and other military targets in target area. ▮▮
4. Raid must take place before 09-20 00:00Z. Raiding aircraft are not to enter the airspace of nonbelligerent countries ▮▮▮▮▮▮▮▮▮▮▮▮▮▮▮▮▮▮▮▮▮▮▮▮▮
5. Undertake subsequent aerial reconnaissance. Report results ▮▮▮▮▮▮▮▮▮▮▮▮▮ to COMAFSTRAT ▮▮▮▮▮▮▮▮▮▮▮ before 09-20 20:00Z.
6. A second raid on the target is not authorized at this time. ▮▮▮▮▮▮▮▮▮▮▮▮▮▮▮▮▮▮▮

Ordnance Used in the Raid on Kŭmgang

September 20

Seq.	Bomb type	Description	Size (lbs.)	Qty.	Delivery
1	GBU-57 MOP	Penetrating	30,000	2	2 B-2A
2	BLU-118/B11	Thermobaric	2,000	4	1 B-2A
3	GBU-43/B MOAB	Airburst	20,000	3	3 MC-130J
4	BLU-117 Mk 84	General	2,000	125	5 B-52J
5	CBU-87	Cluster	1,000	35	2 B-52J
	& CBU-112	Incendiaries	2,000	6	

Total weight of bombs (lbs.)   425,000

Notes:
- The penetrating GBU-57 MOPs and the thermobaric BLU-118/B11s were delivered first by three B-2A Spirits of 393rd Bomb Squadron.
- The airburst GBU-43/B MOABs were delivered next by three MC-130J Commando IIs of the 1st Special Operations Squadron, which flew out of Kadena Air Base, Japan, collected the bombs at Andersen Air Force Base on Guam, and then flew to the target.
- The remaining bombs were delivered in two waves by seven B-52J Stratofortresses of 23rd Bomb Squadron. The first wave of five bombers dropped BLU-117s, while the second wave of two bombers dropped a mix of CBU-87s and CBU-112s. A third bomber carrying additional cluster bombs and incendiaries had to turn back before completing its mission due to engine trouble.

Fires were burning in various places in what was left of the town. A large forest fire was burning to the northeast of the town and a smaller one to the west, both fueled by the month-long draught and scorching temperatures. Various vehicles were parked to the south of the city, likely vehicles of rescue or firefighting teams, and a few tents were visible near the vehicles. The North Koreans were looking for survivors.

At 21:00 on September 20, Washington time (10:00 on September 21 in Kŭmgang), President Anders made a televised address to the nation from the Oval Office. He described the chemical attack on American troops at Kasen, and detailed how many had died or had been injured. He promised a casualty list would be made available once the "families of our brave fallen" had been informed. He then informed the nation of America's response, describing the massive retaliation on the town of Kŭmgang, emphasizing the town's links to the North Korean army. He did not give any estimates of civilian casualties, although he did acknowledge that "civilian casualties were inescapable." Anders explained why he had ordered such a devastating response. An extract from his speech follows:

> The overwhelming nature of our response was necessary to ensure that this war does not escalate, because if it does, so many more will die. ... The North Korean leadership must be convinced of our resolve to prosecute this war even if they again decide to use weapons of mass destruction against us. Their armed forces have recklessly used chemical weapons on our troops. If they do so again, our response will be larger. And if North Korea ever again decides to use nuclear weapons against us, our response will be crushing. ...

A strongly polarized debate followed the President's address, both nationally and internationally. Many were appalled at the loss of civilian life that must have occurred.

The phrases "overkill" and "all out of proportion" were frequently used by news commentators and political pundits. Although no official estimate of civilian casualties has ever been provided, postwar estimates by various military analyst suggest that the number of dead was anywhere between 5,000 and 15,000. Others accepted the President's argument that the North Koreans had to be warned off any further use of weapons of mass destruction. The specter of nuclear war was omnipresent, especially after the attack on Seattle made the human impacts of such a war very real. The debate continues to rage today. Only two things are certain: the North Koreans did not use chemical weapons again during the war, and the town of Kŭmgang and many of its inhabitants no longer exist.

Town of Kŭmgang

Prior to September 20

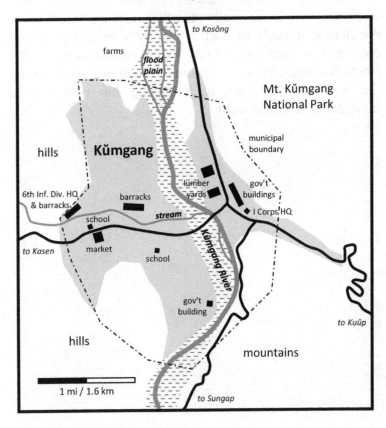

Chapter 21

Breaking the Wall

The blow, wherever struck, must, to be successful, be sudden and heavy.

General Robert E. Lee,
Confederate Army, Civil War.

The troops of the Second Infantry Division had been poised at the DMZ since September 16. As ordered, they had not fired a shot—and they had not been fired upon. The M270 self-propelled rocket launchers of the 210th Field Artillery Brigade sat unused. The Apache attack helicopters of the 2nd Combat Brigade could not fly in support of American soldiers fighting just fifteen miles up the coast at Kosŏng. There were larger political issues that first had to be resolved.

The Second Infantry Division was the core of the prewar ground forces stationed in South Korea. It had a "Stryker" brigade combat team, which was rotated in from various divisions in the United States Infantry Division (in 2033, this brigade was the 1st brigade of the Seventh Infantry Division, stationed in Fort Lewis, Washington). The brigade used the eight-wheeled M1126 Stryker infantry carrier vehicle to make it mobile. The versatile Canadian-made vehicle could be armed with a wide variety of weapons and defense systems, including a 12.7-mm machine gun, a Mk 19 40-mm grenade launcher, a Mk44 Bushmaster II 30-mm chain gun, a 120-mm mortar, or even a 105-mm tank gun (although none of the latter two variants were deployed in South Korea in 2033). The infantry brigade was supported by a field artillery brigade (the 210th) and an aviation brigade (the 2nd).

In addition, as a core element of the division, a brigade was rotated in from the South Korean army. In 2033, this was the 16th Mechanized Infantry Brigade rotated in from the Capital Mechanized Infantry Division. The 16th fielded two battalions of K1 main battle tanks (of the new A3 variant) and a mechanized infantry battalion, which used K200 armored personnel carriers. The invading forces in North Korea were short of tanks, and Eighth Army commander, General Yates, desperately needed the tanks of the South Korean brigade. After the battle of Wŏnsan, the 3rd Armored Brigade only had ten Abrams tanks left. The tanks had been high-priority targets for North Korean soldiers during the battle for Wŏnsan. The 1/66th had been effectively wiped out, and the 1/68th was still regrouping and refitting from its battle damage. The presence of the South Korean 16th brigade was the reason why the Second sat immobile and impotent while other American forces were fighting just a few miles to the north.

Destruction of I Corps

September 17 to 26

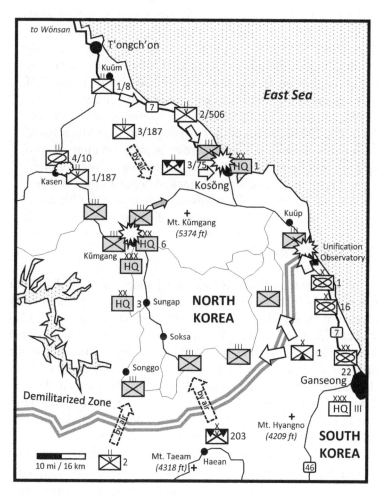

The Anders Administration put a lot of political pressure on President Yeon to allow the 16th brigade to cross the DMZ and participate in the war. Kevin Todd, the United States ambassador to South Korea, recalled the political tension at the time:

> I met with President Yeon or Minister Ryu [Ryu Kun-woo, the Minister of National Defense] either separately or together sixteen times during the war. It was particularly intense after the army [the Second Infantry Division] took up its position on the east coast [of South Korea, north of Ganseong]. I was under enormous pressure from Washington to get President Yeon to approve the use of his forces already attached to our army [the 16th Mechanized Infantry Brigade]. South Korean popular opinion swayed back and forth during the war, depending on our fortunes, and President Yeon's views tracked popular opinion. After Wŏnsan was taken, there was real movement [by President Yeon], and I got some positive indications that the [South Korean] government was about to approve the release of the attached forces.

All that changed after the chemical attack [at Kasen] and our response. At first, Yeon pulled back, and I thought I had lost any chance of an agreement. Then, in the evening of September 21, I was called into his office. Minister Ryu was also present. President Yeon informed me that his cabinet had agreed to release the attached forces. Furthermore, it had authorized other elements of the [South Korean] army on the east coast to participate in the war. I believe that Minister Ryu had a lot to do with this change of heart. I thanked President Yeon and immediately departed to inform Washington about this positive development.

The Anders Administration was indeed overjoyed. The South Korean's were committing an entire division (the Twenty-second) to the war, along with some elite alpine and airmobile troops and two fighter squadrons (a mix of F-15K Slam Eagles, F-35K Lightnings, and KF-16 Falcons, all South Korean variants of American fighters). The only condition set by the South Korean government was that they could be used only in the southeastern region of North Korea.

General Yates was ready to attack across the DMZ as soon as he was approved to do so. The approval came two hours after Ambassador Todd's meeting with President Yeon. Just before 04:00 on September 23, fifteen Stratofortresses from two squadrons (the 20th and the 96th, flying out of Barksdale Air Force Base in Louisiana) dropped four hundred *tons* of bombs on North Korean forces. The bombs landed along a seven-mile coastal strip just north of the DMZ. At 06:00 on the morning of the September 23, some two hours after the bombing raid, American and South Korean forces crossed over the DMZ. Resistance was surprisingly light.

Colonel Curtis Ashby, the commander of the 1st Stryker Brigade Combat Team, recalled:

> After a brief rocket bombardment by the 210th [Field Artillery Brigade], we crossed over on foot and took what was left of the fortifications on the far side [of the DMZ]. There was little opposition. The surviving enemy appeared stunned and surrendered in droves. They were leaderless. Their regimental HQ [headquarters] had been destroyed by our bombers the night before. Their divisional HQ was trapped in Kosŏng and fighting for its life, and their corps HQ had been annihilated by the raid on Kŭmgang. Our engineers [from the 11th Engineer Battalion] cleared a route for us through the debris, and by noon, we were driving up the coastal highway [Highway 7]. Our immediate objective was to take the village of Kuŭp. After we did that, we charged up the highway to relieve our troops fighting in Kosŏng.

The American forces attacking Kosŏng (the 2/506th Infantry Battalion, the 3/75th Ranger Battalion, and the 1/8th Infantry Battalion) were exhausted after seven days of hard fighting in Kosŏng. The town lay in ruins. The enemy comprised of an infantry regiment, well supported by artillery. The enemy forces were supplemented by security and headquarter troops from the First Infantry Division's headquarters and by the town's paramilitary unit, which fought with fanatical abandon. Even with substantial air support from the Navy's two nearby carriers, the battle had devolved into a bloody stalemate. The American forces were too few and too exhausted to finish off the surrounded North Korean forces. This changed with the arrival of South Korean tanks of the 16th Mechanized Infantry Brigade. The K1 main battle tanks of the 81st Tank Battalion drove across a golf course and slammed into the few southern defenders. The North Koreans southern flank disintegrated. The tanks then drove north along Highway 7, linking up with the rangers along the way. With the influx of fresh troops, North Korean morale crumbled, and on September 24, the enemy surrendered and the town was captured.

Major Eustis Petras, the acting commander of the 1/8th Infantry Battalion, remembered walking through the destroyed town after the battle:

There was nothing left of Kosŏng—just rubble and dust. The dust got everywhere, and we had no surplus water available to wash it off. We all looked like ghosts. A few stone walls still stood here and there, but not many. Civilians, all old men and women, picked through the rubble, but I never discovered what for. Food, maybe, or loved ones. Dogs ran free, as did chickens. One rooster, which somehow got to the top of a wall, crowed loud and proud. Everyone nearby stopped to listen. It was the only sound in a town that was deathly quiet. That bird was saying something to the world, that's for sure. Maybe it was simply, "I'm still alive." It was a sentiment that we all felt on that day.

I remember watching some South Korean infantry marching away with North Korean prisoners. The contrast between the stunned, dejected, hungry, thirsty prisoners in their dusty and tattered uniforms and the buoyant South Korean troops in their relatively clean uniforms was striking. The prisoners were very compliant, and they never gave us any trouble. Eighty years of complete deference to authority sure helped us now.

Further west, elite South Korean alpine and airmobile troops crossed the DMZ. The alpine troops of the 1st Mountain Brigade found themselves embroiled in an intense battle with two enemy regiments, which lasted until September 25. In contrast, when the airmobile troops arrived near the villages of Songgo and Soksa, North Korean troops surrendered in droves. At Songgo, the 2nd Air Assault Battalion of six hundred men accepted the surrender of an entire regiment of nearly three thousand enemy soldiers with barely a shot being fired. After questioning their prisoners, the South Koreans discovered that there was a rumor going through the North Korean ranks that Kŭmgang had been destroyed by American nuclear weapons. The enemy troops feared being forced to retreat through radioactive fallout. The South Koreans did nothing to dissuade the North Koreans of this erroneous notion.

By nightfall on September 25, the three divisions of I Corps were surrounded, broken and leaderless. After two weeks of hard fighting, the destruction of I Corps was complete, and all resistance in southeastern North Korea came to an end.

Last Phase of the Battle of Kosŏng

September 23 to 24

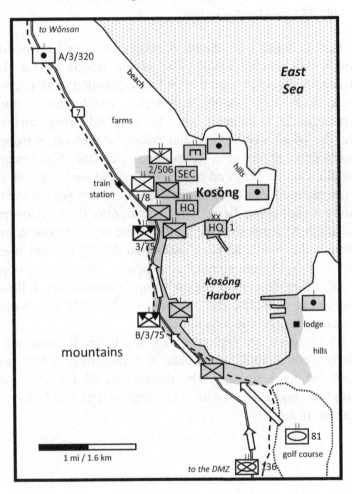

Chapter 22

Through the Mountains

Lead me, follow me, or get out of my way.

General George S. Patton, Jr.,
U.S. Army, World War II.

Although one region of North Korea was secure and one army corps had been destroyed, the North Korean army was far from defeated, and the government of Kim Ji-ho was not giving any indications that it was about to surrender. American forces, now supported by a South Korean division, had to cross the central mountains and capture the North Korean capital. Everyone in the U.S. military was convinced that North Korea would surrender once P'yŏngyang was occupied by American troops. However, three enemy corps protected the capital, and it had taken most of America's available military might to destroy just one.

It was 130 miles by road from Wŏnsan to P'yŏngyang. The most obvious way to get to the capital was on the P'yŏngyang-Wŏnsan Tourist Motorway, which connected the two cities. In peacetime, it was a pleasant three-hour scenic drive through the mountains and farmlands of central North Korea. The four-lane motorway was opened in 1978, and in 2018, it gained the distinction of being North Korea's first toll road (an oddly un-communist approach). By 2033, it was badly potholed and its lane markings had faded away to nothing, but it was the best road there was for crossing the central mountains. Aerial reconnaissance had shown that the North Korean army had set up a strong defensive position across the motorway east of the town of Koksan. The only other option to reach the capital was a windy two-lane, or sometimes just one-lane, road through the mountains.

With the destruction of I Corps and the seemingly inevitable defeat of North Korea, the government of President Yeon removed its restriction that embedded South Korean forces could be used only in southeastern North Korea. In addition, South Korean forces along the western region of the DMZ began to mobilize in preparation to attack "in the near future." Ambassador Todd recalled the change:

> President Yeon's mood had significantly altered. Whereas before he seemed filled with doubt, he now became buoyant and animated. However, I still couldn't get him to agree to provide any more units for our army, or to commit to a date to attack across the western part of the Demilitarized Zone. I believe that he was waiting to see what would happen to our troops when they crossed the mountains. He was not alone. Everyone in South Korea was watching and waiting.

At Camp Humphreys on September 23, Lieutenant General Yates met with Major General Pung Hyun-tae, the commander of South Korea's Twenty-second Infantry Division and Lieutenant General Park Chul-soon, the commander of III Corps (in which the Twenty-second was one of the divisions before it was attached to the Eighth Army). During that meeting, Yates discussed his strategy for crossing the mountains. The result of the meeting was that American and South Korean forces would advance on two axes: one along the motorway and one along the mountain road. The South Koreans would use the former and the Americans would use the latter. On September 24, even before the last of I Corps surrendered, the two columns began to organize themselves. They departed early the next day. Their destination was P'yŏngyang, a sprawling metropolis of 3.3 million inhabitants defended by 130,000 troops and dozens of paramilitary units.

The weather changed on the night of September 24/25. The extreme heat and hazy weather of the previous three weeks broke and a prolonged rainstorm followed. For the next three days, most of the Korean peninsula was subjected to record rainfalls. The Seventh Air Force and the two attached South Korean fighter squadrons were effectively grounded. As a consequence, aerial reconnaissance—a vital component of the advance through the mountain—was not available. The ground troops had to advance the "old-fashioned way," as Lieutenant Marco Brasilia of the 2/14th Cavalry Battalion described it, "by using us grunts on the ground as scouts."

The heavily mechanized troops of South Korea's 55th Mechanized Brigade spearheaded the route along the motorway. Their commander, Brigadier General Lee Beom-soo, was well aware of the strong defensive line near Koksan. However, even before the lead elements of the South Korean column reached that line, they were attacked by enemy forces coming down from the mountains. Five tanks of the 20th Armored Brigade were destroyed by man-portable anti-tank weapons. The South Korean advance slowed to a crawl.

Road to P'yŏngyang

September 25 to 27

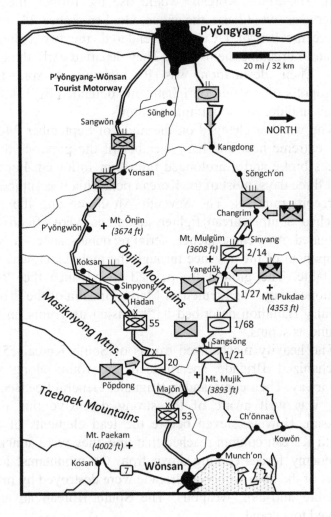

The American forces traveling along the narrow mountain road were spearheaded by the units from the 2nd Brigade Combat Team of the Twenty-Fifth Light Infantry Division, supported by the Abrams tanks of the reformed 1/68th Armor Battalion. The 2nd had emerged relatively intact after its battles in northern Wŏnsan, and so was an obvious choice to lead the advance. At the tip of the spear was the 2/14th Cavalry Squadron, which had seen very little fighting in Wŏnsan.

Lieutenant Brasilia remembered the difficult journey along the winding mountain road:

The road was narrow and potholed, and we constantly had to deal with mudslides blocking the road. Our eight-wheeled Strykers could handle most of them, and we had a platoon of engineers with us to deal with the worst ones. The mudslide really slowed us down a lot. As we drove, we got some harassing fire from various buildings, and that slowed us down even more. Our frequent egresses [leaving the Strykers] to clear out resistance meant that we were soaked all day and all night. Thank God, it was still warm. We were crawling along that road, with a long column trailing behind us. Ahead of us there was nothing but the enemy. We were the closest unit to the capital. That was both exciting and deeply worrying at the same time.

We reached a village called Chagrin—a fitting name, I think [the village's name was actually Changrim]. It was then when the North Koreans really hit us in force. Regiment-strength at least, with some special forces as well. They fought hard, and their snipers were lethal. The captain [Captain James Walser] got one [bullet] in the chest and was casevacked out. The enemy fought us to a standstill, and the column backed up behind us. We were well-and-truly stuck. We badly needed some air support, but the rain just wouldn't let up.

Further back in the column, at the village of Yangdŏk, the North Koreans hit the column hard in a well-coordinated double-flanking attack. The 1/27th Light Infantry Battalion was hit from both the north and south. The southern enemy was just a company of regular infantry, but the northern force consisted of a full battalion of elite special forces.

Private Philip Ward recalled the battle:

We were in a narrow valley with a north-south road coming down into the valley and intersecting our east-west road. It was raining hard, and already dark and gloomy. Night was to fall in about an hour or so. At the crossroads, there was the little village of Yangdŏk, just a few homes nestled in a valley. The point [front] battalion [the 2/14th] had already passed through the crossroads and we were doing the same. Suddenly our column was being hit from both sides. Tim [Private Timofey Indira] and I dived for cover. The whole platoon [3rd Platoon of Alpha Company] was pinned down. We were getting hit from both sides, but the fire was really bad from the north. Intense machine-gun fire. They were pegging [shooting] us one by one. If we lost the crossroads, our lead elements and all of the point battalion would be trapped.

Tim said something like, "I'm going for it," and then he charged up the road to the north, firing from the hip as he went. I thought he was crazy. I laid down some serious cover fire, and the others in our platoon did the same. There was a lot of shooting and then nothing. I left cover and carefully followed where Tim had gone. I passed three machine guns, still on their tripods [likely a Type 82 machine gun, which was North Korea's standard general-purpose machine gun]. Dead [North] Koreans surrounded them. I advanced slowly past them. I could see Tim lying under a bush. He wasn't moving. I came under some serious fire, but I managed to get to him. He had been hit several times, but he was still alive. He had coughed up a lot of blood, and his face was covered in blood. Bullets were flying all around me. I don't know how I didn't get hit. Somehow, I managed to drag Tim back to our lines, and then me and other private carried him over to our medic.

With Tim getting the care he needed, I headed back to our front lines. I later heard that Tim was casevacked out.

Private Indira's solo charge stalled the North Korean attack long enough for the 1/27th to regroup and for two Abrams tanks from the lead elements of the 1/68th to arrive. Private Timofey Indira was awarded the Congressional Medal of Honor for his heroic deed that day. He was twenty-one years old and the second youngest to receive the nation's highest award during the Twenty-first Century. His was only one of three Medals of Honor that were awarded during the Second Korean War, and he was the only one of the three to receive his in person; the other two medals were awarded posthumously. Major Manfred Naylor of the 1/66th Armor Battalion received his medal for his "heroic leadership and sacrifice" during the battle for Wŏnsan, and Sergeant Enrico Giuseppina of the 3/75th Ranger Battalion received his medal for his "courageous and self-sacrificing actions" during the battle for Kosŏng. One of the five bullets that hit Private Indira punctured a lung and severed his spine. He became permanently paralyzed from the waist down. Private Ward received an Army Commendation Medal for his "valiant rescue" of Indira. Ward and Indria remain close friends.

Further to the west, the 2/14th was too busy with its own predicament to concern itself with the problems of others. The fighting around Changrim remained intense throughout the night. However, by early morning an eerie silence fell over the battlefield. Lieutenant Brasilia remembered the "surreal" experience:

It took me a moment to realize that the sounds of gunfire had stopped. We all waited for something to happen. Good or bad, no one knew. I was called over to the CP [company command post]. The new captain [Captain Elijah Johansen] wanted me to take a squad and recon what was in front of us. Two Strykers, one with an M2 [12.7-mm machine gun] and the other with a Bushmaster [a 30-mm chain gun], covered us. Moving cautiously, we headed to the enemy lines. I was really on edge and expected to get shot, but nothing. We arrived at their lines to find them abandoned. My squad went a little way down the road and then we returned. I reported that the enemy had bugged out and the road ahead was open. The captain was pleased about that. I returned to my platoon and hunkered down. Not five minutes later, the big news came through. I was stunned. Everyone in my platoon was.

At 07:25 on September 28, an order from General Sweeny, the commander of United States Forces Korea, was received by all combat units in North Korea. It stated that "all offensive actions by U.S. and allied forces in North Korea are to cease immediately," and that all ground units "are to halt their advance and remain in place." The order did not explain why.

Order to Cease Offensive Operations

September 28

UNITED STATES FORCES KOREA

Classification: UNCLASSIFIED
Transmission: 09-28-33 07:25KT
Confirmation: N/A

AF REC. OFF.
7AF 33/0543/GEN
Rec. 11-21-33

\>> URGENT <<
\>> CEASE ATTACK ORDER <<

To: LTG YATES, COMEIGHTHARMY
    LTG DUNN, COM7AF √
    LTG MOFETTAS, COM5AF
    VADM TRUDEL, COMSEVENTHFLT

From: GEN SWEENY, COMUSFK

Info: ADM SENTSEY, COMINDOPAC

1. All offense operations by U.S. and allied forces in North Korea are to cease immediately.
2. All combat units in and around the Korean peninsula are to change to a defensive posture.
3. All ground units in North Korea are to halt their advance and remain in place.
4. All air units in South Korea are to return to base, except for reconnaissance units and other units as ordered by COMUSFK.
5. All naval units are to withdraw to no less that 250 nm from North Korean coast.
6. All commands will await further communications from COMUSFK or COMINDOPAC

Chapter 23

Chinese Coup

You can have all of the material in the world, but without morale, it is largely ineffective.

General George C. Marshall,
U.S. Army, World War II.

On the evening of September 26, Chinese troops from two combined-arms brigades (the 190th and 191st) of the 79th Group Army crossed the Yalu River. They drove across the border bridge that connected Dandong, China to Sinuiju, North Korea. Evidently, this movement was the signal for Lieutenant General Ahn Mu-yeol, the commander of North Korea's III Corps, to order his men to leave their coastal defense positions north of Namp'o and march on the capital. During the night of September 26/27, the soldiers of III Corps fought the troops from the P'yŏngyang Defense

Command, a large and well-trained army of 70,000 soldiers. However, once it became widely known that the Chinese army had crossed the Yalu River in support of General Ahn, fighting soon ended.

Just after 08:00 on September 27, General Ahn entered the residence of Supreme Leader Kim Ji-ho. Kim had fled, leaving the residence empty and the government without a leader. Ahn declared himself the new "interim" leader of North Korea. Chinese troops entered P'yŏngyang just after 13:00. According to the Chinese media, they were "happily welcomed" by the new North Korean leader and by the "liberated people" of North Korea. In the evening of that same day, additional brigades from the 79th Group Army crossed over into North Korea at various border points. In the north and far northeast, they took control of the cities of Kanggye, Hysen and Ch'ŏngjin. No Chinese unit came into contact with U.S. units. With the exception of the capital region, the Chinese army was active only in the far north of the country.

On the night of September 27/28, Kim Ji-ho was apprehended at a Chinese checkpoint as he attempted to cross the bridge over the Ch'ŏngch'ŏn River at Sinanju. According to Chinese sources, he was on his way north to seek asylum in China. He was detained in Sinanju for a few hours, and then he was transferred to a local government building in Ch'ŏngju and guarded by Chinese troops.

At 05:30 Beijing time on September 28 (06:30 in North Korea and 17:30 on September 27 in Washington), President Guan called President Anders to informed him of the change in North Korean leadership, and that North Korean armed forces would immediately stand down. He further told President Anders that Kim Ji-ho had been detained, and he promised that Kim would be transferred to American custody once the occupational agreement between the U.S. and China had been put into place. Anders assured the Guan that all U.S. and allied forces would "cease offensive operations" and "halt their advance on the North Korean capital." He added that their bilateral agreement on the "temporary occupation" of North Korea "would guide all future American actions."

Immediately after the war, there was a lot of speculation as to why China decided to act on that day. That debate was largely put to rest on November 16, 2033. On that date, CIA Director Valerie Ullman stated in public testimony before the Senate Select Committee on Intelligence:

> It is the considered opinion of our intelligence community, and that of our allies, that China acted when it did because it was observing the general mobilization of South Korean forces. It was concerned that if South Korean forces had to fight their way into North Korea, they might not ever leave once South Korean blood was spilt. The incremental embedment of South Korean forces with our [American] forces on the east coast [of North Korea] was worrisome for the Chinese, but such forces remained under our [American] command. When President Yeon ordered a general mobilization with the intention of crossing the western end of the Demilitarized Zone in force, the Chinese government decided that events had reached a crisis, and that they could no longer delay taking action.

When asked about why the Chinese were not concerned about American troops staying in North Korea, Ullman replied:

> We [in the intelligence community] believe that the Chinese assumed we might stay for some time, but we would not stay forever. We would eventually tire of the occupation and leave. South Koreans, on the other hand, might seek reunification with the North, and that was, and still is, something that the Chinese consider an existential threat to their regional security.

At 07:25 on September 28, the order went out from General Sweeny that all U.S. and allied forces would cease offensive operations. That afternoon, at 14:30, Generals Sweeny, Yates and Dunn and a small contingency of staff officers boarded a Hercules at Osan Air Base flew to the North Korean air base at Kangdong. They were escorted by four Lightnings from the 36th Fighter Squadron.

General Dunn saw firsthand the destruction his command had done to the North Korea air force. He recalled:

Kangdong was inside the capital's air defense network, and we had generally avoided the area. Nevertheless, many buildings were just rubble, and only one of the two runways was still operational. Burnt-out aircraft littered the base.

We exited the Hercules and were met by Chinese and North Korean officials. Our mission was to ensure that all North Korean military and paramilitary units ceased fighting and surrendered to the nearest American or Chinese unit. We discussed the situation in the central mountains and in the north. The Chinese informed us that they were going to secure northern parts of the country, but they assured us that their forces would not approach us [American ground forces].

We met with a number of high-ranking North Korean officers. Some were sullen, some looked relieved, but all were compliant. We never had any issues with them. It all went surprisingly smooth. General Ahn came to our discussions for a short time, but he soon left. I suspected that he had a great many crises to deal with. Near the end of the meeting, the Chinese asked for our assistance in distributing food and medical supplies to the North Korean population. This surprised me. I don't know why. Perhaps it was the unexpected candor. General Sweeny readily agreed to do what we could in that regard.

After four hours of discussions, the three generals flew back to South Korea, leaving a small liaison and signals team behind. Major Daniel Oakes was on that team. He recalled:

My mission was to set up an efficient communication system so that the Chinese and North Korean military leaders could talk to their counterparts in South Korea and back home [in the U.S.]. The North Korean communications network was smashed. Nothing worked, and there was no power. I arranged for four large [portable] generators to be flown in from Osan [Air Base]. I spoke passable Korean, which was one of the reasons why I was chosen for the assignment. My North Korean counterpart, Major Kwan, worked well with me, but our interactions were very formal. He spoke no English at all. There was no ease in our dealings. In fact, they were laced with a palpable tension. Not surprising, I suppose, giving what we had just done to his country.

Back in the central mountains, Lieutenant Brasilia remembered the excitement over the news that the war had ended:

When I undertook that last recon mission, I became the [American non-special forces] soldier who got the closest to the North Korean capital during the war. That's some real bragging rights. When I left on that last mission, we were at war, and our battalion was soon to be heading into an enemy city of over three million people. We were the point battalion, and I didn't rate my chances very high of getting out of the war in one piece.

Just after I got back [from the reconnaissance mission], we got the order to stand down. It took a few moments for what that really meant to sink in. When it did, we started cheering and hugging each other. We had survived. It's difficult to describe the sense of relief that flooded through us on that day. After the hugging and cheering died down, I sat down on a muddy slope, and some others sat down beside me. It was pouring rain. None of us spoke, because we were all lost in our thoughts. I could neither laugh nor cry. I couldn't move. I felt numb and utterly exhausted.

Chapter 24

Endgame

*Man is, and always will be, the supreme element in combat;
and upon the skill, the courage and endurance, and the
fighting heart of the individual soldier, the issue will
ultimately depend.*

General Matthew B. Ridgway,
U.S. Army, World War II.

The war lasted fifty-six days, and ground combat lasted just
eighteen. It was not a long war as wars go, but it was an
intense one, and it was fought with a ferocity that had not
been seen on the battlefield in decades. There was always the
specter of nuclear war to keep everyone on edge.

After the war ended, the first priority for many in the U.S.
military was the return of American prisoners of war. The
lingering ghosts of those "missing-in-action" after the

Vietnam War still haunted many military leaders. There were also thousands of North Korean prisoners who had to be released as soon as possible, because feeding them all was quickly becoming a logistical nightmare.

Lieutenant Jeff Lonigan, a pilot with the 80th Fighter Squadron who got shot down on August 21, remembered the disbelief when he first saw an American soldier:

I had been in prison for thirty-eight days—I kept count. When the warden announced to us all that the war was over and we would be released soon, I didn't believe him. He had told us so many lies before. Anything to make us cooperate. We knew the score. However, this time, it was different. Everyone was suddenly very nice to us. Food rations doubled. We got to talk among ourselves. I now believe that the warden was worried about soon facing war crimes.

For five days, we stayed where we were. Same cells, same food, same guards. On the sixth day, some trucks appeared. My first thought was that we were going to be sent to a secret labor camp in the mountains. I couldn't believe it when an American major climbed out of the lead truck. Soon I was surrounded by Americans. Doctors, medics, officers. It was like I'd gone to heaven. After we gave our names, ranks and units, we were checked out [medically]. Once that was done for all of us, we were loaded on to the trucks and driven to an air base. A Hercules was waiting for us. I wanted to run on to the plane, but I was pretty weak so I just walked slowly up its ramp. Once we were all on board, I collapsed into one of its fold-out seats and couldn't move.

An hour later, we landed at Kunsan. Scotty [the callsign for Captain Frank Schott, Lonigan's wingman] was there to greet me off the plane. We hugged and I cried. A month of fear just evaporated. Scotty helped me to the waiting ambulance. If he had not, I doubt I would've had the strength to make it. I was completely spent, but I was home at last.

The return of the last American prisoners was completed by mid-October. The North Korean officials, with Chinese officials watching closely, accommodated every American request. The thousands of North Korean prisoners were allowed to walk out of the American detention camp if they lived nearby (which many did), or they were transported to Hamhŭng or P'yŏngyang and then released to the nearest North Korean army unit.

The prewar U.S.-China framework agreement on the occupation of North Korea had little in the way of concrete details and simply assigned "temporary occupation zones" to either American or Chinese administration, with the capital being jointly administered. The agreement had not considered the involvement of South Korea. However, on September 29, the South Korean army crossed over the DMZ in force and occupied the southwest region of North Korea. President Yeon had made a speech on that day promising the citizens of South Korea that they would "never again have to live in fear" of North Korean missiles and artillery shells "raining down" on their cities. The South Korean occupation initially caused consternation among the Chinese leadership, and it disrupted the otherwise smooth implementation of the Sino-American occupation agreement.

On October 5, Presidents Anders, Guan and Yeon met via video to discuss the new situation. Anders handed over the administration of the western half of the American zone to South Korea. Yeon promised Guan that his administration would not seek reunification with North Korea, and it would remain inside the region provided by Anders. Guan accepted these assurances and the new reality. Ambassador Todd, who attended the meeting via video, recalled:

Initially, President Guan was extremely agitated about the unilateral occupation of southwest North Korea by South Korean forces. Both President Anders and President Yeon did much to restore the cooperative mood that had been created during President Anders's initial conversations with President Guan. President Yeon assured President Guan that South Korea had no interest in reunification for the foreseeable future and that South Korea's move into North Korea was simply to ensure that no artillery attacks would take place on Seoul or any other border city in the future. The rapport that Presidents Anders and Guan had developed after Seattle and during the subsequent American mobilization really paid dividends during this meeting. President Guan accepted that America could restrain its ally.

By mid-October, U.S., South Korean and Chinese officials began to implement the U.S.-China framework agreement on the temporary occupation zones in North Korea. The southeast zone and a coastal strip in the northeast was administered by the U.S., while the southwest zone was administered by South Korea. The capital region was jointly administered by the U.S. and China, while China administered the rest of the country. China and the U.S. each had observers in all the zones. The puppet government of General Ahn actively assisted in the occupation, particularly in regards to searching for overlooked stocks of chemical weapons. The Chinese government was just as interested in finding and destroying these weapons as were the governments of the United States and South Korea.

The hunt for chemical and nuclear weapons continued until March 31, 2034. Only then was the Anders Administration convinced that it had found all of them. The U.S. Air Force had done a stellar job of destroying chemical-weapon storage facilities, but some secondary facilities survived the bombing campaign. Most of these held only half-a-dozen chemical-loaded artillery shells. All were removed by U.S. or Chinese chemical teams (which were meticulously observed by their counterparts) and destroyed in U.S. or Chinese facilities.

Temporary Occupation Zones

With one notable exception, no intact nuclear weapons were found. A single nuclear warhead was found in the Pup'yŏng facility in northeastern North Korea. It was not in the primary storage facility (which the U.S. Air Force had utterly destroyed), but in the rubble of a "reconditioning" building nearby. It had no delivery system and appeared to have been undergoing maintenance or repair of some sort. It was removed and dismantled by the Chinese technicians under the careful observation by American officials.

By the end of November, crime and black-market activities had become rampant in the U.S. and South Korean zones, and probably much more so in the Chinese zones, although the Chinese government was silent on the issue. All three nations were providing huge sums of money for rebuilding, and it was inevitable that such sums would attract criminal elements. Much was promised about fighting the crime and corruption, but little was actually done.

The U.S. military leadership greatly desired a forward base in North Korea (an Asian equivalent to its base in Guantanamo Bay, Cuba). The U.S. government used the promise of additional reconstruction funds to persuade (many detractors called it *coerce*) the government of General Ahn to permanently cede the Kalma peninsula in Wŏnsan and some nearby islands to the United States. For the American public, a great quantity of American blood had been spilt capturing the strategic site, and many felt it only right to keep what had been so dearly bought. The base, called Joint Base Wonsan-Kalma, was officially opened on June 17, 2034, symbolically on the first anniversary of the attack on Seattle. The base is currently home to a mixed squadron of fighters, reconnaissance drones and transport planes, and to a battalion of infantry and a battalion of engineers, both of which are rotated every six months. The base is provisioned primarily from South Korea by truck along Highway 7, but also by air and sea from Japan and the U.S.[1]

On Okinawa during the 2020s, the U.S. military had learned a lot about maintaining good relations with the local population. In the late 2010s and early 2020s, the local resentment of U.S. military bases on Okinawa flared up, but the military, particularly the Marine Corps, undertook many outreach initiatives and augmented its cultural awareness programs. By 2023, these (along with increased tensions with China at the time) caused the Japanese government to politically pivot. It started to encourage a growth of U.S. military presence on Okinawa and the other islands in the Ryukyu Islands. The U.S. military applied those valuable outreach lessons to its new base at Wŏnsan. A liaison office was set up immediately, and the local city administration was routinely consulted on any issues affecting its citizens. American soldiers, from privates to generals, were required to undertake cultural sensitivity training. The Anders Administration also provided billions of dollars to rebuild Wŏnsan and its environs. As a result of this outreach and largess, the presence of the base became very popular with the locals, and a much-needed source of employment.

---

[1] There was a lengthy and acrimonious debate in Congress as to the name of the base. Some wanted it named after a soldier fallen during the war, and others after various American generals from the First Korean War. No one could agree as to who should be so honored, so in the end, the base was named after its geographical location—a choice which made no one happy. Even then, there was controversy. Some wanted it to be written using the North Korean approach, with a breve over the ŏ, and others wanted it spelled as it would be done in South Korea: *Weonsan*. In the end, the name was Americanized to *Wonsan*, without the breve or the *e*. The joint Army-Air Force base is comprised of Wonsan Air Base and the army base Camp Kalma. Its headquarters are in the Supreme Leader's old palace, and its barracks are on the grounds of the old university. The base also had defensive missile batteries and patrol-boat harbors on four offshore islands. These islands were Sin, Tae, So and Hwangto islands (the spelling of the latter island was Americanized from Hwangt'o by deleting the apostrophe).

Once the Chinese government was satisfied that the
Americans and the South Koreans were following the prewar
occupation framework, it released Kim Ji-ho to American
custody. The exchange took place on November 12 at the
newly reopened P'yŏngyang-Sunan International Airport,
just north of the capital. A Hercules from 36th Airlift
Squadron landed, and a platoon from the Eighth Army's 94th
Military Police Battalion left the plane to meet a Chinese
convoy of three military trucks. Many dignitaries on both
sides were already at the airport. The formal transfer was
jointly officiated by Assistant Secretary Alice Catanzaro of
the State Department's Bureau of East Asian and Pacific
Affairs and her Chinese counterpart, Director Zhu Xiang of
the Department of Asian Affairs in the Chinese Ministry of
Foreign Affairs.

General Dunn was in attendance and remembered the
spectacle:

The Chinese had set it up nicely. Flags were flying—
American, Chinese and North Korean. A Chinese military
band was playing something, but I've no idea what. Lots of
VIPs [very important persons] were in attendance. General
Ahn was there, trying to look important while surrounded
by his Chinese controllers. General Sweeny attended, but
not General Yates. He was far too busy dealing with the
chaos that was North Korea in those days. Thankfully, I was
out of that particular mess. I was fully occupied by getting
the Seventh [Air Force] back up to strength.

A C-130 [Hercules] landed and taxied over. A platoon of
MP's walked down its [rear] ramp. They marched to a place
in front of us and stopped. A convoy of Chinese military
trucks arrived, and a platoon of Chinese soldiers led out
Kim. Jesus, he looked young, just like one of my raw
recruits [Kim had just turned thirty-two]. Surrounded by the
Chinese guards, he looked small ... No, *insignificant* might
be a better description. So much death caused by this one
madman. It makes me furious just to think about it.

Kim Ji-ho was flown to Guam and then directly to Andrews Air Force Base outside of Washington, D.C. Kim was taken to an undisclosed location to await trial. Various politicians from the state of Washington put considerable pressure on the Anders Administration to hold the trial in the Federal Western District Court in Tacoma. Despite this pressure (or perhaps because of it), the Department of Justice eventually decided that the trial would take place in the District of Columbia.

Kim did not face the death penalty—a situation lamented by a great many people. The state of Washington had abolished the death penalty in 2018, and at the federal level, the moratorium on the death penalty (which had been reimposed in 2021 after a two-year suspension by the Trump Administration) was still in place. Emotional arguments were put forward for suspending the moratorium just for Kim's trial, but in the end, the moratorium remained.

The televised trial of the one-time Supreme Leader of North Korea was an international sensation. It lasted from November 6 to 22, 2034. The federal prosecution team relied on the eyewitness testimony of various high-ranking North Korean officers flown to the United States to give evidence, plus an extensive collection of captured documents. The defense team attempted to show the self-serving bias of the witnesses and to establish the vagueness of the documents and their dubious provenance. The jury deliberated for fourteen hours and found Kim guilty of 138,103 counts of first-degree murder (one for each death known to be caused by the bombing of Seattle, as established by the court). He was sentenced to 138,103 consecutive life sentences, with no chance of parole. The once-powerful leader of a sovereign nation is currently serving his sentence in the ADX Administrative Maximum Facility near Florence, Colorado (commonly known as the Florence Supermax Prison). There, Kim is kept in solitary confinement in a seven-foot by twelve-foot cell twenty-three hours a day, and shackled during the one hour of his out-of-cell activity.

Notwithstanding the conviction in an American court, the United Nations wanted Kim Ji-ho to appear before the International Criminal Court, as per the U.N. resolution passed just before the start of the war. The Anders Administration had no interest in letting Kim out of the U.S. After "tortuous" negotiations between the U.S. Department of Justice and U.N. officials, an agreement was finally reached. The untelevised trial took place between May 23 and June 6, 2035, with Kim attending daily by video. Kim was found guilty of crimes against humanity, crimes of aggression, and war crimes, and he was sentenced to life imprisonment. There currently appears to be no interest in either the U.S. or the U.N. to have Kim transferred to the International Criminal Court's detention center (a separate facility within the Hague Penitentiary Institution at Scheveningen, Netherlands). Kim remains in U.S. custody at the Florence Supermax Prison.

In stark contrast to the person who started the war with his nuclear attack on Seattle, the American participants in the conflict were showered with awards, far too many to list here. The leading commanders were each awarded medals for "exceptionally meritorious services in a duty of great responsibility." General Sweeny and Admiral Sentsey each received the Defense Distinguished Service Medal. Lieutenant Generals Yates and Dunn, and Major General Stoltman received their respective service's Distinguished Service Medal, and all three were promoted in rank. The two chemical battalions involved in the war (the 2nd and the 23rd) both received a Presidential Unit Citation, as did two bomb squadrons (the 9th and the 393rd) and two fighter squadron (the 36th and the 525th). Many other units received their respective service's unit citations.

For many, the Second Korean War greatly boosted their subsequent careers, but for many, many more, it was a war that they would rather forget.

Joint Base Wonsan-Kalma

Wonsan Air Base and Camp Kalma

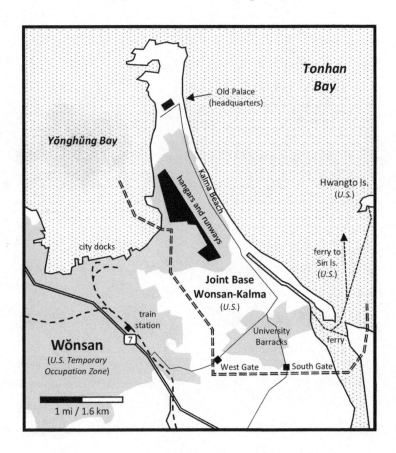

Chapter 25

Unwanted Land

War is never cost-effective. People are killed. To them, the war is total.

General Curtis E. LeMay,
U.S. Air Force, Cold War.

The Chinese government's fear about Korean reunification were unfounded. Poll after poll indicated South Koreans had an overwhelming and profound disinterest in absorbing twenty-six million North Koreans into their modern, prosperous, democratic country. After eight decades of indoctrination, isolation and poverty, North Koreans had nothing in common with South Koreans except a language. President Yeon kept his promise made to President Guan, and he made no effort to go against the clear will of the people of South Korea. However, the South Korean army remained inside North Korea in great strength, and it tightly controlled the southwest occupation zone. The hunt for stocks of weapons of mass destruction by the South Korean army continued long after the American and Chinese forces had ceased their work.

The United States and China, and to a lesser degree, South Korea, provided billions of dollars in reconstruction funding for North Korea. A disproportionally large part of the American funds was focused on Wŏnsan and the southeast region of North Korea, and as intended, this created considerable goodwill in the area around the new U.S. military base. Fairly quickly, Congress became disenchanted with approving more and more funds for rebuilding a country destined to remain in the Chinese political sphere. President Anders, facing a very tight (and ultimately unsuccessful) presidential race in 2036, took his cue from Congress, and in 2035, his administration considerably lessened its requests for future reconstruction funds. As one of his first acts, incoming President Jeffrey Turner cancelled all reconstruction funding in March 2037, except for continued spending on the new base and in the region around Wŏnsan.

The continued military occupation of North Korea became a significant drain on American resources. The occupation of the northeastern coastal strip was transferred to China on April 1, 2034, after only six months of American administration. The occupation of the southeast zone has been slated to end sometime in 2040, and the end of the joint administration of the capital zone is likely to end sometime before 2044. After that, the only American presence inside North Korea will be its military base at Wŏnsan.

The Chinese government continues to support the puppet regime of General Ahn. It is believed that between 2034 and 2037, China spent over fifteen trillion yuan (about two trillion dollars) on North Korean infrastructure and housing. China continues to provide funds to North Korea, although at a much lesser rate. Due to rampant corruption in North Korea, the funds have achieved much less than initially hoped for by the Chinese government. A provocative poll undertaken by the BBC during the summer of 2037, found that only eleven percent of the Chinese people approved of its government's continued spending on North Korea.

And what of the longsuffering North Korean people? The war had decimated their economy and their infrastructure, both of which were barely holding together before the war started. Many parts of the Chinese zone were lawless, particularly in the remote north-central and far-northeast regions. Although the political repression stopped in the American and South Korean zones, food was still in short supply and crime was rampant. Emigration to South Korea was explicitly prohibited by a new South Korean law passed in November 2033.

American casualties, excluding those who died in Seattle, amounted to 5,486 dead and over 12,000 badly wounded. The number of North Korean casualties was considerably higher. The various estimates are steeped in controversy, but the consensus is that between 50,000 and 350,000 North Korean died during the short but intense war, and many more were wounded. The Second Korean War was a tragedy started by one mad dictator and ended through the suffering of hundreds of thousands of people on both sides.

Epilogue

The soldier above all others prays for peace, for it is the soldier who must suffer and bear the deepest wounds and scars of war.

General Douglas MacArthur,
U.S. Army, World War II and First Korean War.

Captain Alan Smith was the pilot on the Globemaster troop-transport plane who first witnessed the nuclear devastation of Seattle. When he returned to McChord Air Force Base, the base was in chaos. With no one to give him orders to the contrary, he rushed to his nearby home and was reunited with his two younger children. On that fateful day, his wife and his eldest son had visited the Space Needle, just north of downtown Seattle. Smith later remembered:

> I feared the worst. I didn't see how anyone could possibly live through that holocaust, but I had to keep it positive for my other children. Thank God that they were too young to

really understand what had happened to their mother and brother.

After six harrowing days, Smith's wife Zoey and his eldest son Adam were located at an aid center set up in the grounds of the University of Washington. Smith was informed that his wife had multiple lacerations, a broken arm, broken ribs, and a concussion. His son had a shattered leg and a deep cut in his thigh. Both were expected to recover. Smith was reunited with his wife and son on July 2, fifteen days after the fateful day. Zoey and Adam were driven to the Smith home in a school bus requisitioned by the Federal Emergency Management Agency. The Smith family believed that their family's ordeal was over. It was not.

Captain Smith piloted his Globemaster during the war. His squadron, the 8th, carried troops from various bases in the U.S. to bases in Okinawa and Guam. Smith also participated in the airborne drop of elements of the 11th Airborne Division. His plane carried Charlie Company of the 3/509th Battalion, to its drop zone west of Wŏnsan. In May 2034, he was promoted to the rank of major and became the deputy commander of the 21st Airlift Squadron based at Travis Air Force Base in California.

On October 3, 2033, a few days after the war ended, Smith returned home to be finally reunited with his wife and children. It was then when Zoey told her husband her bittersweet news. She was just over four-months pregnant, but there were complications. It was news that she had decided to keep from her husband during the war, so that he was "not distracted" and "came back alive." Zoey Smith was five-weeks pregnant when Seattle was destroyed by an atomic bomb and radioactive fallout covered the city.

Smith recalled:

Zoey's pregnancy was not like the other three. I had a persistent sense of dread that just wouldn't go away. I wanted to be excited, but I just couldn't. My unborn child had a truly hellish start to life. Zoey put a brave face on it, but I know that she felt it too.

Although the level of radiation at the Space Needle had not been high enough to affect Zoey Smith or her eldest son (at least not in the short term), it had affected the unborn child that she carried. Although the medical ultrasounds were inconclusive, her obstetrician believed that there were biochemical indications of organ defects. The baby, a girl, was born on January 20, 2034, four weeks premature. She was placed in an infant incubator and spent the first three months of her life in the neonatal intensive care unit at St. Joseph Medical Center in Tacoma. Over her first two years of life, the little girl, who the Smiths named Hope, had four operations on her kidneys and bowels. Fortunately, the prognosis remains good, and Hope should go on to live a nearly normal life. Many babies born in Seattle in the aftermath of the radioactive fallout were not so lucky.

There was another child who was impacted by the momentous events described in this history—and arguably the child's existence caused them. Kim Sang-hui was three-months pregnant when she defected to the United States. The survival of her child in the unstable and bloody regime of her brother was the prime driver behind her decision to abandon North Korea and defect to the U.S. with her husband. The baby would have been born sometime in the latter half of June 2033, around the same time as the nuclear destruction of Seattle. The child, rumored to be a boy, and his parents have been placed in a protection program by the U.S. government, and they are living somewhere in the U.S. under new names. The boy would be the heir to the Kim dynasty. It is interesting to speculate whether or not his parents will one day tell him of his blood-soaked heritage.

Appendices:

Order of Battle for Deployed Units

Appendix A: U.S. and Allied Air Forces

PACIFIC AIR FORCE

Seventh Air Force

8th Wing (*Kunsan, South Korea*)
35th Fighter Squadron (F-35A)
80th Fighter Squadron (F-35A)

51st Wing (*Osan, South Korea*)
25th Fighter Squadron (A-10C)
36th Fighter Squadron (F-35A)

Reinforcements
4th Fighter Squadron (F-35A) (*from 15th Air Force*)
34th Fighter Squadron (F-35A) (*from 15th Air Force*)
355th Fighter Squadron (F-35A) (*from 11th Air Force*)
525th Fighter Squadron (F-22) (*from 11th Air Force*)
Canadian 401st Fighter Squadron (CF-35A) (*from 4th Wing*)

Fifth Air Force

18th Wing (*Kadena, Japan*)
44th Fighter Squadron (F-15EX)
67th Fighter Squadron (F-15EX)
33rd Rescue Squadron (HH-60)
961st Airborne Air Control Squadron (E-7)
909th Air Refueling Squadron (KC-46)

35th Wing (*Misawa, Japan*)
13th Fighter Squadron (F-35A)
14th Fighter Squadron (F-35A)

374th Wing (*Yokota, Japan*)
36th Airlift Squadron (C-130J)

AIR COMBAT COMMAND

Sixteenth Air Force

9th Wing (*Osan, South Korea*)
5th Reconnaissance Squadron (U-2S)

55th Wing (*Kadena, Japan*)
41st Electronic Combat Squadron (EA-37B)
82nd Reconnaissance Squadron (RC-135)

Reinforcements from Fifteenth Air Force
11th Attack Squadron (MQ-9) (*operated from Creech, NV*)
16th Airborne Cmd. Sqn. (E-7)
44th Recon. Sqn. (RQ-170) (*operated from Creech, Nevada*)

SPECIAL OPERATIONS COMMAND

353rd Wing (*Kadena, Japan*)
1st Special Operations Squadron (MC-130J)
17th Special Operations Squadron (MC-130J)
21st Special Operations Sqn. (CV-22) (*Yokota, Japan*)

Reinforcements from 27th Special Operations Wing
3rd Special Op. Sqn. (MQ-9) (*operated from Cannon, NM*)
33rd Special Op. Sqn. (MQ-9) (*operated from Cannon, NM*)

GLOBAL STRIKE COMMAND

Eighth Air Force

2nd Wing (*Barksdale, Louisiana*)
11th Bomb Squadron (B-52J)
20th Bomb Squadron (B-52H)
96th Bomb Squadron (B-52H)

5th Wing (*Minot, North Dakota*)
23rd Bomb Squadron (B-52J)
69th Bomb Squadron (B-52H)

7th Wing (*Dyess, Texas*)
9th Bomb Squadron (B-21)
28th Bomb Squadron (B-1B)

28th Wing (*Ellsworth, South Dakota*)
    34th Bomb Squadron (B-21)
    37th Bomb Squadron (B-1B)

509th Wing (*Whiteman, Missouri*)
    13th Bomb Squadron (B-2A)
    393rd Bomb Squadron (B-2A)

595th Wing (*Offutt, Nebraska*)
    1st Airborne Command Control Squadron (E-4)

AIR MOBILITY COMMAND

Eighteenth Air Force

19th Wing (*Little Rock, Arkansas*)
    41st Airlift Squadron (C-130J)
    53rd Airlift Squadron (C-130J)

22nd Wing (*McConnell, Kansas*)
    344th Refueling Squadron (KC-46A)

60th Wing (*Travis, California*)
    6th Refueling Squadron (KC-10)
    9th Refueling Squadron (KC-10)
    21st Airlift Squadron (C-17A)
    22nd Airlift Squadron (C-5M)

62nd Wing (*McChord, Washington*)
    4th Airlift Squadron (C-17A)
    7th Airlift Squadron (C-17A)
    8th Airlift Squadron (C-17A)

92nd Wing (*Fairchild, Washington*)
    92nd Refueling Squadron (KC-135)
    93rd Refueling Squadron (KC-135)
    97th Refueling Squadron (KC-135)
    384th Refueling Squadron (KC-135)

317th Wing (*Dyess, Texas*)
    39th Airlift Squadron (C-130J)
    40th Airlift Squadron (C-130J)

436th Wing (*Dover, Delaware*)
   3rd Airlift Squadron (C-17A)
   9th Airlift Squadron (C-5M)

437th Wing (*Charleston, South Carolina*)
   14th Airlift Squadron (C-17A)
   15th Airlift Squadron (C-17A)
   16th Airlift Squadron (C-17A)

Canadian 8th Wing (*Trenton, Canada*)
   429th Transport Squadron (CC-177 III)
   436th Transport Squadron (CC-130J)
   437th Transport Squadron (CC-150)

ASSIGNED TO SPACE COMMAND

Fifteenth Air Force

4th Wing (*Seymour Johnson, North Carolina*)
   333rd Fighter Squadron (F-15EX)

REINFORCEMENTS FROM SOUTH KOREAN AIR FORCE

Air Combat Command

11th Fighter Wing (*Daegu, South Korea*) (F-15K)
19th Fighter Wing (*Chungju, South Korea*) (F-35K, KF-16)

Appendix B: U.S. and Allied Naval Forces

SEVENTH FLEET

Seventh Fleet Command and Control (*Yokosuka, Japan*)
   USS *Blue Ridge*, LCC-19

Carrier Strike Group 5 (*Yokosuka, Japan*)
   USS *George Washington*, CVN-73
      Carrier Air Wing 5 (incl. F-35C)
   Destroyer Squadron 15
      USS *Gridley*, DDG-101 (subsequently assigned to AS-7)
      USS *Wayne E. Meyer*, DDG-108

USS *John Finn*, DDG-113 (subsequently assigned to AS-7)
USS *John Basilone*, DDG-122
USS *Jack H. Lucas*, DDG-125
USS *Patrick Gallagher*, DDG-127
USS *Thad Cochran*, DDG-135

Amphibious Squadron 11 (*Sasebo, Japan*)
USS *America*, LHA-6 (incl. F-35Bs)
USS *Green Bay*, LPD-20
USS *Anchorage*, LPD-23
USS *Fort Lauderdale*, LPD-28
USS *Pittsburgh*, LPD-31

REINFORCEMENTS FROM THIRD FLEET

Carrier Strike Group 9 (*San Diego, California*)
USS *Theodore Roosevelt*, CVN-71
Carrier Air Wing 11 (incl. F-35C)
Destroyer Squadron 9 (subsequently assigned to AS-11)
USS *Pinckney*, DDG-91
USS *Daniel Inouye*, DDG-118
USS *Carl M. Leven*, DDG-120
USS *Lenah Sutcliffe Higbee*, DDG-123

Carrier Strike Group 12 (*Kitsap, Washington*)
USS *Gerald R. Ford*, CVN-78
Carrier Air Wing 8 (incl. F-35C)
Destroyer Squadron 2
USS *Howard*, DDG-83
USS *Dewey*, DDG-105
USS *Spruance*, DDG-111
USS *John F. Lehman*, DDG-137

Amphibious Squadron 7 (*San Diego, California*)
USS *Tripoli*, LHA-7 (incl. F-35Bs)
USS *San Diego*, LPD-22
USS *Somerset*, LPD-25
USS *John P. Murtha*, LPD-26
USS *Portland*, LPD-27
USS *Harrisburg*, LPD-30
USS *Philadelphia*, LPD-32

Special Squadron 1 (*San Diego, California*)

USS *Michael Monsoor*, DDG-1001
USS *Lyndon B. Johnson*, DDG-1002

REINFORCEMENTS FROM SECOND FLEET

Carrier Strike Group 2 (*Norfolk, Virginia*)
USS *Enterprise*, CVN-80
Carrier Air Wing 3 (incl. F-35C)
Destroyer Squadron 22
USS *Farragut*, DDG-99
USS *Thomas Hudner*, DDG-116
USS *Telesforo Trinidad*, DDG-139
USS *Thomas G. Kelley*, DDG-140

Carrier Strike Group 8 (*Norfolk, Virginia*)
USS *Harry S. Truman*, CVN-75
Carrier Air Wing 1 (incl. F-35C)
Destroyer Squadron 28
USS *Truxtun*, DDG-103
USS *Gravely*, DDG-107
USS *Jason Dunham*, DDG-109
USS *Norman Scott*, DDG-200

ASSIGNED TO SPACE COMMAND

Destroyer Squadron 26, Fifth Fleet (*Manama, Bahrain*)
USS *Delbert D. Black*, DDG-119
USS *Quentin Walsh*, DDG-132

PACIFIC SUBMARINE FLEET
(*only those submarines deployed to the Western Pacific*)

Submarine Squadron 1 (*Pearl Harbor, Hawaii*)
USS *Hawaii*, SSN 776
USS *Missouri*, SSN-780
USS *Illinois*, SSN-786
USS *Delaware*, SSN-791

Submarine Squadron 7 (*Pearl Harbor, Hawaii*)
USS *Barb*, SSN-804
USS *Wahoo*, SSN-806
USS *Silversides*, SSN-807

Submarine Squadron 11 (*San Diego, California*)
USS *San Francisco*, SSN-810

Submarine Squadron 15 (*Guam*)
USS *Washington*, SSN-787
USS *Vermont*, SSN-792
USS *Arizona*, SSN-803

Submarine Squadron 19 (*Kitsap, Washington*)
USS *North Carolina*, SSN-777

Pacific Fleet Strategic Deterrent, Sub. Sqn. 17 (*Kitsap, Washington*)
USS *Nevada*, SSBN-733
USS *Nebraska*, SSBN-739
USS *Louisiana*, SSBN-743
USS *District of Columbia*, SSBN-826

REINFORCEMENTS FROM ALLIED NAVIES

British Carrier Strike Group 22 (*Portsmouth, England*)
HMS *Prince of Wales*, R09
809 Naval Air Squadron (incl. F-35B)
HMS *Defender*, D36
HMS *Cardiff*, F89
HMS *Birmingham*, F91
HMS *Sheffield*, F92

French Carrier Strike Group 31 (*Brest, France*)
Charles de Gaulle, R91
Le groupe aérien embarqué (incl. Rafale M)
Normandie, D651
Bretagne, D655
Alsace, D656
Lorraine, D657

Canadian Fleet Pacific (*Esquimalt, Canada*)
HMCS *Red River*, FFH-342 (assigned to AS-7)
HMCS *Bow*, FFH-344 (assigned to AS-7)

Allied strategic deterrent submarines (SSBNs)
HMS *Dreadnought*, S32 (*Clyde, Scotland*)
Terrible, S619 (*Brest, France*)

Appendix C: U.S. and Allied Ground Forces

EIGHTH ARMY (*Camp Humphreys, South Korea*)

Eighth Army Headquarters
  1st Signal Brigade
  35th Air Defense Brigade
  65th Medical Brigade
    168th Multifunctional Medical Battalion
  501st Intelligence Brigade
  19th Expeditionary Sustainment Command
    94th Military Police Battalion

17th Aviation Brigade (*Camp Coiner, South Korea*)
  1st Assault Battalion, 501st Aviation Regiment (UH-60A)
  2nd Medium Lift Battalion, 501st Aviation Regiment (CH-47D)
  4th Attack Battalion, 501st Aviation Regt. (AH-1F, OH-58C)
  5th Attack Battalion, 501st Aviation Regt. (AH-1F, OH-58C)

SECOND INFANTRY DIVISION (*Camp Humphreys, South Korea*)

1st Stryker Bde. Combat Team (*rotated in from Seventh Inf. Div.*)
  1st Squadron, 14th Cavalry Regiment
  2nd Battalion, 3rd Infantry Regiment
  5th Battalion, 20th Infantry Regiment
  1st Battalion, 23rd Infantry Regiment
  1st Battalion, 37th Field Artillery Regiment
  23rd Brigade Engineer Battalion

ROK 16th Mech. Inf. Bde. (*rotated in from Capital Mech. Inf. Div.*)
  18th Tank Battalion
  81st Tank Battalion
  136th Mechanized Infantry Battalion

2nd Combat Aviation Brigade
  5th Reconnaissance Sqn., 17th Cavalry Regt. (AH-64E, RQ-7)
  2nd Assault Battalion, 2nd Aviation Regiment (UH-60)
  3rd Support Battalion, 2nd Aviation Regt. (UH-60, CH-47F)
  4th Attack Battalion, 2nd Aviation Regiment (AH-64E)
  Company E, 2nd Aviation Regiment (MQ-1C)

210th Field Artillery Brigade
  1st Battalion, 38th Field Artillery Regiment

6th Battalion, 37th Field Artillery Regiment
5th Bn., 3rd Field Art. Regt. (*rotated in from 17th F. Art. Bde.*)
Battery F (Target Acquisition), 333rd Field Artillery Regiment

2nd Sustainment Brigade
    11th Engineer Battalion
    23rd Chemical Battalion
    2nd Chemical Battalion (*reinforcement from 48th Chem. Bde.*)

AIRBORNE STRIKE FORCE

Eleventh Airborne (arctic) Division (*Fort Richardson, Alaska*)

2nd Infantry Brigade Combat Team
    1st Battalion, 501st Infantry Regiment
    3rd Battalion, 509th Infantry Regiment
    2nd Battalion, 377th Field Artillery Regiment
    6th Brigade Engineer Battalion

Eighty-second Airborne (rapid response) Div. (*Fort Liberty, NC*)

2nd Infantry Brigade Combat Team
    1st Battalion, 325th Infantry Regiment
    2nd Battalion, 325th Infantry Regiment
    2nd Battalion, 508th Infantry Regiment
    1st Battalion, 319th Airborne Field Artillery Regiment
    37th Engineer Battalion

101st Airborne (air assault) Division (*Fort Campbell, Kentucky*)

1st Infantry Brigade Combat Team
    1st Battalion, 327th Infantry Regiment
    2nd Battalion, 327th Infantry Regiment
    1st Battalion, 506th Infantry Regiment
    1st Battalion, 320th Field Artillery Regiment
    2nd Battalion, 44th Air Defense Artillery Regiment
    326th Engineer Battalion

3rd Infantry Brigade Combat Team
    1st Battalion, 187th Infantry Regiment
    3rd Battalion, 187th Infantry Regiment
    2nd Battalion, 506th Infantry Regiment
    3rd Battalion, 320th Field Artillery Regiment

21st Engineer Battalion

INVASION FORCE

Third Marine Expeditionary Force

1st Marine Expeditionary Brigade (*Camp Pendleton, California*)
1st Battalion, 1st Marine Regiment
3rd Assault Amphibian Battalion
1st Light Armored Reconnaissance Battalion
1st Combat Engineer Battalion

3rd Marine Expeditionary Brigade (*Camp Courtney, Okinawa*)
1st Battalion, 4th Regiment
2nd Battalion, 4th Regiment

Twenty-fifth Light Infantry Div. (*Schofield Barracks, Hawaii*)

2nd Brigade Combat Team
2nd Squadron, 14th Cavalry Regiment
1st Battalion, 21st Infantry Regiment
1st Battalion, 27th Infantry Regiment
Alpha Company, 65th Brigade Engineering Battalion

3rd Brigade Combat Team
3rd Squadron, 4th Cavalry Regiment
2nd Battalion, 27th Infantry Regiment
2nd Battalion, 35th Infantry Regiment
3rd Bn., Princess Patricia's Canadian Light Infantry Regt.
Bravo Company, 29th Brigade Engineering Battalion

Airlifted from Fourth Infantry Division (*Fort Carson, Colorado*)

3rd Armored Brigade Combat Team
4th Squadron, 10th Cavalry Regiment
1st Battalion, 66th Armor Regiment
1st Battalion, 68th Armor Regiment
1st Battalion, 8th Infantry Regiment
3rd Battalion, 29th Field Artillery Regiment
588th Engineer Battalion

SPECIAL FORCES

U.S. Special Forces

75th Ranger Regiment (*Fort Moore, Georgia*)
3rd Battalion
Team 3, Regimental Reconnaissance Company

1st Special Forces Group (*Fort Lewis, Washington*)
1st (airborne) Battalion
2nd (airborne) Battalion

Marine Raider Regiment (*Camp Lejeune, North Carolina*)
Alpha Company, 1st Marine Raider Battalion

Naval Special Warfare Group 1 (*Coronado, California*)
SEAL Team 1
SEAL Team 3
SEAL Team 5
SEAL Team 7

REINFORCEMENTS FROM SOUTH KOREAN ARMY

III Corps

22nd Infantry Division
53rd Infantry Brigade
55th Infantry Brigade
56th Infantry Brigade
22nd Artillery Brigade

Independent corps units
1st Mountain Brigade
20th Armored Brigade
102nd Armored Brigade
3rd Engineer Brigade
23rd Security Brigade

VII Maneuver Corps

2nd Quick Response Division
203rd Quick Response (airmobile commando) Brigade

Independent corps units
2nd Air Assault (airmobile) Battalion

South Korean Special Warfare Command
(*known or suspected deployment in North Korea*)

9th Special Forces "Ghost" (reconnaissance) Brigade
51st Battalion
52nd Battalion
53rd Battalion
55th Battalion

13th Special Mission "Black Panther" (decapitation) Brigade
71st Battalion
72nd Battalion
73rd Battalion
75th Battalion

Selected Sources

Government reports

Central Intelligence Agency, 2031. *Analysis of the leadership crisis in North Korea.* Declassified with redactions.

_____, 2033. *Situation in North Korea: weekly summary.* Declassified with redactions. July 15.

_____, 2033. *Situation in North Korea: weekly summary.* Declassified with redactions. August 12.

_____, 2033. *Situation in North Korea: weekly summary.* Declassified with redactions. September 23.

_____, 2034. *Intelligence operations during the recent conflict in North Korea.* Report to Congress. Declassified with redactions. February.

Department of Homeland Security, 2033. *North Korea's involvement in the bombing of Seattle.* Report to the Secretary of Homeland Security, June 30. Declassified with redactions.

_____, 2033. *New security procedures at U.S. ports: guidance for Port Authorities.* Public report, June 29.

Department of State, 2032. *Analysis of Chinese concerns regarding North Korea.* Report to the Secretary of State, July 8. Declassified.

_____, 2033. *Issues of concern for China.* Preparatory material for visit to China by Secretary Bowes, July 30. Declassified with redactions.

Department of Defense, 2028. *History and current status of the North Korean air force and air defense network.* Contract No. F32314-27-R-0017 (Tushingham, M., *et. al.*). March.

_____, 2031. *A comprehensive evaluation of the nuclear, chemical and biological weapons programs of North Korea.* Declassified with redactions.

_____, 2033. *Evaluation of North Korea's military capabilities.* Declassified with redactions. July.

Department of Health, Canada, 2033. *Health assessment of the radioactive fallout on the Lower Mainland of British Columbia.* Report to Parliament by the Minister of Health, June 22.

Department of National Defense, Canada, 2033. *Canadian fighters arrive in South Korea.* Media release, August 1.

_____, 2034. *The role of the Canadian Armed Forces in the recent Korean conflict.* Report to Parliament by the Minister of Defense, March 31.

Federal Bureau of Investigation, 2033. *A compendium of the evidence supporting the role of North Korea in the bombing of Seattle.* Report to the President. Declassified. July 25.

Ministry of Defense, United Kingdom, 2033. *The operations of the Royal Navy's during the Korean conflict: 2033.* Report to Parliament by the Minister of Defense, November 22.

Organization for the Prohibition of Chemical Weapons, 2025. *A global inventory of chemical weapons.* January.

United States Army, 2033. *Review of the battle at Kowŏn, North Korea, September 11 to 13, 2033.* December. Declassified.

United States District Court, District of Columbia, 2034. *United States v. Kim Ji-ho.* Court transcript. November 6 to 22.

United States House of Representatives Committee on Armed Services, 2034. *Testimony of Admiral Lawrence Sentsey, Commander, Indo-Pacific Command, regarding the war in North Korea.* H-04-35/2033.

United States Senate Committee on Foreign Relations, 2034. *Testimony of Ambassador Morris Carver regarding discussions with China prior and during the war in North Korea.* S-13-64/2034.

_____, 2034. *Testimony of Secretary of State Cheryl Bowes regarding relations with South Korea, Japan and China.* S-13-66/2034.

_____, 2034. *Relations with North Korea prior to June 17, 2033.* S-13-78/2034.

United States Senate Select Committee on Intelligence, 2033. *Public testimony of Director Valerie Ullman regarding China's entry into North Korea in September 2033.* S-12-238/2033.

White House, 2033. *Seattle and North Korea: evidence of guilt.* Public report. July 12.

Articles

Baneberry, F.S., and Fortescue, W.R., 2035. *A review of the operations of the USAF during the Korean bombing campaign.* Journal for Military and Strategic Studies. March.

BBC News (website), 2037. *Chinese lose interest in propping up North Korea: new polling results.* January 23.

Carroll, R.S., 2034. *A comprehensive evaluation of American military command at the Battle of Wonsan.* Strategy and Warfare Center.

CBC TV, 2034. *Interview with the Honorable Glen Rathwell, Minister of Foreign Affairs.* June 17.

Fetidin, C.E., and Cortland, C.I., 2029. *A comparison of airlift capacities of heavy-lift cargo aircraft in the U.S. Air Force.* Mitchell Institute of Aerospace Studies.

Gilshaw. J.J., Maj. (USAF, ret.), 2035. *A detailed timeline of U.S. aerial and naval operations on August 4 and 5, 2033.* Journal for Military and Strategic Studies. December.

Hildebrand, X.G., Moon D.-F. and Kay, E., 2035. *An assessment of effectiveness of the USAF bombing campaign over North Korea.* Strategy and Warfare Center.

Jones, M.E.E., *et al.*, 2027. *Cost-benefit analysis of the F-15EX Eagle II compared to the F-35A Lightning II.* RAND Corporation. July.

Kane, F.F, and Hilderbran, E.Q., 2035. *U.S. grand strategy for the Second Korean War.* Institute for the Study of War and Strategy. March.

Kei P.-S., *et al.*, 2036. *The Second Korean War: a retrospective analysis of the U.S. strategies and outcomes.* Institute for National Strategic Studies. November.

Luu H.-S. and Roberts, D., 2034. *The strategic impact of the U.S. Air Force's bombing of North Korea: a critical assessment.* International Institute for Strategic Studies. December.

Makepeace, M.E., 2029. *On the capabilities of the B-21 Raider.* Mitchell Institute of Aerospace Studies.

Markels, T., and Maypole, J.D., 2037. *Anti-submarine warfare by the USN during Second Korean War.* Center for Naval Warfare Studies. March.

New York Times, 2033. *North Korea bombed: night of the bats.* August 5.

Nolt, K.S., *et al.*, 2031. *Weapons and weapon systems available to the Korean People's Army in 2030.* RAND Corporation publications. November.

Norwich, P.L., and Springs, D.D., 2036. *Ground options available to the U.S. Eighth Army after the fall of Wonsan.* Center for Military, Security and Strategic Studies, University of Calgary. April.

Portyanki, K.Z., et. al., 2034. *Assessment of the B-21 performance during the Second Korean War.* Mitchell Institute of Aerospace Studies.

San Diego Union-Tribune, 2033. *Major repairs for Navy carrier: out of the war.* August 9.

SIG Sauer, Inc., 2025: *New reliable weapons for our soldiers: information package on the SIG MCX SPEAR (XM7) rifle and SIG LMG 6.8 (XM250) belt-fed machine gun.* Prospectus.

Tonasket, W.W., 2034. *Ranger operations in eastern North Korea: September 2033.* Journal for Military and Strategic Studies. September.

Washington Post, 2033. *Our soldiers gassed.* September 21.

Woo P., and Edmonds, B.K.A., 2033, *China's new approach to its relationship with the United States.* Center for Strategic and International Studies. May.

Books

Atten, E. (Maj., U.S. Army, ret.), 2035. *From Wonsan to the Mountains.*

Drozdowski, J.A., 2037. *Bomb Them to Hell: The USAF's Bombing Campaign Against North Korea.*

Galton, C., 2036. *Righteous Fury: American Diplomacy in the Aftermath of Seattle.*

Gar, K., and Wilbert, G.F., 2036. *The Case Against North Korea: A Legal Reappraisal.*

Hill, A.D., 2034. *Anders and North Korea: The Politics of War.*

Indris, L.A.E., 2032. *The Korean Caligula.*

Keaney, T.E., 2037. *6/17 Seattle.*

Linkletter, L.S., Jr., (Capt., U.S. Army, ret.), 2035. *Descent into North Korea: Airborne Operations, 2033.*

Moore, M., 2036. *Gas Attack: Kasen and the American Response.*

Nelles Verlag GmbH, 2028. *Nelles Map: Korea, North and South.* 1:1,500,000 scale.

Nyrhila, D.E., 2038. *Invasion at Wonsan.*

O'Connor, M.D. (Col., USAF, ret.), 2036. *Moving an Army: The Eighteenth Air Force and the Second Korean War.*

Soo J.-S., 2035. *North Korea and China: A New Relationship.* English edition.

Suzukawa, K., and Kabel, F., 2037. *Ghosts of Seattle: The United Nations and the Nuclear Destruction of an American City.*

Tackleberry, D.R., Jr. (ed.), 2031. *Jane's Fighting Ships Yearbook, 2031/2032.*

Walker, S., 2005. *Shockwave: Countdown to Hiroshima.*

After-action reports

USAF	US Army	USN
2nd Wing	2nd Sustainment Bde.	Carrier Air Wing 1
4th Wing	10th Cavalry Regt.	Carrier Air Wing 3
5th Wing	14th Cavalry Regt.	Carrier Air Wing 5
7th Wing	27th Infantry Regt.	Carrier Air Wing 8
8th Wing	48th Chemical Bde.	Carrier Air Wing 11
9th Wing	66th Armor Regt.	USS *America*
18th Wing	75th Ranger Regt.	USS *Daniel Inouye*
28th Wing	187th Infantry Regt.	USS *Hawaii*
35th Wing	325th Infantry Regt.	USS *Lyndon B. Johnson*
51st Wing	501st Infantry Regt.	USS *Quentin Walsh*
55th Wing	506th Infantry Regt.	USS *Spruance*
62nd Wing		USS *Theodore Roosevelt*
92nd Wing	USMC	USS *Vermont*
374th Wing	1st Marine Regt.	
509th Wing	4th Marine Regt.	

Interviews and personal correspondence

Ranks and positions are those at the time of the war.

Albright, J.J., Capt., RCAF
Ashby, W.C., Col., US Army
Baquer, I.M.L., Cdr., USN
Beute, R., Pvt., US Army
Beyea, P.E.G., Pvt., USMC
Beyer, L.S., Tech. Sgt., USAF
Brasilia, M.E.E., Lt., US Army
Brown, W., Capt., USAF
Chen, J.X., Pvt., USMC
Cole, J.E., Col., USAF
Cormack, D.T., Col. USAF
Craig, V.G., Tech. Sgt., USAF
Crossman, B.E., Brig. Gen., USAF
De Silva, C.M.E., Maj., US Army
Dunn, L.A., Lt. Gen., USAF
Eddy, F.B., Lt., US Army
Emon, A.J.P., Mstr. Sgt., USAF
Finick, B., Cdn. PR to NATO
Galanis, H.C., Cpl., US Army
Halmahera, J.H., Lt., USAF
Hunt, J.D., Lt. Cdr. (Dr.), USN
Kozelek, D.B., Lt., USAF
Lindstrom, T.J., Sr. Agent, FBI
Lonigan, J.R., Lt., USAF
Lowry, R.W., Jr., Maj., USMC
MacFarlane, B.W., Lt. Col., RCA

McAdams, T.C., UK
Mendez, E., Capt. USAF
Miller, G.F., Lt., USN
Nagle, W.F., Pvt., USMC
Neilson, S., Lt., USAF
Oakes, D.Y., Jr., Maj., US Army
Petras, E., Maj., US Army
Rathwell, N.J., Tech. Sgt., USAF
Rojas, F.E.A, Col., USAF
Schoelrok, C.R., Cdr. USN
Schott, F.M., Capt., USAF
Smith, A.C., Capt., USAF
Sutton, M.E., Capt., USAF
Swarbrick, L.Y.J., Lt., RCAF
Todd, K.R., US Ambas. to ROK
Trang, C.P., Col., USAF
Trautman, D.W., Cdr., USN
Van Dusen, B., Pvt., US Army
Ward, P., Pvt., US Army
Waters, L.M., Cpl., USMC
Williston, B., Cdr., USN
Wiltz, M.S., Maj., USAF
Whitechurch, D.E., Gen., USSF
Wu, J., Lt., USN
Yellen, C.V., Lt., USAF
Zeligs, A.W., Cdr., USN

About the Author

Mark Tushingham has accumulated a library of hundreds of books on military matters. This collection covers battles on land, at sea and in the air, campaigns, strategy, weaponry, and logistics, as well as the genius and the blunders of military leadership.

His first novel was *Hotter than Hell*, a speculative military fiction published in 2005. The book created a national controversy in 2006. At that time, he was acknowledged in the media as "a keen student of military matters" and being "able to recreate [modern warfare] vividly."

Since then, Tushingham has written a second speculative military fiction novel, *Hell on Earth*, a military science fiction novel, *Defenseless*, a historical caper novel set in World War II, *Inspired and Dedicated Thief*, and other novels in the genres of science fiction, fantasy and crime. His latest speculative military fiction is his Battle 2033 series: *Battle for the Taiwan Strait 2033*, *Battle for the Baltic States 2033*, and *Battle for North Korea 2033*.

Tushingham's novels are praised as "fast-paced," "gripping" and "engrossing." The one compliment from readers for which he strives is "I couldn't put the book down."

Novels by Mark Tushingham

"Gripping" – *Charlottetown Guardian*

SPECULATIVE MILITARY FICTION
Hotter than Hell
Hell on Earth
Battle for the Taiwan Strait 2033
Battle for the Baltic States 2033
Battle for North Korea 2033

SCIENCE FICTION
Defenseless
Second Awakening
Beyond Ageless
Uplift 40

FANTASY
The Gifts of Faeries
The Dreams of Faeries

CRIME
Inspired and Dedicated Thief
Blue Ice Dead

CHILDREN'S BEDTIME STORY
The Great Trek of the Churkahs
The Long Search of the Churkahs

NON-FICTION
Good Government: A Voter's Guide

These books may be purchased through Amazon.
Electronic Kindle editions are also available.

Follow on Instagram *@fairycrosspublishing*
and X (Twitter) *@Mark_Tushingham*

Made in United States
Orlando, FL
06 December 2024

54980364R00173